THE MOCHE WARRIOR

Mystery . . . made in Peru.
Lara explores sacred burial grounds steeped in
riches—and fraught with danger . . .

"With its setting shifting from Toronto to New York to Peru, this engaging story is a passport to adventure . . . richly woven descriptions . . . fascinating and vividly presented subject matter, and [an] artfully crafted plot." —*Booklist*

THE MALTESE GODDESS

Murder casts a shadow
on the island of Malta as
ancient legend and modern intrigue collide . . .

"A pleasant blend of past civilizations and present intrigue."
—*The Toronto Star*

"Exotically absorbing and culturally colorful."
—*Midwest Book Review*

THE XIBALBA MURDERS

Arthur Ellis Award Nominee
for Best First Novel

Lara is drawn to the lush jungles of Mexico
to uncover the secrets of the Mayan underworld
known as Xibalba . . .

"A successful mystery—and series: a smart, appealing, funny, brave, and vulnerable protagonist and a complex, entertaining, and rational plot." —*The London Free Press* (Ontario)

Berkley Prime Crime Books
by Lyn Hamilton

THE XIBALBA MURDERS
THE MALTESE GODDESS
THE MOCHE WARRIOR
THE CELTIC RIDDLE
THE AFRICAN QUEST
THE ETRUSCAN CHIMERA
THE THAI AMULET
THE MAGYAR VENUS
THE MOAI MURDERS
THE ORKNEY SCROLL

THE
Orkney Scroll

LYN HAMILTON

BERKLEY PRIME CRIME, NEW YORK

THE BERKLEY PUBLISHING GROUP
Published by the Penguin Group
Penguin Group (USA) Inc.
375 Hudson Street, New York, New York 10014, USA
Penguin Group (Canada), 90 Eglinton Avenue East, Suite 700, Toronto, Ontario M4P 2Y3, Canada
(a division of Pearson Penguin Canada Inc.)
Penguin Books Ltd., 80 Strand, London WC2R 0RL, England
Penguin Group Ireland, 25 St. Stephen's Green, Dublin 2, Ireland (a division of Penguin Books Ltd.)
Penguin Group (Australia), 250 Camberwell Road, Camberwell, Victoria 3124, Australia
(a division of Pearson Australia Group Pty. Ltd.)
Penguin Books India Pvt. Ltd., 11 Community Centre, Panchsheel Park, New Delhi—110 017, India
Penguin Group (NZ), 67 Apollo Drive, Mairangi Bay, Auckland 1310, New Zealand
(a division of Pearson New Zealand Ltd.)
Penguin Books (South Africa) (Pty.) Ltd., 24 Sturdee Avenue, Rosebank, Johannesburg 2196,
South Africa

Penguin Books Ltd., Registered Offices: 80 Strand, London WC2R 0RL, England

THE ORKNEY SCROLL

A Berkley Prime Crime Book / published by arrangement with the author

PRINTING HISTORY
Berkley Prime Crime hardcover edition / April 2006
Berkley Prime Crime mass-market edition / February 2007

Copyright © 2006 by Lyn Hamilton.
Excerpt from *The Chinese Alchemist* copyright © 2007 by Lyn Hamilton.
Cover image of Ancient World Map by Rob Atkins / Getty Images.
Cover photograph of Gurness Broch Tower by Sigurd Towrie.
Cover design by Richard Hasselberger.
Interior text design by Kristin del Rosario.

ISBN: 978-0-425-21431-2

BERKLEY ® PRIME CRIME
Berkley Prime Crime Books are published by The Berkley Publishing Group,
a division of Penguin Group (USA) Inc.,
375 Hudson Street, New York, New York 10014.
The name BERKLEY PRIME CRIME and the BERKLEY PRIME CRIME design
are trademarks belonging to Penguin Group (USA) Inc.

PRINTED IN THE UNITED STATES OF AMERICA

10 9 8 7 6 5 4 3 2 1

For my father, much missed,
JOHN BORDEN HAMILTON
May 16, 1913–November 24, 2005

Acknowledgments

As always, I owe a debt of gratitude to many people, notably Chris Mathers and Denise Bellamy for their advice on legal issues. For their friendship, advice, and support I thank fellow mystery writers Mary Jane Maffini, Claudia Bishop, and Rhys Bowen. As always, my sister Cheryl is first reader and best critic. Those who would like to learn more about the adventures of the real Viking Earls of Orkney could read the Orkneyinga Saga. The translation I like is by Hermann Pálsson and Paul Edwards. While I've tried to mimic some of the features of the real sagas, Bjarni the Wanderer is, like all the characters in the present, a figment of my overwrought imagination.

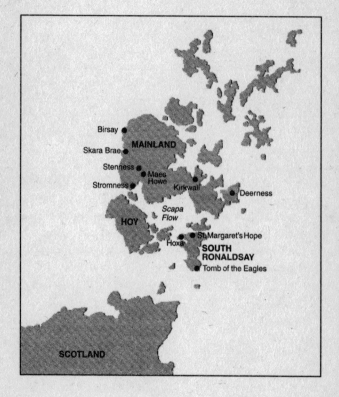

Birsay

Skara Brae

Stenness

MAINLAND

Maes
Howe

Stromness

Kirkwall

Deerness

*Scapa
Flow*

HOY

St Margaret's Hope

Hoxa

**SOUTH
RONALDSAY**

Tomb of the Eagles

SCOTLAND

Prologue

Before he went mad, Bjarni the Wanderer hid the cauldron in the tomb of the orcs. It's an intriguing declaration to be sure, one that requires more than a little explication, and in some ways an irritating way to put finis to a story. For some, though, it is a beginning rather than an end, a statement of such promise that hopes and dreams are pinned on it, as if believing would make it so. To decide whether you come down on the side of the dreamers or the skeptics or rather somewhere in between, you will have to go back to the beginning, and that means more than nine hundred years.

I do not know if Bjarni's saga is true. My grandfather used to say that it was not inconsistent with the facts. You will perhaps not see this as a ringing endorsement, but then you didn't know my grandfather. I can tell you that the tale has been passed down through my family for longer than anyone can remember. My grandfather believed that at first the story would have been transmitted orally, the structure and cadence of the poem being an aid to the memory, so that it would always be accurately told. At some *time, no one knows when, it was written down, possibly in Norn, but more likely first in Latin, stories of this sort appealing to twelfth-century clerics it seems, then passed from one generation to the next. It was my grandfather who translated it from Latin. That was how I learned my letters, by copying the story in a notebook, actually several of them, my grandfather watching to make sure that I made no error, left nothing out. And that, I suppose, is why we have the story still, copied over and over again by successive generations. I think for some of us, the preservation of Bjarni's saga became a sacred trust.*

I suppose over all that time liberties were taken with it, errors of omission and commission both, so much so that its true meaning may well be lost. Then again, perhaps not. It is possible I am the last to treasure it. My sons have no interest in it. One doesn't understand it. The other believes it to be of no worth. Still, I have hopes for one of my granddaughters. She's a restless spirit, but she comes by that honestly, a true descendant of Bjarni the Wanderer. She used to like me to tell her the story, and demanded that I recite it with her. I will leave the notebooks to her when I die.

So now that you've heard the requisite disclaimers, the attempt, however feeble to encourage you to view everything I say with some suspicion, do you still want to hear the story of Bjarni Haraldsson? Of course you do. Who could resist a tale that ends with the words, before he went mad Bjarni the Wanderer hid the cauldron in the tomb of the orcs?

Chapter 1

OF TREVOR WYLIE it was often said that he was a rogue and you should keep your hand firmly on your wallet when he was in the vicinity, but that you couldn't be upset with him for long. Somebody, though, stayed angry long enough to kill him.

Trevor lost his life over a piece of furniture, at least that's the way it looked, although it didn't take long for any of us to figure out there was a lot to Trevor that wasn't the way it appeared. The object in question was a desk, or rather more correctly a writing cabinet, and for a short time it belonged to a lawyer by the name of Blair Baldwin. Trevor was the antique dealer who sold it to him. In contrast to the charming Trevor, Baldwin was a difficult man to like. That was because he was arrogant and had a hellish temper which he unleashed at the slightest provocation, usually in front of a TV camera. At one point in time though, I think Blair considered me a friend.

I first met Blair in my early days as an antique dealer when he turned up in the doorway of McClintoch & Swain with a piece of cameo glass carefully wrapped in tissue, a vase he'd spent a lot of money to acquire because he believed it to be by the master of Art Nouveau glass, Emile Gallé. Blair's law offices were down the street from my shop, and I expect he dropped by in part to show his acquisition off to someone who would appreciate it, but also looking to me to corroborate his find. Baldwin's difficult reputation had preceded him, and so it was with some reluctance that I had to point out to him that somewhere between the factory in Romania where the vase had been manufactured and his hands, someone had managed to grind off the letters TIP which would have indicated that the piece was done in the style of Gallé, but not by Gallé.

It was a tense moment, but Baldwin took it with amazingly good grace. He paid close attention as I showed him what to watch for, had a careful look through the magnifying glass I offered, and asked if there were books on the subject I could recommend. At the end of his visit, it was no longer Mr. Baldwin and Ms. McClintoch, but rather Blair and Lara, and later, it became Blair and "babe." Not that I was happy about the "babe," mind you, but Blair was a really good customer. He'd suggested that first day that if I saw anything I thought he might like, I should give him a call. Baldwin was absolutely addicted to Art Nouveau, and for many years I was fortunate to feed his habit. I say fortunate because he had the wherewithal to buy pretty much whatever he fancied, having been hugely successful defending some pretty unsavory characters. He lived in a spectacular house, big enough to accommodate whatever he bought, and paid whatever he had to for something he fancied. Blair Bazillionaire, we called him at McClintoch & Swain.

I've had mixed feelings over the years about Baldwin. I'd seen him way too often strutting his stuff for the cameras outside a courthouse, fingers hooked under his suspenders so that he looked as if he were about to take flight, and crowing about how he'd got some scum off on a technicality. Not that he called them scum, of course. That would be editorializing on my part. I believe "my wronged client" was the term he used.

Still, when business was slow at McClintoch & Swain, slow here being used as a euphemism for on the verge of bankruptcy, Baldwin seemed to know it, and he always purchased something spectacular close to month end, whether he needed it or not. He recommended me to his wealthy pals, many of whom became regulars at the shop. When his wife Betsy left him, being the lawyer he was, he could have tied her up in knots forever, legally speaking, but he didn't, and they seem to have parted reasonably amicably, at least from my perspective, she with what I'd call a small fortune to see her through. There was obviously more than one side to Blair Bazillionaire.

As for antiques, over the years he developed a pretty good eye. After that first unfortunate episode, he wasn't often fooled. He'd expressed his displeasure over the Gallé by tossing it into my wastebasket, which fortunately was full, allowing me to retrieve it in one piece after he'd left. I have it still. It's lovely, really, no matter who made it, but then I didn't pay a fortune for it as Baldwin had. He still relied on me for a second opinion on the big ticket items, and that is why I was called to Scot Free, Trevor Wylie's antique shop to have a look at something special Blair was thinking of buying.

I was late, having spent an unexpected hour or two with the local police force. It turned out I was merely the latest victim of a rash of robberies of antique shops in my neighborhood, something the constable attributed to the opening of a Goth bar just down the street. I wasn't so sure. For one thing, my sort-of stepdaughter Jennifer patronized the bar, and she said it was just a bunch of people who liked to wear black and talk about themselves. For another, this looked like theft to order to me: someone wanted a pair of eighteenth-century candlesticks and sent a rather professional crew to get it. The thieves had used glass cutters at the back door, bypassed all sorts of expensive merchandise and had taken only the candlesticks. They got out before the security company was able to respond. I was not in a good mood.

The appointment with Blair and Trevor did not start out well. First, I had to push my way past a very large Doberman in Trevor's doorway: by large I mean we were almost eyeball to eyeball, a somewhat intimidating way to start. The dog's owner, who was about as wide as he was high and would have looked more at home keeping the riffraff at bay at the door of the aforementioned Goth bar than in an antique shop, was admiring a not particularly appealing bronze lamppost, and obviously eavesdropping at the same time.

Blair was impatiently tapping his fingers on Trevor's front counter and looked as if he were about to tear my face off for my tardiness. Trevor, on the other hand, resembled the proverbial cat that swallowed the canary, and I just knew he was going to lord his find, whatever it was, over me.

"You're late, babe," Baldwin said, through clenched teeth, as a rather scruffy looking individual in a rumpled beige suit with bicycle clips holding his pant legs edged past the Doberman and into the shop. The new visitor didn't look as if he belonged there any more than the bouncer did. Given the time I'd just spent with the police on the subject of robberies, I viewed him with some suspicion.

"This is going to blow you away, hen," Trevor said, kissing me on both cheeks. Trevor was from Scotland and looked and sounded a little like a young Sean Connery, which is probably why I tolerated him. "Hen" is, I believe, Glasgow slang for any female. All this hen and babe stuff was making me nauseous. "This way," he said, indicating the back room. The man with the bicycle clips, trying to look nonchalant, tripped over a pair of flatirons and almost fell down.

"Are we ready to be impressed?" Trevor asked, hand on a sheet that covered a fairly substantial object of some kind, maybe four feet high and three wide. Baldwin swallowed hard and nodded.

"Lara?" Trevor said.

All this drama was getting on my nerves. "Get on with it, Trevor," I said. "Although maybe you want to close the door?" I could see both Mr. Doberman and Mr. Bicycle Clips edging toward the office. When Trevor went to the doorway, Bicycle Clips clomped up the stairs to the shop's second floor.

"No one to guard the merchandise, I'm afraid. So . . . lights," he said, flicking a switch that turned a little spotlight on the object. "Gloves," he added handing both Blair and me a pair.

"Ta dah!" Trevor exclaimed, as he swept the covering away.

After all this, I didn't expect to be impressed, but this piece just blew me away. Standing under the spotlight was a single piece of furniture, a writing desk, or rather a writing cabinet. It was exquisite, ebonized wood, mahogany, and when you opened the doors, which Trevor did with a flourish, there was a lovely leaded glass panel, and some perfect inlaid woodwork. There were slots, pigeonholes for papers, and drawers that opened beautifully. Beside me, Baldwin made little squeaking sounds.

"It can't be, can it?" I said, turning to Trevor.

"I wasn't sure when I found it," he replied. "I took a chance, but I'm convinced it is."

"Babe?" Baldwin managed to say.

"It looks to be the right age," I said carefully. "The style is definitely Glasgow School. I'd have to do some research."

"I've done it already," Trevor said, handing me a file. "Be my guest." Baldwin impatiently leaned over my shoulder as I opened it.

There was only one sheet of paper in the file. It was a drawing of the desk in question, complete with exact specifications. And it was initialed: CRM/MMM.

"Good lord," Baldwin gasped and sank into a chair.

"Charles Rennie Mackintosh," Trevor said. "Margaret Macdonald Mackintosh."

"Are you all right, Blair?" I said. "You aren't going into shock or anything, are you?"

"I'll make tea," Trevor said. "And perk it up a bit with this." This was a bottle of rather fine single malt scotch. Trevor was feeling pretty cocky.

"I know this looks convincing," I said. "But it isn't definitive."

"There's more," Trevor said, bringing a book down from a shelf above his desk and opening it. "Here's something similar. Take your time."

"How much?" Baldwin said.

"Blair!" I cautioned. The book in question was a very good text on Art Nouveau, an international style that emerged about 1890 and was highly popular until it burned itself out in about 1904, but which had names associated with it—like Tiffany and Lalique—that remain famous today. Several brilliant individuals were part of this movement, of which Glasgow's Charles Rennie Mackintosh was one. Mackintosh, while not terribly favored in Britain at the time, was a huge influence on European designers like Josef Hoffman and the Weiner Werkstatte. His work, like the Art Nouveau movement itself, was something of a flash in the pan, but after some decades of neglect is now much sought-after. Very occasionally a piece comes on the market. Trevor had marked a page in the book with a yellow sticky and there was a photograph of a writing cabinet similar, but not absolutely identical to the one in front of me, in the book.

"I think Mackintosh made two to this design," Trevor said. "That is not, after all, unprecedented. He sometimes made a second piece for himself when he'd been commissioned to design something for a client."

"Where did you find it?" I said, nodding toward the cabinet.

"I was on my regular trip in Scotland," Trevor said. "One of my pickers told me that an old lady was holding a contents sale on the weekend and might have some interesting stuff. I went over early, and had a look, and charmed her into selling the piece to me, a couple of pieces, actually. The other one didn't pan out. This one did. Lucky for me. If it hadn't, I'd have been royally screwed. I paid a lot for it, way too much if my hunch wasn't right. But that's the business we're in, eh, hen?"

"I suppose. Where'd you find the drawing?"

"In the right-hand drawer! Can you believe it? It was under about a hundred years' worth of liner paper. I didn't find it until later."

"It could still be a copy," I said. Trevor's exuberance was trying, or maybe I was just jealous.

"It could, but it isn't," Trevor said. "I'm convinced of it. Charles designed and built the furniture. His wife Margaret did the stained glass. It has her stamp all over it. You'll notice it's in remarkable condition, just a bit of wear on one of the drawers and the legs."

"How much?" Baldwin repeated.

"One very similar sold at auction in the late nineteen-nineties for something in the neighborhood of one-point-five million U.S.," Trevor said. "But I'm prepared to negotiate." As he said one-point-five million, there was a crash upstairs and some scuffling. Mr. Bicycle Clips had apparently tripped over something else. I would have been up the stairs in a flash. Trevor ignored it.

"Babe?" Baldwin said.

"I don't know, Blair," I said. "All I can say at this moment is that I can't find anything wrong with it."

"I'm sure we can work something out," Trevor said, winking at me. At that very moment the phone rang. "Sorry," Trevor said. "I should take this. You two can chat. Dez!" he said into the phone. "You got my message?" Blair paled. There may be a lot of Dez's in the world, but only one who would be calling Trevor right at this minute. Desmond Crane was also a lawyer, and Crane and Baldwin often found themselves on the opposite sides of various lawsuits. Word was the antipathy they displayed toward each other in court was absolutely genuine: they disliked one another intensely. It did strike me as a little overly convenient that Dez had chosen this very moment to call, but perhaps Trevor had suggested the time, all part of the plan to entice Blair to buy on the spot.

"Do you think it's genuine?" Blair asked quietly.

"I think it could be," I said, albeit reluctantly. I really wanted more time.

"It may still be available," Trevor said, looking right at Baldwin. "I'm talking to Blair right now."

"I'll take it!" Blair said.

Trevor nodded and smiled in our general direction. "Call you back, Dez," he said. "Sorry."

"I'm off," I said. I didn't want to know what Blair was going to pay for this passion of his, and I sure didn't want to find myself in the middle of a dustup between Baldwin and Crane. After all, both were customers.

"I'll be at the Stane later," Trevor called as I dodged past the Doberman again. "If you'll join me, hen, I'll stand you to a single malt or three."

I didn't take up Trevor's offer of a scotch at the Stane, or rather The Dwarfie Stane, his favorite bar, there being only so much gloating I can stand in one day. I did see him a few days later, however. Baldwin, never one to quietly enjoy a victory over a competitor, held a rather grand cocktail party in his Rosedale mansion to show off his purchase. Trevor came with his latest girlfriend, Willow somebody or other. There was no point trying to remember her last name. If the relationship followed the normal course, she wouldn't be around long enough for it to matter. She had the standard

Trevor girlfriend look, long dark hair and even longer legs, a certain innocence of expression. Like most of them, she had an unusual name. McClintoch & Swain was represented by both me and my business partner—and ex-husband—Clive Swain. I brought my life partner, Rob Luczka, as my date, and Clive brought his, my best friend Moira Meller.

Blair's home was a shrine to Art Nouveau. It was a little over the top, but far be it for me to criticize, given I'd helped him to acquire a lot of it. Even the powder room walls had been covered in genuine Art Nouveau fabric. Not a copy, the real thing. Every room was a little museum, decorated to the point of excess and beyond. He had pieces from many of the masters of Art Nouveau, including some lovely furnishings by Josef Hoffmann, Carlos Bugatti, Henry van de Velde, and Victor Horta among others, and now, of course, he had a Charles Rennie Mackintosh. In the smaller items, he had much from Steuben and Tiffany, Sèvres and Meissen and many lesser known but still important pieces dating to the period, and of course, determined as Blair was to erase his first mistake, a few genuine pieces of Gallé glass. All were carefully placed, and artfully lit, none more so than the Mackintosh writing cabinet which was on a raised platform in an alcove off the living room all by itself. It was, to continue the shrine analogy, the holy of holies in Blair's residence, the spot where he placed his prized possession of the moment.

I idly wondered what had happened to the objects previously displayed there. At one time the alcove had held a Josef Hoffman walnut-veneered sideboard, another time a rather unusual carved wood chair by Antoni Gaudi no less. I hadn't seen either of those pieces in awhile. I wondered if he sold stuff he got tired of, or simply stored it in the basement, which would be unfortunate. Blair had paid just over a hundred thousand for that one chair, which was a deal considering how unique it was. He'd got it for a few tens of thousands less than the going rate because it had a very small cigarette burn on the seat. A shame really, which is perhaps why the chair was nowhere to be seen anymore. The Mackintosh writing cabinet was, if not his proudest acquisition, then perhaps his most extravagant. Blair was a Collector, with a capital *C*.

"Do you like this stuff?" Rob asked as we wandered from room to room. "All these swirls on everything?"

"I do, but not all in one place. I prefer a home to be a little more relaxed," I replied. "Consistency can be a virtue of course, but rigid adherence to one particular design aesthetic may not be an entirely good idea if you have to live with it. There comes a point where it's just too much, and with Art Nouveau, that point may come sooner rather than later. I haven't told Blair that, of course. I'm not that stupid. Actually maybe I am. I did tell him once early on that he might consider mixing stuff up a little. I believe all he said was 'babe' in a pained tone."

"Personally, I believe a home decorated entirely in one style is the product of a diseased mind," Clive said. He does, too. A house like this makes Clive, who is the designer of our team, nauseous. Given his surroundings, on this particular occasion, he was holding up rather well.

"I think I'd have to agree with you there, Clive," Rob said. This was something. Rob and Clive agreed about once every year or so. "The desk thing is nice, though. It seems cleaner in design."

"Yes, Mackintosh's furniture is more pleasingly geometric than most of the pieces from that period."

"It's the bugs on everything I wonder about," Moira said.

"But that's the point, you see," I interjected. "Art Nouveau appeared in the late nineteenth century as a reaction to industrialization, the mass production of everything. The people who espoused it believed objects should be made by hand, by artists and real craftspeople, and the motifs went back to nature, tendrils, leaves, insects and crustaceans, organic designs really."

"Okay, but who wants to eat off platters with bugs on them?" Rob said.

"Just about everybody, apparently," Clive said. "Have you seen the way people are attacking the mounds of shrimps and oysters and lobster, to say nothing of the gallons of real champagne being swilled? You can fault Blair's design sense, but you can't complain about the food."

He was right. The party was an extravagant event. Blair didn't seem to know how to do anything in a quiet way. I confess I do not enjoy parties like this, but both Blair and Trevor were so excited about the Mackintosh it would have been churlish to refuse to attend, and furthermore, as Clive is always pointing out, it is good for business for us to be seen in such company. Everybody, but everybody was there: media types, film stars, the usual hangers-on, titans of industry, various civic leaders, including the mayor, and even the chief of police, which was a bit of a surprise, considering how a fair number of Blair's legal successes must have galled him and how many of Blair's clients, some of whom looked to be auditioning for a part in *The Sopranos*, were also in attendance.

"Didn't I arrest that guy for something?" Rob said. He's a Mountie, an officer in the Royal Canadian Mounted Police, so he can ask questions like that.

"Arrest whom?"

"The guy on the far side of the buffet table scarfing down all the shrimp. What is he doing here? I'm sure I arrested him for something."

"If you didn't, you should have. Anyone who wears a green suit like that deserves to languish in a dungeon forever," Clive said.

"You are such a design snob, Clive," Moira said.

"Yes, I am. Someone has to try to set some aesthetic standards for this great city of ours. Tough job, I'll grant you. Ah, Trevor, there you are. Nice sale. We at McClintoch and Swain are consumed with envy."

"What? Oh, thank you, Clive," Trevor said, before he hastily moved on to the next room.

"What's eating him, I wonder?" Clive asked. "It's not every day I hand out a compliment. I expected him to be revoltingly cheerful, if not downright triumphant about the whole thing, and he just looks kind of nervous. Maybe he's having a fight with his girlfriend. Attractive one, that. What's her name? Balsam or something?"

"Willow, you twit," Moira said, giving him a dig in the ribs.

"Well, I knew it was a tree."

"Is that Desmond Crane?" Rob said. "The lawyer who competes with Baldwin to get the most slime off on technicalities? It is Crane, isn't it?"

It was. On Dez's arm was his wife Leanna, who was tipsy as usual. The two lawyers' dislike for each other both in court and out didn't stop Blair from inviting him and Dez from showing up.

"I can't believe you've brought me here," Rob said. Usually he is very amiable about the social events I ask him to accompany me to, finding something interesting in all of them to talk about later. Now he sounded grumpy.

"I came to that Christmas party at one of your police pal's home, you know, the one where the host looked down the front of my dress the whole time, and some young kid drank so much he almost puked on my suede shoes. You were perhaps thinking I would accompany you again this year?"

"Great party," he said, giving my waist a little squeeze. "I think I'll go and have some shrimp if that sleazeball left any for the rest of us."

Dez steered his wife over to the writing cabinet, where they both looked at it carefully, or at least he did. "Nice," he said to Trevor, sending a cheery wave in my direction. For some reason I expected more than that, Dez being almost as competitive and arrogant as Blair. Perhaps he was determined not to show his disappointment at being bested by Baldwin. So unperturbed by the Mackintosh being in his rival's hands was Dez that I found myself wondering if the telephone call to Trevor at the very moment Blair was deciding whether or not to purchase the cabinet had been faked, with someone else entirely on the line. Faked or not it had had the desired effect on Blair. There didn't seem to be any way that I could ask Dez, and it didn't really make any difference anyway. Blair was going to buy the cabinet that day no matter what it cost. I was also very curious to know what Blair had paid for it, but I didn't know how to ask that question directly either, and my subtle attempts to find out from both Trevor and Blair had been roundly ignored.

In truth, most people paid the writing cabinet scant attention, being more interested in the food, drink, and company. It caught my eye often, though. There was something about it that bothered me, a feeling that I put down to my ambivalence on the subject of ownership of such a beautiful piece. While I'd love to sell just about anybody an antique for any reason at all, should my advice be asked, it will always be to buy something you like and something you'll use. You wouldn't catch me slapping my laptop and coffee mug down on a one-point-five million writing cabinet, believe me. Perhaps more importantly, while Blair was obviously enthralled and that was nice, I always feel that something of this quality, created by the hand of a master like Mackintosh, really belongs to everyone, not just one bazillionaire. I was hoping that after he'd had it for a while, Blair could be persuaded to donate it to an art museum. I was sure there would be many who would prize it.

One who clearly was not only interested but also covetous was the curator of the furniture galleries at the Cottingham Museum. Blair was either rubbing Stanfield Roberts's nose in it, since the Cottingham was probably eager to have such a piece in its collection, or he was genuinely pleased to show off his acquisition to a man who would certainly agree with me that the Mackintosh belonged in a museum. Stanfield had barely had time to blurt out the required social niceties in the entrance hall before he rocketed right over to the writing cabinet. He posed, there is no other word for it, looking very artistic and interested, his chin resting on his left hand, while the elbow was supported by his right. Finally, after a few minutes of contemplation, he approached the cabinet and had a much closer look. After examining it carefully, he stepped back with a very slight smile on his face. I didn't know whether this meant he was thrilled to be in the presence of such a wonderful piece, or something else. I do know that Trevor watched his every move and gesture.

"I'd love to have a closer look, privately," Stanfield said to Blair who approached him. "I wouldn't dream of doing it now, with everyone here, but might I come over some time this week?"

"Of course," Blair said. "You and your colleagues at the Cottingham are always welcome to study my collection." For a man who had pulled himself up by his bootstraps, this must have been a rather important moment for Blair.

"I look forward to it," Stanfield said, but for some reason he looked amused rather than pleased.

As the evening wore on, Leanna, who by this time was really plastered, managed to weave her way over to Blair and immediately spilled some champagne on his jacket, which clearly annoyed him. I can't say I've ever seen Leanna completely sober, but then I only ran into her at events like this. It may well be that she is sober on numerous occasions, but this wasn't one of them. Clive liked to call her Leanna the Lush—not to her face of course.

As Blair tried to sponge his jacket off with a cocktail napkin, Leanna leaned over and whispered something in his ear, then started pulling on his arm. Blair shook his head, but she persisted, finally leading him over to the writing cabinet. She peered at everything, opening and closing the doors and the drawers before Dez came and dragged her away. After she left, Blair stood stock-still staring at the cabinet for a full minute, I'd say, and then, his face dark as thunder, he went over to speak to Stanfield Roberts of the Cottingham. Both men went over to the cabinet for a brief consultation, before Blair quickly left the room, as the party rolled on without him.

I was standing with Rob, Clive, and Moira in the crowd not far from the cabinet when Blair returned. He was carrying an axe. He walked up to the writing cabinet, swung the blade, and in a few short seconds had hacked it into several pieces. Jaws dropped, hands flew to mouths, and several people started heading for the door. "Wylie!" Blair shouted, looking around the room. "Where are you, you bastard?"

But Trevor was nowhere to be seen. Blair then turned his attention elsewhere. "You!"—he pointed right at me—"are either a crook, too, or incompetent. Either way, you're finished, babe!" He looked for a moment as if he were going to come right over waving the axe, but Rob stepped between us. Instead, Blair picked up the biggest piece of the furniture, walked to the French doors that opened on to a patio and began to throw the furniture out piece by piece.

"Outta here!" Clive said.

"I'm with you," Rob replied.

"Just a minute . . ." I said, looking at the furniture as it flew out the door, but Clive grabbed one arm and Rob the other, and together they hustled me out the front door.

One thing we all agreed on, as we sat around my dining room table eating the lovely dinner Rob had cooked, was that as parties went, that one was a dud. All of them, Rob, Moira, and even Clive tried to cheer me up, being the lovely people they are. They were very solicitous, but in a rather irritating way. "You can't be right every time, hon," Rob said in a soothing tone, after I'd gone on and on about it. What bothered me most, as I told them at least a hundred times, was that several of our customers were at the party. What, I asked, would they think?

"He didn't give you the time you needed to make a proper assessment," Moira said. "You told him it wasn't definite."

Surprisingly only Clive, who is usually the bane of my

existence even if I'm still in business with him, and who spends most of his time, I'm convinced, trying to come up with ways to annoy me, said anything remotely comforting. "I'd like to see a piece of that wood," he said after a couple of glasses of wine.

"Why would you want to do that?" Moira asked.

"I didn't get a chance to get close to it at the party, what with everybody else drooling over it. I'm just wondering," he said.

"Wondering what?" Moira said. "And no one was drooling over the furniture. They were drooling over the oysters and champagne, and jockeying for position with the celebs, just as you were."

"Stanfield Roberts was drooling. I'm thinking Lara doesn't make a lot of bad calls, except perhaps divorcing me. I'd just like to see the wood for myself." Considering Clive stood to lose as much as I did if our customers were put off by Baldwin's accusation, I thought this comment was very generous of him.

"Do you think Baldwin destroyed the real deal thinking it was a fake?" Rob said. "That would be a bad mistake to make, wouldn't it? I mean, I don't know anything about antique furniture, but it looked good to me."

"It was a beautiful piece of furniture, and even if it was a fake. Blair shouldn't have done that. And if it was real Charles Rennie Mackintosh, he should be charged with something for destroying it, shouldn't he?" Moira asked. She directed her question to Rob, who as a Mountie is supposed to know this kind of thing.

"I'm not sure," Rob said. "He owned it, and I don't know of any heritage legislation that would protect it under the circumstances. He sure could be made a fool of, though, and

Lara would be exonerated. We would make certain of that. But is that what you're saying, Clive?"

"I don't know what I'm saying," Clive said. "I guess I'm thinking maybe we were a little hasty in dragging Lara out of there before she could get a closer look. I'd just like to see a piece of that thing for myself."

I decided that it was still a good idea to have a look at a piece of wood, which is why I found myself early the next morning hiding out in a hole in the cedar hedge surrounding Blair Baldwin's home. I'd been there when Baldwin had chosen one of his six cars for the day. He had this turntable device in his huge garage, so that he pressed a button until the right car was facing out. It made me think of an aircraft carrier, and I can't even imagine how much this all cost. In any event, he'd chosen a silver Porsche and driven off in a spray of gravel. A few minutes later the maid had swept the patio where large chunks of furniture had been tossed the previous night. They weren't there now. The yard was the picture of good gardening practice. There wasn't a blade of grass out of place, and just about no chance the gardener had missed a piece of furniture.

There was, however, a large Dumpster at the back, and I was formulating a plan that entailed a dash across the yard, or perhaps a dodge up from the laneway behind, followed by an athletic scaling of the Dumpster, whereupon I would find a piece of writing cabinet right on top and make my getaway. It was a ridiculous idea, I know, and I felt like a complete idiot hunched over in the hedge. I also had no idea what I would say if someone in the house saw me and called the police.

While I stood there gamely trying to convince myself I could do this, a large disposal truck came up the drive, picked up the Dumpster, and emptied it into the back. I heard the compactor come on, and despaired. Trevor's writing cabinet might or might not be a fake. I would never know. I could have cried. Instead, I stood there, crouched over in the branches, watching as the Dumpster backed down the drive.

And then there it was: a chunk of wood, thrown free, perhaps as the Dumpster had been tipped. I crashed through the hedge, sprinted to the driveway, grabbed the wood and within minutes was coming through the back door to McClintoch & Swain.

"Is that new perfume? You smell like a Christmas tree," Clive said. "And did you know you have scratches on your face?"

"Writing cabinet," I said, holding my treasure aloft.

"Well done!" he said. "A good-sized piece, too, with the lock, no less. Turn on that light!"

"Mahogany," I said.

"Yes," he agreed. "Old wood. Beautiful finish. All hand work. Rather well done."

"Yes. Master craftsman, for sure."

"Too bad about that lock," he said.

"It is," I agreed.

"When do you figure it was manufactured? Maybe fifteen minutes ago?"

"Something like that." I was trying to keep my tone light, but in truth I was absolutely mortified.

"Amazed you'd not see that," he said. "You must have been feeling really pressured by Blair Bazillionaire, or was it charmed by Trevor the Rogue?"

"I checked the lock," I replied. "I don't know how I missed it."

Clive was silent for a moment. "It's okay," he said finally, patting my shoulder. "We'll survive."

I really hate it when Clive is nice to me, and the only person I could think to take it out on was Trevor, who surely deserved it. "Trevor had lots of time to look at the lock. I'm going to take this over to Scot Free for a little chat."

"Are you going to hit him with it?"

"Maybe. After that I am going to get Blair his money back, on the assumption Trevor won't do it willingly, and that Blair will be too proud to ask."

"Be careful," he said. "This is bad enough as it is."

The door to Scot Free was open, and the bell jangled, but Trevor did not show his face. Perhaps he'd seen me coming and quite correctly surmised that I wasn't happy. I went partway up the stairs to the second floor and called his name, but silence greeted me.

I headed straight for the office, had a quick look around to make sure I was alone and then started through Trevor's desk. There had to be something there that would tell me what I needed to know. You would never call Trevor a tidy person, nor a particularly efficient record-keeper, but he at least kept his customs forms and shipping documents in one file and his diary seemed up-to-date. By referencing the dates of his trip to Scotland, and some bills of lading later, I was able to find the documents for a large shipment from Glasgow. There were dozens of items listed, and I was just making my way through them, when I noticed an envelope, unstamped, addressed to me. I was about to open it when I heard a creak in the ceiling over my head.

"Trevor, you little worm!" I said, heading for the stairs. But it wasn't Trevor. It was Mr. Bicycle Clips peering over the railing, his glasses now held together at the bridge of his nose with what looked to be duct tape. "What are you doing here creeping about?" I demanded.

"The same thing you are," he replied belligerently.

"And what might that be?" I said.

"Snooping around," he said. "I could see you from up here, going through the stuff in the desk."

"I was looking for this," I said, holding up the envelope. "It's addressed to me. I told Trevor I'd pick it up."

The man had the good graces at least to look embarrassed. "You took a long time finding it," he said, finally.

"That's because Trevor didn't leave it where he said he would," I replied, compounding my lie without so much as a qualm. "Now where is Trevor and why are you snooping around?"

"I have no idea where he is," the man said. "I'm just looking around. I like this shop."

"You were eavesdropping when I was here last," I said. "I don't believe you."

"I don't believe you either," he said.

"I'm calling the police," I said, turning and walking toward the office.

"I'm just trying to help my grandmother," he said.

"Your grandmother?" I said, my voice dripping with disbelief.

"Honest," he said. "It belonged—belongs!—to my grandmother. See," he added, pulling out his wallet. "I have a photo of her with it." I looked at the picture he proffered. It was the Mackintosh, and there was a very nice looking older woman standing beside it. "She wasn't completely, you know—she suffered from dementia, and that slime Trevor Wylie sweet-talked her into selling it to him before anyone could stop her. She wasn't ready to sell and didn't remember what she had. Trevor had a truck backed up to her door within an hour. He knew exactly what he had, and he paid her much, much less than it was worth. She didn't have a receipt or anything, and he paid cash, but she thought he was from Toronto, even though he sounded Scottish, and she knew his name was Trevor. We can't afford a private investigator, so I flew over and here I am. I thought if I explained about my grandmother he'd reconsider. She needs the money. It was to pay for her care. I don't know whether you are in this scam with Wylie, but if you are. . . ." He looked as if he were about to cry.

"I'm not," I said. "And I'm sorry about your grandmother. The truth is, though, that she may have done as well as she could on the deal. It was a fake. I suppose you know that."

"A fake?" he said. "It is not."

"Yes," I said. "It was."

"It is!" he said. "What do you mean by was? Don't you mean is?"

"I mean it's gone. It has been destroyed. Whatever it was, it is no longer."

"No!" he exclaimed. "You can't be serious."

"I'm afraid I am. I'm sorry about your grandmother. Trevor shouldn't have done that, but it wasn't the genuine article."

"But it was!" he said again.

"Several people were fooled by it," I said. "Several of us," I added. I was going to have to learn to live with this.

"We won't know now, will we? Who destroyed it?" he said.

"A man by the name of Blair Baldwin. Trevor sold it to him, and I guess he was a little peeved when he found out it was a fake."

"I'll kill him," the man said.

"Kill whom?" I said. Like Trevor, his s's sounded more like *sh*, which reminded me of Sean Connery once again, but there the resemblance stopped. He was neither old nor young, maybe forty, rather thin and pale, and in his khaki pants complete with bicycle clips, which added a comical twist, he looked kind of harmless. I didn't think he was the killing sort.

"Maybe both of them," he said. "Or maybe not." He looked completely dejected.

"I'm Lara," I said. "I really am sorry about your grandmother and this whole business." *You have no idea how sorry*, I thought.

"Percy," he said after a moment's hesitation. "Are you going to open it?" he asked pointing at the envelope.

There was a note inside scribbled on lined paper. *Hen*— the note began. I was liking this hen business less and less all the time. *I know you're mad at me. But I've had a spot of bother lately, and lo and behold there's a way out. I'm not going to let this opportunity pass me by. Don't bother looking for me. I've too much of a head start. Cheers, Trev*

"What does he say?" Percy asked.

"I have no idea what he's talking about," I said. "But it is very irritating. I think we need to find him. Did you look closely upstairs?"

"He's not there. Nobody's here. Can I read it?" he asked, pointing at the letter.

"Be my guest."

"Is this all there is?" he asked when he'd finished. "Nothing else in the envelope?"

"Nothing," I said. "He's here somewhere you know. How carefully did you look upstairs?"

"There's nobody up there," he replied. "Anyway, that letter sounds as if he's taken off to parts unknown."

"He's here," I repeated. "Unless you broke in here."

"I did not!" Percy said indignantly. "The door was unlocked."

"So he's here," I said. "Believe me, antique dealers do not leave their stores unattended, even for two minutes. I mean stuff gets stolen even when we're there."

"Maybe he wanted it to look as if he were coming right back," Percy said.

"He hasn't left," I said, pointing to the envelope with my name on it. "See, no stamps. He'd have mailed this first."

"I thought you said he asked you to pick it up," Percy said.

I hate it when I trip over my own lies. "Neither of us is exactly innocent. Come on," I said. Percy looked chagrined and meekly followed me up the stairs. There we opened every seaman's chest and blanket box, armoire and credenza, or at least I did. I peered behind the large pieces, under the beds. No Trevor.

While I was doing this, Percy kept opening and closing drawers in a most annoying way, and then rechecking every place I looked. "He's not hiding in a drawer, Percy," I said.

"Oh," he said. "I know. I was just checking for clues."

"Downstairs," I sighed. We did the same search on the main floor. Still no Trevor.

"I told you," Percy said. "He's not here."

"I expect there's a basement," I said.

"Okay," he sighed. "I'm game if you are."

The door that led to the basement was locked, but it didn't take long to find the key in Trevor's desk. A nasty open staircase with no railing led down to a rather dark and dingy place. I was a woman on a mission, though, so down I went, followed closely by Percy. The place was just generally unpleasant, damp and vaguely sewerlike, and it looked pretty empty except for a worktable with a broken chair on it, several mousetraps in the corners, and cobwebs here and there. I was regretting this excursion very much, but wasn't going to admit it. There was nothing of interest in the first room, nor in the second, even behind the furnace. In the third room, the light switch didn't work.

"I don't want to go any farther," Percy whined. "I don't think he'd stay down here. Anyway, it smells bad. Let's go back."

"Oh, for heaven's sake, Percy, it's just a basement. There was a flashlight on the shelf in the first room. Go and get it." He did what he was told. The flashlight wasn't much to speak of, but I stepped into the room anyway and swung the beam around.

Trevor was there, not that I got any satisfaction from being right. I may not have known what that self-serving gibberish in Trevor's letter was all about, but I was reasonably sure that having an axe buried in what was left of his skull was not what he'd meant by head start.

Chapter 2

My family traces its roots in Orkney back almost a thousand years to one Bjarni, son of Harald, also known as Bjarni the Wanderer. Bjarni came from a good family in Norway and journeyed to Orkney during the time of Earl Sigurd the Stout, who gave him land in Tankerness. Bjarni, you see, was Earl Sigurd's man, a warrior as well as a farmer. In Orkney, in those days, there were three social classes: the wealthy and powerful earls who inherited their estates; free farmers and warriors of which Bjarni was one; and thralls or serfs who worked the land. Bjarni spent the winters in Orkney, but every summer, he joined Sigurd's raiding parties to Caithness, the Hebrides, and as far away as Ireland. They were looking for booty, of course, but also for land, trying to extend the power of the earls of Orkney throughout the British Isles. There's a story about Sigurd, that his Irish mother, a sorceress, made him a magical raven banner: whoever carried the banner would die, but victory would go to the man before whom it flew. It was in Ireland that Sigurd died, and it's said he himself was carrying the banner.

True or not, it was then Bjarni's fortunes changed. Sigurd had four sons in all, but one of them, who would later be Earl Thorfinn the Mighty, one of the greatest earls of Orkney, was still a lad at the time. The other three, Sumarlidi, Brusi, and Einar took over Orkney when Sigurd died. They were a fractious lot, especially Einar, known as Wry-Mouth, and not disposed to share the land equally. As often happened in those days the competition turned bloody.

Rivalries both within families and without were intense in those days, and power changed hands often, making it rather easy to find oneself on the wrong side of a political struggle. And so it was with Bjarni. Bjarni sided with Earl Brusi in the dispute over the control of Orkney and killed Thorvald the Stubborn, one of Einar's men, in the struggle. While Bjarni offered to make a settlement over the killing of Thorvald, and to hold a great feast in the earl's honor, Einar, a hard man, was not disposed to accept it. Men of goodwill interceded on Bjarni's behalf, but to no avail. Einar's men came for him and burned down his house, but Bjarni, having been warned of the attack, was able to make his escape with the help of some like-minded men.

A family conference was held and there was much discussion about what was to be done. Finally Oddi, Bjarni's brother spoke. "I'm not blaming you for what you've done, Bjarni. Thorvald the Stubborn deserved what he got. But it seems to me if you stay around here, your head and your shoulders will soon be parted. I'm thinking a voyage of some distance and some duration might be in order here. I say we take two longboats, and some men who are willing, and head for Scotland. It may be that those who care for Sigurd's young lad, Thorfinn, can intercede on our behalf with Einar, persuade him to have a change of heart. In the meantime, we will be out of harm's way. We won't be the first to leave Orkney because of Einar. Nor will we be the last."

All agreed that this was the best course of action. And so it was that Bjarni, Oddi, and some of their kin, including the skald or "poet," Svein the Wiry set off in two longboats on a voyage that would take some of them farther than they ever dreamed.

You are thinking I am making this up, which I can certainly understand, but you'll find the stories of Sigurd the Stout, his sons Brusi and Einar, Sumarlidi and Thorfinn if you look. The lives of all of them are there for anyone to see in the pages of the Orkneyinga Saga. As I've said, our story is not inconsistent with the facts. True, you'll not be finding Bjarni the Wanderer or his brother Oddi in the saga. No, you'll not be finding them.

You DIDN'T NEED a degree in criminology to guess the number one murder suspect in the death of Trevor Wylie. After all, Blair Bazillionaire had been swinging an axe about in front of approximately seventy-five people, one of whom was the chief of police. Not that anything was said about an axe-murderer, mind you, that being evidence the police were keeping to themselves. It was suggested strongly to me that I do the same.

For a while, though, it seemed to me that I was spending as much time at the local police station as Blair was. Like Blair, I had to be fingerprinted. The police said it was to eliminate mine from the many at the scene, which made sense, I suppose, given my prints were all over just about everything, even a half-empty coffee cup I'd moved so that I could get at Trevor's files. Blair's prints were all over the same things mine were, with one unfortunate addition: the axe. Neither Blair nor the staff at his residence were able to produce the axe he'd so publicly used to chop up the furniture, so while it couldn't be proven definitely, it pretty much looked as if the same one had been used to chop up Trevor's head.

It looked open and shut as they say, and not good at all for Blair, and just about everything I said to Detective Ian Singh only made it worse.

"Take me through this," Singh said, after I'd explained that I'd gone to Scot Free to discuss Baldwin's purchase of the writing cabinet. "Baldwin was a good customer, and you went with him to Trevor Wylie's establishment to check out this desk that Baldwin wanted to buy."

"I met him there, yes."

"You thought it was genuine, the desk, I mean."

"I thought it might be," I said, reluctantly.

"And Baldwin bought it on your say so."

"I guess so." This was going to be really painful. "I did point out I'd like to do more research."

"And Baldwin later found it to be a fake."

"Yes."

"Did you tell him it was?"

"No. I don't know who told him."

"But it was a fake."

"I think so. I did manage to get a piece of it, after it was chopped up, and had a good look. The lock used was not consistent with the supposed age of the cabinet. It was brand-new, in fact." I really hoped he didn't ask me how I got that piece of wood. I still had the scratches.

"How much was the desk thing worth?"

"Under the circumstances not much," I said. "A few thousand, maybe. It was a nice piece regardless of who made it."

"Let me rephrase the question. How much would it have been worth if it was genuine?"

"A similar one sold for a million and a half not that long ago." Trevor had been right about that. I'd checked it myself later.

Singh's eyebrows went up. "So, in your opinion, Baldwin, thinking it was genuine, might have paid well over a million for it."

"I guess so. I don't know, though. I left before they discussed price."

"I'd like to ask you a few questions about your relationship with Baldwin."

"He was a longtime customer, at least ten years."

"He bought a lot of merchandise from you over those ten years?"

"Yes."

"How did he normally pay?"

"What?"

"How did he pay for this merchandise?"

"The usual way. Check, credit card, cash."

"How often did he pay cash?"

"I can't recall. From time to time, I guess, for the smaller purchases."

"Can you recall the largest purchase he paid cash for?"

"Not really."

"Would he have paid, say, a hundred thousand in cash?"

"Hardly. We don't carry that kind of merchandise often. He might give us a couple of hundred dollars in cash, on occasion, maybe four hundred? Anything over that, and he wrote a check or paid by card. Why are you asking this?"

"Just part of our investigation," Singh said.

"Surely it's academic. He couldn't have paid cash for the writing cabinet," I said. "Could he?"

Singh didn't answer. Instead, he went on to ask about the

evening at Baldwin's, which we went over in excruciating detail, and then back to my unfortunate discovery of the body.

"The shop was empty when you got there," he said.

"It was. No, it wasn't, but I thought it was. There was a customer upstairs."

"So you waited."

"Yes."

"As did this customer wait with you?"

"Yes."

"And then you both went looking for him."

"Yes. The shop was open. I thought Trevor had to be there somewhere. You don't just go out and leave the merchandise for all takers. For one thing, there have been a number of robberies at antique stores around here. So far there have been no arrests."

Singh ignored the jibe. "And this customer, what did you say his name was? Percy?"

"Yes. He looked for Trevor, too."

"Percy who?"

"I don't know. We didn't get that far."

"So, you and this fellow with whom you are on a first-name-only basis decided to look in the basement?"

"Yes."

"Isn't that a little odd?"

"As I said, Trevor had to be there. I mean, what if he'd had an accident and fallen down there?"

"An accident," he repeated, and he almost smiled. "And this Percy came downstairs with you."

"I didn't want to go by myself," I said. That was partly true, I suppose.

"And when you found Trevor, then what?"

"I ran upstairs and called nine-one-one."

"And Percy?"

"He ran outside. I don't think he was feeling well." Actually, he'd made little retching sounds and dashed up the stairs.

"I don't suppose you know where Percy might be found," Singh said.

"I told you already that I don't. He said he'd flown in from Scotland recently. That's all I know."

"But you saw him in the shop before, the day you went to look at the desk I believe you said."

"Yes. Is he a suspect?"

"We have only your word that he exists," Singh said. "But on the assumption your story is true, he would of course be of interest to us. You did say he was there when you got there?"

"Yes." I was certain Percy hadn't killed Trevor. He was such a timid-looking man. Furthermore, killing Trevor wasn't going to get his Granny's writing cabinet back. I hadn't seen him at the party either, so how would he have known about the axe business, and how would he get the axe? I said none of this to Singh.

"Did you see Wylie socially?" Singh asked.

"There's a bunch of shop owners in the neighborhood who get together for drinks from time to time, maybe once a month. We talk about issues affecting the area and whine about business and stuff. Both Trevor and I are, were, part of it. Trevor liked The Dwarfie Stane. It's a bar named for some tomb in Scotland. Maybe you know it. It's the place that has a hundred different single malt scotches, or something like that. We often get together there. Trevor was working his way through all one hundred. Other than that, I'd see him

every now and then at parties. We had some clients in common."

"Did you like Wylie?"

"He was very charming," I said. "And I liked him well
enough up until that cabinet turned out to be a fake."

"About this friendly little note Trevor left for you,"
Singh said. "What did you think the note meant?"

"I have no idea. I thought he was just being a jerk."

"Wylie could be a jerk, could he?"

"I thought so."

"But you spent a lot of time with him."

"No, I didn't. I told you already that I saw him only occasionally."

"Your fingerprints are on every piece of furniture in the
place."

"I was looking for him."

"In the furniture?"

"Yes, in the furniture. I thought he was hiding from me."

"You didn't by any chance receive a—what shall we call
it?—a commission on the sale of this desk?"

"I did not!" I said.

"Would you not perhaps have felt entitled to a . . .
um . . . commission? It was on your say so that Baldwin
bought the desk."

"I did not bring Baldwin to Trevor. Trevor called him all
by himself. If there were to be a finder's fee, it would only be
paid if I brought Baldwin to Trevor. Even then, I would not
have asked for a commission. Baldwin was a good client. He
asked for my help from time to time, and I gave it, free."

"I guess it was worth what he paid for it," Singh said. I
took that to be payback for my remark about the lack of arrests, and I suppose I deserved it. "So no discreet palming of

an envelope filled with cash? A little undeclared and there-fore tax-free income?" he said. "If so, I'd report it now if I were you."

"There was absolutely no commission, tax-free or other-wise," I said. "Nor was it expected."

"You have received nothing of any sort from Wylie?"

"I have not."

"Assuming what you say is true, you must have been just a little annoyed with Wylie yourself."

"I was," I said. "But I don't axe people, if that is what you are implying. Do I need my lawyer?"

"Up to you."

"You know what?" I said, rising from my chair. "I don't believe you can keep me here, and I'm tired of all these questions that imply I am a murderer, a liar, or a thief. So let's just say this discussion is over."

"Please sit down," he said. "Nobody is accusing you of anything. Did anyone else see this Percy?"

"There was just the two of us there. Blair might remem-ber him because he was there when Blair and I first went to look at the cabinet. Just a minute: there was another person there, too, that first time, a rather unlikely-looking person to be interested in antiques. He had a big dog, a Doberman."

"A Doberman? Was this strange-looking person about the same height as the dog and maybe as wide?"

"Yes," I said. "You know him?"

"I might," Singh said. "You do meet the most unusual people." He made a note on the pad in front of him. "If this man with the dog is who I think it is, then you really keep bad company, Ms. McClintoch."

"I wasn't the one keeping company with this person," I said.

"I suppose," he said.

"I'm leaving now," I said rising from my chair and heading for the door.

"I require some of that free advice of yours," he said to my back.

"I guess whatever advice I'd give you will be worth what you pay for it then," I retorted, but I stopped my retreat.

"There is no record of a transaction between Baldwin and Wylie," Singh continued.

"What are you saying?" I said.

"I'm saying it's not just Percy that's missing. No check has cleared Baldwin's bank accounts, at least not the bank accounts we know about, nor has there been a significant deposit in the order of magnitude we're talking about here, in Wylie's. There isn't a credit card transaction on any of the cards we can find for Baldwin either. Wylie had about eighty dollars on him when he died. We've searched his house and the shop. No cash."

"So if Baldwin hadn't yet paid for it, why did he get so annoyed about the fake?" I asked. "Or are you saying he had other accounts, offshore or something?"

"I need you to go with one of my forensics people to look at Wylie's records," he said. I said nothing. There was obviously no point in asking a question, because Singh had already demonstrated he wasn't for answering any of them. "Forensic accountant, that is," he added.

"Baldwin couldn't have paid cash, could he?" I said. "That's what you were getting at when you asked how Blair paid for merchandise. It would be way too much."

"We need you to identify the records pertaining to this desk thing. We can't find any record for it, either."

"It's probably not called a desk," I said.

"That would be why we need your help," Singh said. "You cannot be compelled to assist, but perhaps you might like to do so."

"I might not," I said.

"My mistake," he said. "I assumed given your relationship with a fellow law enforcement professional . . ."

"What has my relationship with Rob Luczka have to do with it?" But he had me. I could hear Rob's speech now, something along the lines of how honest citizens needed to come forward to assist police in their investigations or we would all go to hell in a hand basket or something. "Okay," I said. "When?"

"How about right now?" Singh said.

About thirty minutes later I found myself sitting once again at Trevor's desk, going through his papers. This time I wasn't snooping, or rather I was now snooping officially, in the company of a policewoman by the name of Anna Chan. Chan was an accountant as well as a police officer, and she struck me as rather good at both.

"I can't find any reference to a desk in these documents," she said.

"That's because it's a writing cabinet," I said. "Or rather it was a writing cabinet. A desk, well, we all know what a desk is. A writing cabinet has doors that you open to reveal the work surface and the drawers. This one had beautiful inlaid work, leaded glass. It was really lovely. So we'd be looking for a different listing."

"So can you find it?" she asked.

The office looked pretty much the way it had when I'd left it to find the elusive Percy upstairs. I handed Anna the relevant files right away. I had, after all, been looking at them before.

"You found those rather fast," she said, with a hint of suspicion in her voice.

"They were right on the top of the desk," I said. "Trevor must have been working with them when . . . you know." I glanced toward the basement door.

"I've checked the declared value for customs," she said in a disapproving tone a few minutes later. "There is nothing listed anywhere close to a million dollars. I suppose our customs officials are concentrating on finding terrorists and weapons, not furniture that is seriously undervalued."

"That doesn't make Trevor a criminal," I said. "The reason this was supposed to be worth as much as it was rested entirely on the claim that it was by one of the masters of the Arts and Crafts movement, Charles Rennie Mackintosh. Trevor, when he bought it, might have wanted it to be Mackintosh, but he wouldn't necessarily have known that it was. He would have to do his research. So he would have valued it at what he paid for it, which was probably a decent sum for a writing cabinet, but a pittance for Mackintosh. People take chances on this kind of thing all the time. It doesn't make them dishonest."

"Tell that to the poor sod he ripped off," she said.

"Not entirely fair," I said. "Trevor did his research. The owner didn't." I felt a stab of sympathy for the nice old woman with dementia in Percy's photograph, but still I continued. "Trevor took a chance. He paid to ship it. If it wasn't what he thought it might be, he'd be out a lot of money. If you're going to sell something like this, then maybe you have to do some work to find out about it. If you don't, then people prepared to take a chance may be the winners. I wouldn't knowingly rip somebody off, but I might take a chance on something, and win, and I wouldn't be too happy if the owner came back to me and claimed I'd ripped him off. Now let's have a look at all this stuff."

"He seems to have done better shipping back to Scotland," she said a few minutes later.

"We ship all over the world. I can only assume Trevor did the same."

"For your sake I hope you have this kind of business. This one is valued at just under a million bucks. It's a chair. It must have been some chair!"

"Wow! Let me see." I looked at the paperwork she showed me. "I guess Trevor was doing better than I thought."

"Not exactly," she said, pulling out another file. "Looks to me as if he shipped it but he only got a commission, just under ten thousand, plus shipping and handling. So that means he sold it for someone else, I presume."

"I guess so."

"Would that be unusual?"

"Not unprecedented. We take some pieces on consignment from time to time. The markup is usually pretty good."

"Would one percent or so be considered good in your business?"

"For consignment, no, but the percentage would be lower on a high-ticket item."

"But not that low."

"I guess not."

A few minutes later Anna spoke again. "Baldwin," she said. "Why am I not surprised?"

"Baldwin what?"

"It was Baldwin's million-dollar chair. He cashed a check for nine hundred and fifty thousand, and paid Baldwin, less the small commission and expenses."

"Blair had a chair worth nine hundred and fifty thousand? Not from me."

"Too bad."

"I'll say. Let me see." It looked to me as if Anna were right. The chair was marked as museum quality, which it would have to have been. The merchandise was delivered to a dealer in Glasgow. There was a copy of both checks in the file.

"Is there really such a thing as a nine-hundred-and-fifty-thousand-dollar chair in real life?" she asked.

"Obviously, there is. Not in my league. I helped Blair buy an Antoni Gaudi chair for something over a hundred thousand once."

"That's nowhere near this one. Name one chair that would be worth that much."

"King Tut's throne?" I said. I was being facetious of course, but I was also making a point.

"You found that desk thing yet?" she said.

"Not yet." In fact, it took a couple of hours going through Trevor's files. I'd known Trevor for years, but never this intimately. I felt as if I were going through his underwear drawer. To make matters worse, I couldn't keep my eyes off the door to the basement, and half expected Trevor's ghost to come floating past. It was not a pleasant experience. I tried to concentrate.

Trevor had specialized in Scottish antiques, obviously, given his background and the name of his store, and when I'd first known him he'd gone to Scotland at least three times a year. In the past year, however, he'd gone only once, and that was about six months earlier. He'd shipped back a container of furniture at that time, which had arrived about three months before. There wasn't anything specifically referred to as a writing cabinet in that shipment, but there was something I was reasonably certain was it, a lacquered mahogany cupboard. The dimensions were about right. Its value was listed as $15,000 U.S. I pointed it out to Chan.

"You think this is it?" she said.

"I think so. There isn't anything else that qualifies."

"Nice markup if Wylie got over a million for it."

"I guess he hadn't been doing too well financially," I said. "Up until the transaction with Baldwin."

"Why would you think that?" she said.

"He only made one trip this year to Scotland, which would indicate he wasn't selling enough to make another trip."

"Hmmm," she said. Another police officer not inclined to answer my questions. When I thought about it, though, I realized that wasn't right. I'd had to check invoices and receipts as well, and he wasn't doing too badly. He didn't have any employees, just minded the shop himself, and while the rent in the neighborhood was considerable, as I very well knew, he'd managed to sell a decent amount of merchandise.

"I wonder what this is," I said aloud a few minutes later.

"What?" she said.

"Another shipment from Scotland about a month later. It's only one piece, though."

"And that would be unusual because?"

"I don't know," I said. "I suppose it just didn't make the container, for some reason. It's expensive to ship one piece all by itself, that's all." But that wasn't really it. This shipment was for one black cabinet, valued at $10,000 U.S. "I guess this one could be the writing cabinet, too. It got here about eight weeks ago. That would have given him a few weeks to get it out of customs, do the research, and approach Baldwin. I'm sorry, but I think it could be either of these."

"If you had to choose one?"

"I don't know. Have you found receipts or invoices for this trip? There might be more information there."

"Wylie did keep all the paperwork for that trip in one file. Let me see. Here," she said, a few minutes later. "A receipt from an antique shop on George's Square in Glasgow called J.A. Macdonald and Sons Antiques, for the right amount, and it refers to it as a lacquer cupboard."

"Let's see," I said. "This looks like it, and you're right, when you do the currency conversion, it's about fifteen thousand dollars. Is there something for the other one?"

"Not that I can find," she said. "Hold on. It's in another file. This one is for someone by the name of, well, I can't read the name, it's handwritten, but the address is, are you ready for this? St. Margaret's Hope. Where do you think that is?"

"I have no idea. I think that has to be the one, though. Percy, the man Detective Singh does not believe exists, said the cabinet was purchased from his grandmother, and the first one we found was purchased from an antique dealer. I wonder if St. Margaret's Hope is near Glasgow. So my vote is with the second one. It's called a cabinet, for one thing, and I don't think Trevor would have waited four months to contact Baldwin once he knew what he had."

"But he didn't have it, right? He would need some time to set up the scam?"

"Right," I said. "Something that should be said here is that there is a very real possibility that Trevor was fooled, too, that he was the victim of the scam and not its perpetrator."

"I don't think so," Chan said.

"Why not? You don't know that," I protested. "Have a look around. The furniture in this place is good quality. It's genuine. It's not overpriced. It's not inexpensive, but it's worth what you pay for it."

"I wouldn't know," she said.

"I would. There is nothing I can see here that indicates Trevor was a crook."

"Except the Mackintosh," she said.

I was trying to think of a suitable retort when Chan's cell phone rang. After a word or two, she told me that my statement was ready, and that Singh was wondering if I'd mind stopping by the station to sign it. "I will later," I replied. "A bunch of us are getting together at Trevor's favorite bar, The Dwarfie Stane, for a bit of a wake. I'll stop by after that." Chan relayed the message.

"You haven't told me why you're sure Trevor wasn't fooled along with me," I said.

"No," she said, and that was it.

The gang was already at the Stane when I got there. Mc-Clintoch & Swain was well represented, as we had a part-time employee, a student, to close up the shop. Clive came, as did Alex Stewart, our part-time employee and friend. Moira, who owns the Meller Spa came, too, looking perfect as usual. She was sporting a very chic haircut, very short all over. It suited her, even if the circumstances weren't the greatest. Moira's had some health problems, chemotherapy, in fact. Elena, the craft store owner was there, as was Kayleigh, who'd bought the linens shop a year earlier. A local restauranteur by the name of Kostas dropped by, as did several others I didn't know very well. Even Dan, who had once owned an independent bookstore in the area, showed up, back from his new home in Florida. I was very happy to see them all, particularly because not one person mentioned the affair of the fake Mackintosh, at least not at first.

The first round was on the house. We all had Highland Park Single Malt, Trevor's favorite. "Here's to Trevor Wylie," Rendall Sinclair, the publican, said. "He had his faults, but his choice of whisky wasn't one of them." It was a good toast, and kept the event from being too maudlin, and soon everyone was sharing their favorite story about Trevor. I decided that, under the circumstances, I wasn't about to contribute to this, but the tales, tall some of them, were funny, and I found myself warming to Trevor a little once again.

When I thought about it, though, all the stories had one thing in common. Elena was telling a story about how she'd been bested by Trevor in some business dealing or other. "I could have killed him," she concluded. "Oops! I didn't mean that." Everyone assured her they knew that, that it was just an expression.

"Why would anyone want to murder Trevor?" Dan said.

Clive opened his mouth to speak, but I gave him a look that should have turned him to stone. Moira added a jab in the ribs.

"Were you going to say something, Clive?" Dan asked.

"I was just going to suggest we order some snacks," Clive said. Moira smiled at me.

But that had been the nub of it, surely. Trevor, for all his charm, was always getting the better of people, always taking shortcuts of some kind at other people's expense, but doing it in such a way we all forgave him. Except for one person, whoever that might be. Trevor had taken his little escapades just one step too far, with someone who was not

THE ORKNEY SCROLL 47

only immune to his charm, but had a short fuse. Someone like Blair Bazillionaire.

As I listened in a rather subdued fashion to the conversations around me, I thought about Anna Chan's conviction that Trevor knew what he had, and her comment about his needing time to set up the scam. It occurred to me that I'd been seeing rather more of Trevor in the last couple of months than at any time previously. He'd regularly made dates at the bar for the shopkeeper's association we'd set up in the neighborhood, and in fact had to all intents and purposes become the leader of the group, which was fine with the rest of us. Dan the bookseller had done it for a while, but he'd closed up shop when one of the big chains had opened up nearby and retired to Florida. After that the group had languished until Trevor had taken an interest. Was there, I wondered, something more to Trevor's enthusiasm than met the eye? In other words, had he been setting me up for the two months since the second cabinet had arrived? I was losing my edge, charmed by a guy who looked like Sean Connery. Any warm feelings engendered by the wake evaporated. *I should sell my half of the business to Clive*, I thought. *I should follow Dan to Florida*.

The Dwarfie Stane was a very pleasant place, rather modern in design despite being named after some ancient tomb, with lots of comfortable chairs and alcoves, and a beautiful granite-topped bar with lots of mirror and chrome to show off the single malts, of which there were many. I had a sense that someone was watching me, and sure enough, sitting facing the bar but watching in the mirror was Detective Singh. I'd heard about police attending the funeral of a murder victim, but not the wake. This did not improve my mood any. This seemed rather tasteless of him to me, but then everything was making me crabby these days, something Clive and Rob had both pointed out to me. I walked right up to the bar, told Rendall I'd like to buy the next round, and then said, "Hello, Detective Singh. Off-duty are we?" He had a glass of something in front of him, but it might well have been soda, and a folded newspaper.

"Seen the late edition of the paper?" Singh said. I could tell that Rendall had not only heard, but was interested in the conversation.

"Not yet," I replied. He unfolded the newspaper to the top of the front page and slid it along the counter toward me. "Axe Murderer at Large," the headline screamed.

"Only one person other than our small team at the station knew about the axe," he said.

"Two, including Percy," I said. "I have told no one."

"The elusive Percy," he snorted. "Well, it doesn't matter now. If it did, you wouldn't be sitting here swigging single malt. You'd be down at the station with me."

At this point I just wanted to go home, but I went back to the group, not wanting to seem rude. As I sat there, who should come in but Percy himself. "Percy," I said, standing up. He turned at the sound of my voice, then sprinted back out the door. It took me a minute to climb over everybody, wedged as I was in the middle of a large sofa, and behind a long table, but as soon as I was able, I, too, was out the door and running down the street in the direction I thought he'd gone. I caught sight of his head a couple of times, but it was soon pretty clear I'd lost him. I made my way back slowly, peering into the shops that were still open, of which there were not many, and going into my own to say good night to Ben, our student. Detective Singh was standing at the door of the Stane when I got back.

"Lose somebody?" he said.

"Percy," I replied. "The guy who doesn't exist?"

"Really," Singh said. It wasn't a question. He didn't believe me.

"Yes, really," I replied

"How convenient," he said. "Just when I'm in the neighborhood."

"Come on! You can't help but have noticed he ran away when I called his name."

"Not that I saw," he said, returning to his seat at the bar. I decided it was time to go home and went to the bar to pay my tab.

"Lara," Rendall said, appearing from the back. "Call for you. You can take it my office. I'll show you the way."

That seemed a bit odd to me, given I have a cell phone, but I followed Rendall down a corridor and into a back room. "There's no phone call," he said. "I need your advice. First, that guy you went chasing after. He's been in here a fair bit. He was asking about you. He's Orcadian, and . . ."

"What's Orcadian?" I said.

"From Orkney. It's the name of the place that attracted him I'm sure. The Dwarfie Stane is a tomb on the island of Hoy in Orkney. He was also asking about a fellow Orcadian called Trevor Wylie."

"I thought Trevor was from Glasgow," I said.

"Not originally. He was born on the Mainland."

"The Mainland of what?"

"Mainland, Orkney."

"I'm not sure I know exactly where Orkney is," I said. "All I know is that wherever it is, Trevor was glad to have left it."

"Dull as dishwater is what he called it."

"That doesn't sound like Trevor."

"Aye. Perhaps I edited it for your delicate ears. Boring as shite is what he said."

"That sounds more like it. So where is Orkney?"

"Group of Scottish islands and too small a place for our Trevor. The thing is I told that fellow where to find Trevor. You don't think . . ."

"That he killed Trevor? No, I don't. He looked pretty harmless to me," I said. "His name is Percy, right?"

"That's not the name I recall. Arthur, that's what it was."

"Are you sure?" I said, but it was a stupid question. Like all good publicans, Rendall didn't forget a name.

"I'm pretty sure it was Arthur. Do you think I should tell the police?"

"I don't think it would help," I said. "Singh, the policeman at the bar, didn't believe there was anyone by the name of Percy at Trevor's place, and if you tell him the name is Arthur, he'll be really skeptical. But you decide. As far as I'm concerned, we never had this conversation."

"What conversation?" he said. "You're not worried he was asking who you are?"

"Not really. I'm just as suspicious of him as he is of me."

"I told him you owned an antique shop down the street. He seemed to be satisfied by that."

"Okay. It's not a secret. You wouldn't happen to know of a place called St. Margaret's Hope, would you?"

"Indeed, I do. Lovely little town on South Ronaldsay. You should visit Orkney some time."

"I just might do that," I said.

My day ended as it began, at the police station with Singh. I arrived there at the same time that Betsy Baldwin, Blair's ex-wife did. She, too, came to sign a statement and gave me a tight little smile. I'd always liked Betsy and was sorry when she and Blair parted. I didn't think it looked good for Blair that she was there.

In what I can only describe as a stroke of bad luck, our exit from the station coincided with the arrival of Blair, hand-cuffed and surrounded by dozens of reporters and cameras. The media was all over this one, in all its gore. Through the chaos, though, Blair saw me. "This is your fault," he hissed, as the crowd swept past. I noticed he hadn't called me "babe."

"I wonder how he knew about my statement," Betsy sighed. "I didn't want to give it, not that I had any choice. They knew."

"Sorry?"

"He blames me for his being pulled in for questioning, but I don't know how he'd know what I said," she replied.

"I think he was blaming me," I said. "He thinks I misled him on something."

"I'm sure he meant me," she said. "The police looked into his background and discovered I'd once called them about his violent behavior. He hit me, you know. More than once. That's why I left him."

"I had no idea," I said. "I'm sorry."

"That's why he didn't contest the divorce. I agreed to shut up about it, and he paid up big. Now, though, with the police all over this, I didn't have much of a choice. He has such a temper. There were times when I was afraid he was going to kill me, and for sure he hurt me a lot. Now maybe he has killed someone. I think my statement will be rather damning. I'm sorry he blames me, though. I did love him. Still do." I left it at that. I knew Blair had meant me, but it seemed a rather silly argument to have with her under the circumstances.

Chapter 3

Before I proceed with the tale, there are one or two facts you should know about Bjarni, germane to the subject at hand. First, Bjarni Haraldsson was a Viking. Please do not misunderstand me. Viking is not an ethnic term, despite the way we use it now. Some say it is derived from vik, the word for a "bay" or "cove." I don't agree. I believe it to be what we might call a job description. Ethnically, Bjarni was Norse. The word Viking refers to a specific activity, and that activity when you come right down to it was raiding. In other words, Vikings were pirates, and the term suited Bjarni and his friends rather well. Oh, they'd trade if it suited them. If not they just took what they needed. Every spring, when the weather was good and the sowing done, all able men headed out on raiding parties to see what they could find. Sometimes they went in autumn after the harvest as well. They had the fastest ships on the sea, light, with shallow drafts that allowed them to beach almost anywhere, and they were exceedingly adept sailors and fierce and skilled fighters. They came in fast, looted, burned, raped in increas-

ingly violent attacks, and then moved on. No wonder they were feared wherever they went. No wonder prayers rang out from pulpits across Europe asking that the faithful be saved from the Viking scourge.

The second salient point is that Bjarni was a pagan. While Earl Sigurd the Stout had converted to Christianity, Bjarni had not accepted the new faith. Wiser people than I have made the point that Christianity was not a natural fit for a Viking. Their code was different. Men fought together, raided together, and their loyalty was to those with whom they fought, and to those who behaved in a way that merited it. Family was extraordinarily important. Blood ties were sacred for the Vikings. If you killed someone's kin, the victim's entire family was obliged, and to say nothing of inclined, to kill you. An eye for an eye was really the code of the Viking. Turning the other cheek wasn't something a proud Viking was too likely to do, and the idea of the meek inheriting the earth would seem merely laughable. Still by Bjarni's time, Christianity was being accepted all over the Viking world and under some duress in Orkney. Earl Sigurd converted only because Olaf Tryggvason, King of Norway, forced him to be baptized. It was either that or have his head cut off by Olaf. Sigurd had to promise that everyone on Orkney would be baptized. We don't know whether Bjarni was baptized or not, but we do know that he clung obstinately to his belief in the old gods of northern Europe.

I suppose we would say now that Bjarni was something of a throwback, a relic of some earlier more violent time, when the earls of Orkney and their Norwegian kings dreamt of a Norse-Orcadian dominion throughout what is now the British Isles. Whether they knew it or not, those hopes died with Sigurd in Ireland at the Battle of Clontarf.

At the very least Bjarni was out of touch with his times. The world of a thousand years ago was rapidly changing. The Vikings were gradually settling down. For example, those in Northern France, the people we now know as Normans, were pretty firmly established. Other peoples were doing the same. The Magyars, those marauding horsemen who had terrorized much of Europe, were now settling peacefully in the area we know as Hungary. And monks, now finding it less necessary to protect their treasures from the heathen hordes, were flexing power, both spiritual and political. It was only in Britain that the Vikings still had the power to instill fear, and even there life was changing. While life on Orkney had for well over a hundred years been one last raid after another, and one battle after another, too, even Sigurd's grandfather, the aptly named Thorfinn Skull-Splitter had managed to die of old age, rather than from his wounds. It was not just the old religion to which Bjarni clung, it was the old ways as well.

But to continue with his story: those sailing from Orkney usually waited for good conditions in the spring, but Bjarni was not in a position to time his exit to fair weather. He left in February, kissing his wife Frakokk and two sons good-bye, and promising to return. Neither he nor they had any idea what was in store for our Bjarni.

THREE EVENTS OF some significance occurred in rapid succession that night following the wake at the Stane. The first was that while I was dreaming about disembodied heads, Blair was officially charged with the murder of Trevor Wylie. The second was that sometime in the wee hours, perhaps while the police were congratulating themselves on a quick resolution to the murder, McClintoch & Swain suffered another break-in. So, as it turned out, did Scot Free, Trevor's shop, an event that was to annoy Detective Singh no end.

The third was that I had this little epiphany, somewhere around 3 AM. Even though I didn't want to, I was replaying the business about the writing cabinet, a rather unpleasant habit I'd developed. I suppose it was better than dreaming about Trevor's head, but it was exhausting nonetheless. I tried to picture the cabinet, going back over in my mind the examination, one I thought I had been careful about the first time I saw it in Trevor's store. I imagined myself opening the doors, looking at the leaded glass and then the wood, the dovetailing, the finish, and then the lock. I was sure the lock was fine.

I then went back over my conversation with the elusive Percy, or Arthur, or whatever he was called. When I'd told him the cabinet was a fake, we'd got into one of those "Is, too; Is not" conversations. Clearly he had been convinced of the authenticity of his grandmother's writing cabinet. But the piece of it I'd foolishly and painfully crawled through a hedge to get, said it wasn't. Wrong lock, no doubt about it.

Then I went over in my mind the documentation I'd searched for on behalf of Anna Chan. There had been one lacquered mahogany cupboard, valued at fifteen thousand dollars, in the big shipment from Scotland, purchased from an antique dealer on George Square in Glasgow by the name of John A. Macdonald & Sons. There had been a second shipment with only one object, a black cabinet valued at ten thousand dollars from somewhere called St. Margaret's Hope. Who could forget a name like that? So there were two black cabinets, and I'd had a difficult time deciding which would have been the one I'd seen in Trevor's store. What if the cabinet Trevor had shown to Blair and me that fateful day had been a real Mackintosh? What if there was a second cabinet, a forgery? What if Blair had paid for the real one, but received the fake? I knew that was unlikely. Forging furniture is very difficult to do. Still, I had to wonder.

I called the police station expecting to leave a voice mail for Singh, but got the man himself. He sounded tired, but jubilant. He told me that Blair had been charged and that he appreciated my assistance. I told him I thought there were two cabinets.

"Isn't that a little unlikely?" he asked. "I've been reading up on your man Charles Rennie Mackintosh. Never heard of him until now, but I see he's famous. It sounds like a lot of work to forge a second desk thing."

"Not if you can sell it twice," I said.

"Interesting," he said. "Bait and switch. But it doesn't make any difference, does it? Wylie may have shown you and Baldwin the real deal, but he delivered the fake. That's still a motive for murder. It may say something about Trevor's ethics, but it doesn't change the fact Baldwin took an axe to Trevor's head. It doesn't make any difference to the case."

"It makes a difference to me," I said.

"I can see that. Your credibility as an antique dealer is on the line, so it would be better for you if the one you saw was authentic."

"Surely it does show that something else was going on here," I said.

"I'll tell you exactly what was going on, because it will be public information in the morning. Trevor Wylie had a gambling problem, by which I mean he couldn't stop, and he owed almost eight hundred thousand to someone, who, when he couldn't collect, sold the debt for fifty cents on the dollar to a guy who likes to intimidate his prey by showing up with his Doberman. That, you see, was why I was interested in your comment about the man with the dog. We'll be having a little chat with this guy, whose name is Douglas Sykes, better known as Dog, as soon as we can find him, and I'm willing to bet Trevor paid him in cash, which is the only thing he accepts, just before he died. You understand how it works, right? Man with Doberman pays the original lender half, in other words four hundred grand, and then sets out to collect the full amount, which is how he makes his money. Wylie was about to get himself very badly hurt if he didn't come up with the money, so he concocted this scheme to sell a fake Mackintosh to Baldwin, for cash, and presto, he's out of trouble."

"Maybe the man with the Doberman killed Trevor."

"Not good for business. You rough them up to scare them, but you keep them alive so they can pay up and then rack up more debts."

"I guess so," I said. "But you don't know this for a fact."

"Guess nothing. Safe money says that's the way it is. Thanks for calling me, though. Hold on a sec."

I waited. He had put his hand over the mouthpiece, so all I could hear was a muffled conversation. "McClintoch and Swain in Yorkville," he said finally. "That's you, right?"

"Right."

"Sorry to have to tell you you've had a break-in," he said. "You might want to go over there now." There was a pause. "You're kidding," he said. "Shit!"

"What?"

"Sorry," he said. "It seems the perps hitting antique stores are at it again. Wylie's shop has been broken into as well. Okay, I'm on my way."

My partner, Rob, who lives right next door and who spends a lot of time working nights, was pulling into his parking spot as I came out. When I told him what had happened, he very generously insisted on coming with me, even though he looked as if he could use some sleep.

The shop was in some disarray this time, rather different from the time before when it was left in perfect order except for the missing candlesticks. It hadn't been trashed, though, I'll say that. It's just that every drawer, credenza, chest, and cabinet in the place had been opened and left that way. The office had fared worse than that, with every drawer having been emptied.

Singh showed up as I was surveying the place. "What's missing?" he said.

"I'm not sure. I don't see anything. We'll have to do an inventory tomorrow."

"We'll dust for prints," he sighed. "Here and at Wylie's. If it makes you feel any better, his place looks worse. Fortunately, Anna Chan took the files with her when she left yesterday. I suppose you're going to tell me that it was Percy looking for his grandmother's chest."

"No," I said. "I don't think he'd be looking in an armoire for a writing cabinet. But somebody was certainly looking for something."

"Money," he said. "Did they get any?"

"I don't think it was money. There's only the petty cash, and the box hasn't even been opened. The lock wouldn't hold up to much prying, either."

I saw Rob looking around. "Someone was looking for something very specific," he said. "How did they get in?"

"No visible signs of entry," Singh replied.

"So someone with a key?" I said. "I don't think so. There's just Clive, Alex, Ben, our student, and me. I'd vouch for all of us. In any event, anyone with a key would know the combination to the security system."

"How fast did the security company respond?"

"We were here in about six minutes," Singh said. "I don't know how long they waited to call us."

"A lot of activity here for six minutes," Rob said.

"What are you saying?" I said.

"Either you could use a new security company or someone was hiding in the store when it closed."

"You mean the alarm went off when they left?"

"Maybe. Let's go home," Rob said. "There's nothing you can do now."

"I'd better call Clive and warn him," I said.

"I'd appreciate it if you'd cast your eyes over Wylie's place later, let me know if you think anything's missing," Singh said. "Say ten o'clock, so I can go home and have a shower.

"Sure," I said.

THE SUN WAS just coming up when we got home, so I made breakfast for Rob. It was the least I could do. I told him my thoughts on the writing cabinet. He was very nice about it, but I knew he thought it completely unlikely. He told me I should forget the whole business and just get on with my life.

"Does Blair's arrest not look a little too pat to you?" I asked Rob. "I mean, Blair uses an axe in front of dozens of people, including the chief of police, and then uses the same axe on Trevor? Did he think no one would remember the axe business? He's smarter than that."

"You're assuming it was premeditated," Rob said. "Maybe he went to the store to get his money back, and Trevor refused to give it to him."

"He went to the store with an axe?" I said.

"I guess that's why he's charged with murder," he said. "Maybe he just intended to scare him, and Trevor was his usual cocky self."

"Blair's a lawyer," I said. "He's gotten some pretty sleazy people off."

"You can say that again," Rob said. "Some of them were guilty as sin."

"Maybe one of these sleazy types had a grudge against him and framed him for it."

"Or maybe one of the sleazy people did the job for him," Rob replied. "Some of them at least must feel they owe him big time."

"The police can't find any record of a check or credit card transaction," I said. "I mean they can't even prove that Blair paid for the thing. There's that business about Trevor owing eight hundred thousand dollars to his bookie, of course. I get the impression the police think Trevor took cash and paid off the debt."

"Eight hundred thousand in cash?" Rob said. "Then Blair has more problems than a murder charge."

"Meaning what?"

"Nice law-abiding people like you and me don't have that much cash around," he said.

"But he's very rich."

"If he came into your store and offered you, say, a hundred grand for something, would you accept payment in cash?"

"No," I said. "I know that significant sums of money like that have to be reported."

"Exactly," he said.

"But Trevor needed cash to pay his gambling debts. Maybe he gave Blair the deal of a lifetime, at least what would have qualified as that if the cabinet had been genuine Mackintosh. It's worth a lot more than eight hundred thousand. Blair would think it was a really great deal and pay the cash."

"Think this through, Lara. Honest people do not keep that kind of cash around. Have you ever thought how much space that kind of money takes up? Let's say it's in fifties, hundreds being hard to spend sometimes. So each bundle of one hundred bills is five thousand dollars. You'd need one hundred and sixty bundles of fifties. Four hundred if it's in twenties, which most people want. You don't just throw that in a shopping bag and take it to your favorite antique dealer, now do you? Good deal or not, Blair had money he shouldn't have."

"What are you saying?"

"I'm saying he must have had a reason to have so much cash on hand, and it would tend to be an illegal one." Rob should know, of course. Right at this moment he was running a restaurant. He knows nothing about the restaurant business. He does know about money laundering, however, and that was what he was doing, hoping, of course, to catch some bad guys doing it. He tells me he is making pots of money by laundering illicit cash, but that he still hasn't nailed down what he calls the substantive offense, the crime, in other words, that resulted in all this money that needs to be laundered. He was given this assignment because he's of Ukrainian descent, and apparently there were some Ukrainians in town who were interested in doing business of this sort. What do I know? I was just not entirely happy he had to consort with people like this, who in my opinion probably would kill you if you looked at them wrong. Still I was not prepared to concede the point.

"He's a lawyer," I said.

"And your point is?"

"I don't know," I said. "Maybe he has an aversion to paying income tax. Singh seems to think I'd accept cash so I wouldn't have to declare it. Maybe Blair does that. I just think it's all too pat. Blair has a temper, certainly, but I just don't see him as a murderer."

"That may be because you don't want to."

"Isn't it time you got some sleep?" I said.

"Sorry, I'm coming down hard on you, aren't I? Baldwin was the defense lawyer in a case that I worked on. I know the guy was guilty, and Blair got him off, and believe me, our streets are more dangerous as a result. I'm accusing you of bias, and I should be pointing the finger at myself."

"I'm just in a bad mood because I missed the lock," I said. "And for sure I'm sympathetic about how you feel about all the slime Blair got off. But you know somebody has to defend them. That's the way our system works, even if it's galling from time to time. Furthermore, Blair told me once about how he grew up poor, and when he wanted to go to university his grandfather took a bundle of cash out from under the mattress and gave it to him. Don't roll your eyes! I know rags to riches is a cliché. His grandfather's wad of cash paid for his first year of university and he was able to take it from there. His grandfather believed in cash, and maybe Blair does, too. Okay, so he has more cash than other people. I understand what you're saying, but just having it does not make you a criminal. Surely it's what you do with it that counts."

"Where I come from it's not only what you do with it, but where you got it in the first place," he said. "But I take your point. I can't assume because he gets slugs off he's a slug himself. Nor can I assume that because he has cash, he was doing something illegal, or that he sank an axe into Trevor's head. I stand corrected, or at least moderately chastised."

"Thank you. I appreciate that concession. Now, you get some sleep, and I'll go to the shop, and maybe we'll have an early dinner before you head out to catch bad guys."

"Great idea. Promise we won't discuss Baldwin, Wylie, or locks, okay?" he said.

"Absolutely not," I said. "I still think there were two writing cabinets, though."

"Call Ben and ask him if there was a chance someone hid out in the shop," he said. "That idea I'm sticking to." So I did. Ben told me that he had been in the office just before closing when he heard the bell that rings when someone enters or exits, but when he went out there was no one there. He said he looked in both showrooms but saw no one, and assumed that someone had looked in and then left right away. He was devastated to think he might have missed a thief, but I told him it could have happened to any of us. I told him I didn't think anything much had been taken, and that was to prove correct.

Singh was right about Trevor's shop. It really was a mess. Furniture had been overturned, drawers pulled out of everything. The place essentially had been trashed. Singh and I just stood in the middle of the chaos and looked around.

"I don't think I can tell you much of anything in this mess," I said. "There may be stuff missing, but I'm not sure I could say."

"I can understand that," he said. "And I guess it doesn't matter that much with Wylie dead. He won't be complaining, will he?"

"Does this look like a different thief to you?" I said.

"Hate to think we have two of them," he said. "But yes, it does."

"I'm glad mine was neater," I said. "And you're right, it's a good thing the records were removed yesterday or it would be days before we got them straightened out."

"I know it's a long shot," Singh said, "but have a look around."

As I did so, a piece of paper caught my eye. It was face-down in the middle of the room, but it looked like a check. I picked it up, took one look, and handed it to Singh.

"Tell me again about how Trevor used the money Blair gave him to pay off the guy with the dog, or rather the man called Dog," I said. The piece of paper in question was a check, dated the day I'd gone to the store with Blair, payable to Scot Free Antiques and signed by Blair, for eight hundred thousand dollars. It was not the first time I'd thought that Trevor had chosen a very stupid name for his store, unless, of course, he planned to give away antiques, but this was not the issue right at this moment.

"It doesn't change anything," Singh said. It was beginning to sound like his mantra.

"It does sort of take the edge off the motive," I said. "If Trevor hadn't cashed this yet, then why would Blair kill him?"

"He killed him," Singh said, simply as he pulled out a plastic bag and put the check into it. "Don't know how we missed this the first time."

"I expect Trevor hid it somewhere until he could take it

to the bank, except that he didn't get there. It just got dislodged, wherever it was, in the break-in."

"How long would you hold on to a check like this? It doesn't do much for your theory that there were two of these desks, either," Singh said.

"You're just bitter." I could hardly wait to rush home and tell Rob that he'd been completely wrong about Blair having illicit cash hanging about in huge piles, and that he had misjudged the man, as had Singh. My small moment of righteous indignation did not last long, however. Despite what I'd thought, the check made Blair look even guiltier, if that was possible. It turned out the check number was out of sequence: in other words, after Trevor was dead and Blair under suspicion, Blair had signed a check and backdated it to the day he'd purchased the cabinet. The two checks with numbers immediately before it were dated after Trevor died. It looked as if Blair had arranged to have someone break into Trevor's shop and leave it there in a faked robbery. If so, it had been really dumb of Blair not to think about the numbers on the checks, although he claimed, according to Singh, that he had postdated a couple of checks that he was sending through the mail. The trouble with that one was that when the police went through the recycling bin of one of the check recipients, they found the envelope, postmarked after Trevor had died. It seemed incredibly inept for a man of Blair's obvious intelligence, but once again the police were back to having no record of the transaction.

Anna Chan, who continued to phone me from time to time with questions about Trevor's paperwork, told me they'd caught the man who'd trashed Trevor's place, although not mine, I'm afraid. His name was Woody somebody or other, some lowlife Blair had successfully represented on a charge of a particularly vicious house invasion. Apparently Woody's gratitude extended to planting the check at Blair's request, but not as far as lying about it when caught. It seemed pretty open-and-shut, as they say, at this point, and a rather inept attempt to subvert the course of justice on Blair's part.

Percy never showed up again, not even at The Dwarfie Stane. Rendall had promised he'd call me if he did. It was as if he'd never existed.

I tried just to get on with life, to forget it, but that was very hard to do. For one thing Blair's journey through the justice system was very big news, and every court appearance, however brief, filled the newspapers with lurid headlines about the Skull-Splitter killer, and much was made of there having been a dispute over a piece of furniture. Stanfield Roberts, the curator at the Cottingham who'd been at Blair's ill-fated party, was quoted about unscrupulous antique dealers. Fortunately my name didn't come into it, but that didn't make me feel any better, as my role, however anonymous in the whole sordid business, continued to rankle. I alternated between being sure I'd been right about the cabinet and being completely down on myself for my ineptitude. It had to be that I was so besotted by either the cabinet or by Blair's money or Trevor's charm that I missed something as obvious as the lock. At my age!

My self-flagellation on the subject of the lock was made worse by my conviction that Blair was not the murderer. It was, as I kept saying to anyone who would listen, just too pat. I also clung to the notion that the saga of the two cabinets was crucial to my understanding of what had really happened. There was absolutely no concrete support of any kind for this feeling of mine, which just made me more upset.

Various people continued to try to cheer me up; the rest avoided me. I could hardly blame them. I was rather tiresome on the subject. Mention locks, for example, or even a word that rhymed with it, like shock, or bring up the subject of Scotland, or furniture, something it's easy enough to do when you're an antique dealer, or heaven forbid, utter the word forgery, and I was off on a little tirade. I did mention to Clive and Moira that I thought there might have been two cabinets, and while they seemed enthusiastic, I knew they really thought I was just rationalizing my mistake, and I only felt worse. Clive went on being nice to me, a situation I found intolerable. Moira tried a lecture or two. "Self worth is not measured by how many antiques you identify correctly," she intoned. I didn't retort that lack of self worth might be measured in the number of times you'd got something so wrong another person had been killed because of it, but that was what I was thinking.

What surprised me was that all of this didn't affect our business adversely. In fact, business had rarely been better. That was almost entirely due to Desmond Crane, who may or may not have been in competition with Blair for the writing cabinet. Shortly after Blair was charged, Dez, who had never been a customer in the same league as Blair, although he did buy from us occasionally, came into the shop, had a look around, and then asked me if I would consider decorating his daughter Tiffany's condo.

"I bought her a little place as a graduation present," he said. By little, I was soon to learn, he meant about two thousand square feet, which is bigger than my house. "She loves antiques, unlike my son who won't look at anything designed before the year 2000," he said. "And she has absolutely no furniture, because she lived at home during her years at university. Will you come and have a look?"

"I'd love to, Mr. Crane," I replied. "But you do know I was involved in that business with Blair and Trevor Wylie?"

He gave a dismissive wave of his hand. "I'm sure it wasn't your fault," he said. "And please call me Dez." I suppose he could afford to be magnanimous, given that his chief rival for all those high profile and lucrative court cases was out of commission. "Let's make an appointment to meet at the condo. It's a surprise. She'll be back from her summer job in about four weeks. Can you do it?"

Of course I could. It was a huge success, too. It was actually Clive who did most of the work. I find the antiques, but he's the designer. Tiffany had inherited her grandmother's china, which her mother, Leanna the Lush, said Tiffany loved, and Clive picked up the colors in that for the walls and the accents. We ransacked our showrooms and warehouse for furniture and carpets, silverware, art for the walls. What we didn't have, I went to auctions and found. Clive and I were both there when Dez and Leanna, who reeked of stale booze, brought Tiffany over, and after she commented on what a smashing place it was, we handed her the keys. Tiffany cried, Dez and Leanna cried, and I could have cried, but with relief, too. Even Tiffany's brother Carter—Clive maintains that Carter's real name is Cartier and that he and his sister are named for their parents' favorite places to shop—asked me if I thought he could mix a few antique pieces with his modern furniture. When I said yes, he came over to the store and bought a huge armoire for his stereo system and another for his kitchen. Soon people Dez had referred to us started buying stuff, too.

"There is one small problem with all this business Dez has sent our way," Clive said.

"We have no merchandise?" I said.

"Exactly," he said. "This is a nice problem to have, I know, but we aren't going to have stock for the Christmas season, which is not good at all. How will we take advantage of that ridiculous time of year when everyone waits until the last minute to shop and is therefore forced to spend obscene amounts of money at McClintoch and Swain if we don't have anything to sell? We're okay on the Asian stuff, but Crane and his friends and relatives have almost cleaned out our European collection. I've been over to the warehouse, and it's practically empty."

"Relax. It's only August," I said. "I'll e-mail our pickers and agents in Europe and head over there next week, assuming, that is, that Detective Singh will let me go. If I do it right away, there'll be plenty of time to get it here."

"It's too bad you have to make an extra trip," he said. "I know you did double-duty here while Moira was having chemo."

"I don't mind," I said. "I'll e-mail our people in Italy and France, and maybe Ireland, and see what they can come up with on short notice. I'll head out as soon as I hear back."

"I've got to hand it to you, Lara," Clive said. "I thought we were doomed, but you've pulled it out of the bag."

"Mmm," I said. The truth was that while I was publicly rehabilitated, privately I still felt like dirt. A week or two far away from home seemed like a very good idea to me.

That might have been the end of it, had I not become better acquainted with Willow Laurier, Trevor's last girlfriend. We'd been introduced at Blair Bazillionaire's ill-fated cocktail party, and I'd seen her briefly at Trevor's funeral, but we'd not exchanged more than a few words. Still, I knew her well enough to know that it was she who was sneaking into the alley beside Trevor's former store at about one in the morning one warm August night.

I'd been working very late trying to get everything organized for my trip to Europe and was locking up and heading for my car when I saw her. She wasn't good at stealth, obviously, because she stood under a street light for a minute or two looking up and down the street in a rather furtive fashion, before darting into the alley. A few minutes later a dim light, most likely a flashlight given the way it moved through the shop, glowed in the window.

There was only one way out, really, either through the back alley which led nowhere but out to the street again, or the front door which deposited you right on the street. I found myself a perch on a stone wall across the road and waited.

At least twenty minutes passed, and Willow had not yet appeared. Worse yet, the roving light was gone. My imagination, already inclined to the macabre where that store was concerned, started working overtime. What if Willow had fallen in the darkness, was lying there, and would be until the landlord showed up, heaven knows when. Or, and this was a really unpleasant thought, a murderer had been waiting there for her. That was ridiculous, I knew. Blair Bazillionaire had not been granted bail, given the horrendous nature of the murder and the fact that with all his money, he was considered a flight risk. Still I wasn't convinced Blair had done it, so maybe, improbable though it might be, the real axe murderer had returned to the scene of the crime at the very moment Willow decided to enter it. I did not want to go into the store at night, or any time for that matter. But after almost half an hour, Willow still hadn't shown up.

Very reluctantly, I went down the alley and tried the back door. It was unlocked, which seemed rather careless of her. I hesitated in the doorway for a few seconds, slid my hand along the wall in a vain attempt to find a light switch. By now my eyes were adjusting. There was some street light filtering through the front window, and much to my regret, a light in the basement, which probably explained why I couldn't see it from the street. Fighting back nausea, to say nothing of terror, I went to the top of the stairs.

"Willow?" I said. "It's Lara McClintoch." There was no sound. "Willow?" I said again. Still no reply. There was nothing for it: I was going to have to go down.

She was standing in the back room where I'd found Trevor's body, and she was crying. "Leave me alone," she sobbed.

"Willow," I said. "I am not going to leave you alone. You shouldn't be here. First of all, it's illegal, and furthermore, it is not nice down here. You really have to come upstairs. I'm going to take you for a coffee, or maybe something a little stronger."

"I've looked everywhere," she said. "Even behind the furnace. I've looked for signs the floor has been dug up and new floor put down. I've looked in every piece of furniture upstairs. I even looked to see if it would be possible to hide stuff in these pipes."

"Willow," I said. "What are you looking for?"

"I thought he loved me," she burbled on as if I didn't exist. "He said he did."

"I'm sure in his way he did," I said in a soothing tone.

"Don't patronize me," she said, turning on me. "I know he was a first-class jerk. What I really want to know is where did he put the money?"

"The money?"

"Look," she said. "You may think I'm naïve, but I'm not. I'm not overcome with grief, either. Even if I might have been, I found his packed suitcase and in it the airline ticket: an around-the-world ticket. You know what those things cost? Thousands! Almost exactly what I lent him a week before he died. I know he was planning to make a run for it. He'd only booked the first leg of it, to Orkney via Glasgow, and after that, parts unknown."

"A fugitive, you mean?" I said.

"Exactly right," she replied. "So where, I ask you, is the money? He made a big score, didn't he, with that fake desk thing? Hundreds of thousands of dollars? So where is it?"

"The police say he was a compulsive and unlucky gambler. They think he paid off his debts to a bookie with it."

"I guess that's what they meant with all their questions about what Trevor did in his spare time, is it? I knew he played the horses, and he sometimes went to a casino. I went with him a couple of times. I liked the shows. But there had to be more. He was heading out, but not with me. I knew there was something going on, but I never thought he'd run out on me."

"Maybe he was going to ask you to come with him?"

"There was only one airline ticket," she said. "He was leaving me."

"Perhaps he thought, given his gambling problem, that he should do you a favor?"

"There you go again, patronizing me," she said. "He was a rat."

"You're right. I'm sorry. He pulled the wool over my eyes, too, in a different way of course."

"He convinced you it was the real deal?" she said. "That desk thing?"

"Writing cabinet," I said. "Why does everybody have so much trouble with the name? Come on, let's get out of here. The police have been all through the place. There is no stash of cash here."

"If it is, I can't find it," she said. "But if not here, where?"

"I'm trying to tell you there may not be any."

"There is," she insisted.

"Look, Blair Baldwin claims to have paid eight hundred thousand dollars for the writing cabinet. The police say that's pretty much what Trevor owed his bookie. He took the cash, paid the bookie, and that's it. If he was leaving, he was leaving broke."

"I don't believe it," she said. "We only have Baldwin's word for the eight hundred thousand. What if he paid more than that? A lot more than that?"

"Possible," I said.

"Exactly. That thing, the writing cabinet, was worth more than eight hundred grand, wasn't it? I mean if it had been real?"

"Yes."

"So where's the rest of the money?"

"But Baldwin said . . ."

"He's an axe murderer," she interrupted. "Why would we believe him?"

"Good point. We don't know he's the murderer for sure,

and I rather think maybe he isn't. However, I've been thinking . . . Could we discuss this upstairs? This place is creeping me out. In fact, could we discuss this at the all-night coffee shop down the street?"

"What have you been thinking?"

"I'll tell you when we are out of here. How did you get in?"

"Key," she said. "If it weren't for that yellow police stuff across the door, it would almost be legal."

"Almost," I agreed, as we locked up the store and headed back to the street.

With a couple of decaf cappuccinos in front of us, we went back to our chat. "I've had the feeling, and I may be rationalizing, that there were two writing cabinets," I said.

"I'm not sure what you mean."

"There was a real Mackintosh writing cabinet, shown to me and to Baldwin. And there was another one, a forgery that was delivered to Baldwin, the one he chopped up at the party."

"So we're looking not for money, but for a second writing cabinet?" she said. "I'm still not getting this."

"Maybe Trevor sold the Mackintosh twice," I said. "Maybe he showed the real one to two different people, sold it to both of them, and shipped the fake to Baldwin, and the real one to someone else."

"Like who?" she said.

"I don't know. I realize thinking that there is someone out there forging Charles Rennie Mackintosh furniture is a little far-fetched, but no more so than a huge amount of cash hidden in the basement." The person who was most likely to have the cabinet was, of course, Desmond Crane. I'd been to Crane's home several times lately and hadn't seen it, but then it would be rather foolish of him to have it on display while I was present."

"And the reason you think there were two is?"

"Percy was convinced it was real. I'm not the only one who thought so."

"Who is Percy?"

"Percy's grandmother once owned the cabinet. Percy or Arthur, that is."

"Who is Arthur?"

"He's Percy. He told me his name was Percy and he told Rendall at the Stane his name was Arthur."

"Two different names? He sounds about as reliable as an axe murderer," she said. "Wouldn't it be difficult to make an exact copy? Wouldn't you have to completely dismantle the original in order to do so?"

"Very difficult, but a lot easier if you had the complete drawings and specifications, which Trevor did, and if you'd seen the original, also possible in this case. That and a few photographs, and some paint chips that matched and you'd be away. The color wouldn't have to be absolutely exact anyway, because you would never see the two pieces together."

"I knew it!" she said. "There is money somewhere. Lots of it."

"It isn't in the shop. As my partner the RCMP officer has pointed out, that kind of cash takes up a fair amount of space. And for sure it isn't in Trevor's bank account. I think it was irresponsible of him to not have a will, but I know the landlord, and he's told me he is going to auction off Trevor's merchandise for back payment of rent as soon as the police and the courts will let him."

"I lent Trevor rent money from time to time," she said. "Quite often, now that I think about it. The creep owes me quite a fair chunk of cash, and I'd like it back. No chance of that, I guess. I have no record of it. I mean we practically lived together. Why would I ask him for a receipt? I tried approaching the lawyer the court appointed, but it doesn't look good. He went on about when people die without a will, the money would go first to a spouse, and if there isn't one, and I guess I don't qualify, then they look down first, by which I think he meant children, then up to parents, and then out almost indefinitely to relatives, you know siblings, then cousins."

"Did Trevor have siblings or close relatives?"

"He's never mentioned any, but they'll probably come up with somebody. Still, I figured I was played for a fool, and at the very least, I'd like my money back. I suppose I could plead my case with whomever they find out there to give the money to. I mean you never know: unlikely as it is, I might find a decent human being. That would make them quite unlike Trevor. So I'm thinking if I find the money it would make my life simpler."

"If you found the money, you'd have to turn it over to the police," I said.

"I know, but it might be about ten thousand short when I did," she said. "I was saving that money for a down payment on a house. You probably think that's terrible of me to even contemplate keeping some of it."

"No. If I could find some way of salvaging my reputation as an antique dealer at the expense of Trevor, I'd do it in a flash."

She smiled at last. "He had a way with women, didn't he? I thought he looked and sounded a little like Sean Connery."

"I did, too. I think that's why I let him get away with stuff."

"Like what?"

"Stealing good customers right from under my nose."

"Do you have a card?" she asked. "I'd like to stay in touch if I may."

"Of course. Give me yours as well. Is your name really Willow by the way?"

"Yes, it is. I don't have a card," she said. "I'm a dental hygienist. You don't need a card for that. But I'll give you my number. I'm thinking we might collaborate."

"On what?"

"Salvaging your reputation and recovering my cash. I figure there would have to be at least a reward for its return, don't you? Where do we start?"

"I wouldn't mind a chance to visit Scotland, to go to John A. Macdonald Antiques on George Square in Glasgow and see what they have to say for themselves. Maybe even go to Orkney. You can't generalize, of course, but if a piece of furniture is forged, it does tend to have been in the country of origin of the authentic piece. I'll be in the general area anyway, so maybe I'll just pop up there and talk to them."

The tiny part of my rational brain that was still functioning, the part that had been banished to a position floating somewhere near the unpleasantly bright neon light fixture in that coffee shop, looked down on two sadly deluded, if not delusional, women and wept.

Chapter 4

Bjarni had some choices to make in terms of where he should go. He could go back to Norway, of course. It was where he was born, and he still had kin there. But he wasn't sure in what favor he'd be viewed, or whether Einar's ties were stronger than his, and frankly retracing his steps does not appear to be something Bjarni liked to do. He knew, of course, of the route via the Shetlands and Faroes to Iceland, and he probably had kin there. Icelandic ships put in at Orkney, and Bjarni doubtless knew all about the land of fire and ice, the harsh and unforgiving terrain, and the long cold nights. Iceland fared rather poorly in comparison to the lush and fertile lands of Orkney, it had to be said, even if it did have an air of adventure to it. It did not take him long to decide Iceland was not somewhere he wanted to go. He'd heard rumors, too, of lands even farther west and even less hospitable. So Bjarni heeded his brother's advice and took the route he knew as well as any other, to the west, to the lands where he'd raided every year with Sigurd, and where he thought some support in his difficulties with Einar might lie.

And so Bjarni headed for Caithness in northern Scotland. Caithness fell under the control of the earls of Orkney some of the time and was fertile hunting ground for loot most of the time. Indeed, the Orkney earl credited with taking Caithness was an earlier Earl Sigurd, this one known as Sigurd the Powerful. There is a legend about this Sigurd, that he died because he tied his vanquished enemy's severed head to his saddle. The dead man bit Sigurd's leg and Sigurd succumbed to the wound. A good story to be sure, and probably not true, but it does give some idea of the animosity that existed between the Vikings on one side and the Picts and Scots on the other.

At this particular juncture, Caithness and neighboring Sutherland to the south belonged to Einar's youngest brother, Thorfinn, who had been given it by his grandfather King Malcolm of Scotland. The boy was too young to rule but advisors were appointed by the king. A number of Orkney men who had suffered under Einar's tyranny, or like Bjarni had provoked his wrath, had gone to Caithness to enjoy the support of young Thorfinn.

But this would not be true for Bjarni. You've probably already guessed by now that Bjarni was of somewhat intemperate disposition, rather prone to setting disputes with his Viking axe rather than negotiation. He had left Orkney a little short of provisions, given his haste, and so he did what he'd always done: he helped himself to what he needed. The trouble was he met with some resistance in the form of the brother of one of Thorfinn's advisors. Bjarni emerged from the little set-to as the victor, but it didn't do him much good. The brother was dead, and Bjarni was once again on the run.

GLASGOW IS CHARLES Rennie Mackintosh's city. It was here that he was born, where he studied at the Glasgow School of Art, and here that he formed the Glasgow Four, with fellow draftsman Herbert McNair, and two sisters, Frances and Margaret Macdonald, both members of a group of women art students who called themselves, rather fetchingly, the Immortals. The Four developed a unique body of work, an unusual design aesthetic, which is often now referred to as Glasgow School, a subset of the Arts and Crafts movement, and indeed of Art Nouveau. Herbert went on to marry Frances, and Charles married Margaret, who collaborated with her husband from that time on.

Mackintosh's work is everywhere in Glasgow, having finally achieved the hometown recognition denied him during his lifetime. Not that Mackintosh was deterred by this lack of acceptance while he lived: he boldly laid claim to being Scotland's greatest architect. True or not, the remaining examples of his work have become places of some modest pilgrimage for those who love Arts and Crafts design. Mackintosh's designs for furniture, textiles, posters, lighting, clocks, and so on, are now much admired and indeed coveted. You can eat Scottish salmon on brown bread in the faithfully reproduced Willow Tearooms that Mackintosh designed for Miss Catherine Cranston. You can walk the hallowed halls of the Glasgow School of Art where Mackintosh not only studied, but which he later designed when new quarters were called for. You can see the rooms in which he and Margaret lived, every piece of furniture designed by them, carefully reconstructed in the Hunterian Art Gallery. You will have barely scratched the surface.

I did all of these things. I went to every place that exhibited authentic Mackintosh. I talked to every expert I could find. I peered at every detail, most particularly the locks. I came away convinced that the first cabinet I'd seen was authentic.

While I had no trouble finding Charles Rennie Mackintosh's ghost in Glasgow, what I couldn't find was the real John A. Macdonald Antiques. Not on George Square, the address on the receipt in Trevor's files, nor anywhere else for that matter. In my heart of hearts, I knew I wasn't going to find them. I just wasn't prepared to admit it. Before I left home on the buying trip, I'd checked Glasgow telephone listings on the Internet and had done a dealer search on the British Antique Dealers' Association Website, as well as on other Websites that featured Scottish antique dealers. No John A. Macdonald Antiques.

Still, my optimistic, or perhaps desperate, little soul had decided if I went there I'd find them. Once I'd convinced myself of the notion that I had not been wrong about the writing cabinet, further self-delusion was not only possible, but essentially effortless.

Glasgow had not been a regular stopping place for me, and I had been looking forward to it. It has a reputation for being one of the, if not the, most stylish city in Britain—edgy, fashionable, and exciting. I had not had time to put my usual careful plans in place for the trip, given the events of the spring and summer, so it was rather more haphazard than usual: I started in Rome, moved on through Tuscany, the south of France, Paris, then over to Ireland, before ending up in London. All along I took digital photos of the merchandise I'd purchased and e-mailed them to Clive so he would first of all know I was on the job, and secondly that he'd have something to show anyone who thought our showroom looked a little bare. From London, I called him to say I couldn't get a flight back right away, so was going to head for the English countryside for a couple of days for a break. He was actually nice about it, which just served to make me feel guilty, although not guilty enough to forego my intended excursion to Charles Rennie Mackintosh country.

The trouble was, while Glasgow was every bit as interesting as everyone says it is, I got absolutely nowhere on my mission. Indeed it was one step forward, two or three steps back. After walking around George Square twice—it's a rather impressive place except for rather tatty-looking tents set up in the middle of it for some conference or other—and thence along George Street, and West George Street, too, all without success, I entered the premises of the one antique dealer I could find in the immediate vicinity of George Square, one Lester Campbell, Antiquarian.

"I have a client in Toronto," I said, after we'd been through the social niceties, and I'd had a brief look around his shop which was rather posh, just the place to look for outrageously expensive furniture. "Someone who is most enchanted by Charles Rennie Mackintosh. He will buy anything by Mackintosh. Do you know of something on the market?"

"I don't," Lester Campbell said. "I wish I did. I'd be only too happy to have a client like that."

"Anybody with a private collection who might be prevailed upon to sell part of it? My client is not without means."

"No, again. There are lots of reproductions and copies out there, and I suppose a few downright fakes, you know," he said. In fact I did know that only too well. "The odd piece comes up from time to time. There was a very nice writing cabinet from the mid- to late nineteen-nineties that fetched a rather becoming price at auction."

"Yes, about one-point-five million U.S. if I recall. My client wouldn't even blink at that price. Unfortunately that was before he started collecting. He has come to this passion of his relatively recently."

"Aren't you the lucky one?" he replied.

"Yes, indeed," I said, with an inward cringe. "This is not the kind of antique I usually carry, but I was given the name of an antique dealer here in Glasgow who dealt in Mackintosh, so I thought I'd look him up. For some reason, I can't seem to locate him. John A. Macdonald?"

"Never heard of him," Campbell said.

"Nobody has," I said. "Strange that."

"Strange, indeed. Perhaps someone is having you on?"

"Could be," I said. "Annoying that."

"I hope it didn't cost you money," he said.

"Not money, no. Reputation, maybe."

"Ah," he replied.

"You have my card," I said. "If you hear of anything, would you let me know?" I tried not to sound too out of sorts even if the inescapable conclusion was that if the invoice for the black cupboard was a fake, then so, too, was the cabinet.

"Of course," he replied. "Here is my card as well."

I had a brief look at it and looked again. The name was wrong, which is to say, it was clearly marked as Lester Campbell, Antiquarian, but the typeface was similar to what I recalled on the invoice from John A. Macdonald. Now there is no law that says you can't use the same typeface as another dealer, but this one was a bit unusual. It was designed to look like handwritten script. "Are you sure you've never heard of John A. Macdonald Antiques?"

"Absolutely certain. Do you want me to check the British Antique Dealer's listings for you?"

"I've done that. I'm baffled."

I must have looked rather dejected as I headed for the door, because as I reached it, he called me back. "You wouldn't be planning to stay over a day or two would you?"

"I could, I suppose."

"You might want to consider a little charity," he said, reaching to pick up a card on the counter and waving it at me.

"Charity?"

"There's a fund-raiser tomorrow night," he said. "It's being held at the residence of Robert Alexander and his wife, Maya. He's a big man about town, philanthropist obviously. He's paying the shot for the evening, so all proceeds go to charity. He's also a big collector, furniture, paintings, the works. If anybody has a Mackintosh or three, it would be him. And he can often be persuaded to sell them if he wants to make a big gesture for one of his favorite causes. I expect there's a ticket or two left."

"Thank you," I said, taking the card. "I just may go to that. Will I see you there?"

"You will," he replied. "You have to stay in with these kind of people."

"You do," I agreed, thinking about the last big party of a customer I'd attended. "I owe you for this."

"Yes, you do," he agreed. "See you there. I'll introduce you to the Alexanders if the opportunity arises."

If I couldn't find the elusive, if not entirely fictional John A. Macdonald, I did find Percy Bicycle Clips. Not that it helped any, mind you. In fact, it put me in a really foul mood. He was riding his bicycle, of course, his jacket flapping around behind him, and I hailed a cab the minute I saw him. "See that fellow on a bicycle?" I said to the driver. "I think he's a friend from Toronto. Can you see if you can catch up to him for me?"

It wasn't as easy as it might be. Percy cycled along at a fairly good clip, and he didn't have to sit in traffic. The cab driver was a pro, however, and managed to keep him in sight. Then Percy wheeled on to Buchanan Street which unfortunately had been blocked off to traffic.

The cab driver, never one to give up, apparently, whipped along a parallel street and then pulled up on Argyll where it crossed Buchanan. I handed the driver the fare and stepped out of the cab as Percy wheeled up. "Percy," I said. "Remember me?"

Percy made to turn around, but I had my hand on his handlebars and to get away he was going to have to drag me with him, which would have caused quite a scene in this very busy shopping area. "Let go," he said.

"I won't! I want to talk to you."

He tried to pull the bicycle away from me, but I held firm. "If I talk to you, will you leave me alone?" he said, defeated.

"I guess so. If I let go and you make a run for it, I'm going to scream thief at the top of my lungs. Just so you know."

"I understand," he said, pushing his glasses up on his nose nervously.

"Do you want to go for a coffee?"

"No. Just say what you want to say."

"I'm trying to track down the source of the writing cabinet," I said. "You say it was your grandmother's, but there is an invoice and receipt for it, from an antique dealer here in Glasgow by the name of John A. Macdonald."

Percy looked perplexed. "An antique dealer here?"

"Yes. So I'm wondering if the cabinet, the one you showed me a picture of, really belonged to your grandmother."

"The cabinet?" he said.

"The cabinet in the photo of your grandmother, if that's who she is, the one that's possibly worth one-point-five million."

"One-point-five million what?" he said.

"U.S. dollars," I said.

"That thing was worth one-point-five million?" he said.

"If it was real it was," I said.

"Real what?" he said.

"Charles Rennie Mackintosh. What else?"

"Whoa," he said.

"You were looking for it," I said.

"Well, yes, I guess I was."

"You guess? I have this idea there were two, so I'm interested in your grandmother, where she might be, some way of getting in touch with her."

"Two what?" he said.

"Two writing cabinets," I said, in a rather impatient tone. Apparently I could not stay calm on this subject.

"Two of these things worth a million and a half? Is that each, or for both of them?"

"One was worth that much. The other was a fake."

"A fake," he repeated.

"Don't play dumb with me. You told me your grandmother didn't know what it was worth."

"I did," he replied. Then inexplicably he started to laugh.

"What is so funny here?" I asked, after watching him chortle for a while. He couldn't reply because he was laughing too hard. "Are you going to let me in on this little joke?"

"I knew he had it," he said at last. "That guy with his head chopped up."

"Trevor Wylie," I said, through gritted teeth. "You didn't kill him, did you?"

"Nooo," he said. "Did you?"

"No. You did run away."

"I suppose," he said, calming down a little. "I felt sick. I didn't want to get involved, either. It might have derailed my quest."

"Your quest? What were you doing in the shop?" I said, as he started giggling again.

"Same thing you were, I expect," he said. "Or maybe not. You're telling me that there are two of those things. Or rather were two of those things. One was destroyed, right, but there is another?"

"That's my theory anyway."

"So the one that was destroyed was a fake," he went on.

"I think so. It had a new lock."

"A lock," he said in a perplexed tone.

"Never mind. Look, I'm going to tell you what I think happened. You'll think I'm crazy, but hear me out." So I told him. I told him how embarrassed I was about making a mistake, but then started to think I hadn't, how Trevor had needed money to cover his gambling debts, and that selling the one cabinet may have covered his debts but didn't put him any further ahead, and that whether he had intended to do so at first or not, the presence of a second cabinet had been too much for him, and he'd baited Blair Baldwin with the real one, shipped him the fake, and then sold the first a second time. I told him I was in Scotland trying to prove there had been two cabinets even if everybody else in the world thought I was nuts. Percy listened as I rattled on and on.

"So it's possible the real one is still out there?" he said, when I'd finished.

"I think so."

"Where?"

"It could be anywhere."

"But it's in Canada?"

"Probably. Both the real one and the fake were brought over from either Glasgow or Orkney or both. Trevor needed to have both of them for this to work."

"First you raise my hopes, and then you dash them," he said. "I guess I might as well go home." With that he hopped on his bike and rode away. I just stood there too depressed to make good on a threat to yell thief. It took me a minute to realize I still didn't know his name!

So that was two illusions shattered. I'd half thought that Percy, once found, would confirm something about the real writing cabinet and maybe even point me in the right direction for getting to the bottom of this mess. Now I found that he hadn't a clue about its value, even if he'd shown me a picture of his grandmother standing in front of it. Clearly he was not the person to confirm that the cabinet I had seen was authentic. He was on a quest, to use his quaint expression, but not for the same reasons I was. Maybe he really just wanted to help his grandmother retrieve a piece of furniture the family thought had sentimental value. Maybe telling him what it was worth was going to make my own little quest harder. It was in a rather grumpy state of mind that I went to the party the following day.

Tickets for this exclusive little event that Robert and Maya Alexander were hosting were five hundred pounds each, a rather breathtaking sum for a few shrimp and a couple of small glasses of champagne. But still there was the charity, a new drop-in center for drug addicts, and, of course, the cachet. Cachet does not come cheap. Neither, of course, does obsession, at least certainly not mine. Every day that I persisted in my hunt for the sources of two writing cabinets put a bigger and bigger dent in my wallet.

On the bright side, transportation was included, a bus that picked up those of us with tickets on George Square and then took us out into the countryside. I had no idea where I was, but it was very pleasant wherever it was with fine views of water and a rather splendid home.

With the exception of the Scottish accents, the ticket prices and the admirable fact that no one was chopping up the furniture, the party seemed remarkably similar to one I had attended earlier in the summer. There were important-looking people, even if I didn't know who they were, the requisite number of fawning hangers-on, and enough food to feed a small country.

Still, the house was spectacular. The invitation had said the affair was limited to a mere one hundred guests, and like Blair's, this place could hold them. Unlike Blair's, which was the living embodiment of his rather obsessive love of Art Nouveau, this home was furnished in a much more at-tractive and eclectic fashion. I liked it a lot better than Blair's, even if I hadn't made a cent on it. The art and the furnishings were of exceedingly good quality, but they had been chosen by someone with a good eye for the whole. Pieces were put together because they looked good that way, not because they belonged to a particular school of design or period. It was also, I suppose, more relaxed because of the country vistas with the lights of the city visible only in the distance.

I was very happy to see Lester Campbell arrive, given he was the only person I knew at the party, and one of only two people, if one could include Percy Bicycle Clips, that I knew in all of Glasgow. He had waved and was making his way toward me when there was some clinking of glasses, and a woman's voice, amplified by a microphone, could be heard above the din.

"Could I have your attention for just one minute," the voice said, and I moved into the main room to see an earnest-looking woman of about thirty at a small podium. "I don't want to interrupt this lovely party, but I cannot let the occasion pass without a heartfelt thank-you to our hosts, Robert and Maya Alexander." There was an enthusiastic round of applause. "You all know, I'm sure, what a terrible problem drugs are in Scotland, in Edinburgh particularly, but also here in Glasgow. The suffering these drugs cause for individuals and their loved ones, the huge costs, social and economic to our community, must be addressed. And Robert and Maya are doing something about it, supporting as they have our new center in a very significant way. I don't know what we'd do without you, Robert and Maya, and others like you. I'd like to thank all of you for coming, and I'd like to ask Robert to say a few words."

To a second round of applause, a rather attractive man of about fifty, with lovely silver hair and dark eyes took the microphone. "Thank you, Dorothy," he said. "I want you to know that how delighted Maya and I are to be able to help even in a small way."

"Hardly small," Lester whispered to me. "He's given them a million pounds."

While Robert was talking, Maya, delighted to be able to help or not, hung back a bit, shy perhaps. She was wearing a lovely silk dress, but what really caught my eye was her gorgeous necklace. It was simple but beautifully designed, with what looked at this distance to be garnets and pearls. I have a weakness for antique jewelry. We don't carry much of it in the shop, and I can't afford the good stuff for myself, so I usually just admire it from afar, as I was doing now. People think jewelry has to have lots of precious stones to be worth much, but an antique with great design and a good designer or manufacturer can be costly even with just semiprecious stones. I'd seen one very similar at home, in fact. Blair Bazillionaire had been thinking of buying it for his wife, but they broke up soon after, so I guess that hadn't happened. The one he'd been looking at was worth about ten thousand dollars, so there was no way I was going to buy it if he didn't. Let's face it, my lifestyle doesn't involve enough sparkling social events to justify jewelry worth even a tenth of that price.

"We are relatively new to this community," Alexander continued. "Ten years, I think. And you've been most welcoming, considering I'm English and my wife's American— not at all what I heard about Scottish reserve." People applauded a bit more. "Well, perhaps at bit reserved, at least at first, but not nearly as bad as we expected." Everyone laughed. "And there is no question Scotland has been good to us. Who would have thought a boy from Liverpool, a former army captain, a kid who joined the army just to get a cheap education and see the world, would end up with a house like this, and a spectacular wife like Maya!"

"You're a captain of industry now, Robert," someone called out, as Robert kissed Maya's hand and everyone applauded.

"We wanted to repay the community in some way. We are so glad to have been able to make even a small contribution to helping make our streets a little safer. We thought about it a great deal before making a decision as to how we

could best help. Dorothy is very persuasive, believe me."
Everybody laughed and clapped, and Dorothy blushed. "Seriously now, it's the least we could do, and really, the thanks
go to each of you," Alexander continued. "Maya and I are
perfectly aware that you can find champagne and Scottish
salmon for less at other establishments." More laughter
greeted that comment. "Please enjoy the evening. Our
home is at your disposal, although we do hope you won't
stay the night."

"Pleasant fellow," I said, turning to Lester. "Nice sense of
humor."

"Yes, but don't get on his bad side," Lester replied. "You
don't go from army captain to millionaire many times over
by being nice to everybody."

"I suppose not."

"Have you had the beautiful homes tour?"

"I was just starting to have a look around when the
speeches started."

"I'll escort you, shall I? An antique dealer's guided tour?
Let's get some more of that vastly overpriced champagne to
take with us."

Lester was very amusing and also very knowledgeable. It
was fun, really, seeing the place through his eyes, and he
seemed to enjoy it, too. I knew enough about the stuff he'd
sold to the Alexanders to make the appropriate appreciative
noises, and so he was happy as a clam. They had clearly
spent millions on the place, but all in very good taste, and
Lester had helped him do it. It made me think of my former
relationship with Blair. I wished I could be as proud of that
as Lester seemed to be.

The house really was open for everyone to see. I was in
heaven. I love open houses. I drop in at real estate open

houses all the time, just to see how other people live. I insisted upon looking in every corner, every bathroom, any room that wasn't locked, and there really weren't any that I could find. Yes, there were people who were obviously making sure we guests didn't abscond with the Meissen porcelain, but it was all very tastefully done. You'd hardly guess the gorgeous young people in artistic black were security guards.

Upstairs there were many bedrooms. The master bedroom was all Art Deco, and really spectacular with a huge balcony that ran the length of the room. There was also an upstairs den, and in it a couple of Charles Rennie Mackintosh chairs, both with neat little signs on them asking us to please refrain from sitting on them and a bookcase, also Mackintosh. *Bingo*, I thought.

"I see you do know your Mackintosh," Lester said, as I walked right over to them.

"I've become something of an expert in the last few weeks," I said. "Did you sell them these?"

"I regret to say I didn't. In fact, this is the first time I've seen them." He peered at them carefully. "Undoubtedly authentic."

"Authentic, I'm sure, but I must say those chairs look uncomfortable. What do you bet even their owner doesn't sit in them?"

"They were designed to be uncomfortable. Miss Cranston, for whose tearooms Mackintosh designed these chairs, thought her staff sat around too much, so she asked him to design uncomfortable furniture for the staff room."

I laughed. "You obviously know a lot about this."

"I'm Glaswegian," he said. "I love the way he has these doors on the bookcase. Every detail is perfect. All that hand

work. You just never see something like this these days.
Look at these hinges and the lock."

"Oh, believe me, I have," I said. "I wish I had a photograph of the writing cabinet," I added half to myself.

"What writing cabinet?"

"Umm, I mean the kind of writing cabinet my client
would be interested in. Maybe Alexander has one in his
basement or something."

"Why don't you get a book on Mackintosh and copy a
photo of something similar so you'll have something to
show?" Lester said. "I'd be happy to take it to Alexander for
you, for only a small commission if he sells it to you."

"I'll do that. Have we seen the whole place?"

"Just about," he replied. "Now, come and meet a few
people."

Lester knew everybody. He introduced me to various people whose names I would never remember, and finally, in the
dying minutes of the soirée, he introduced me to the Alexanders themselves. We were admiring what Lester referred to
as the garden room, furnished with lovely old rattan with
lots of orchids everywhere, when the Alexanders walked in.

"Lester!" Robert said. "Good of you to come."

"Entirely my pleasure. May I present Lara McClintoch,"
Lester said. "Ms. McClintoch is an antique dealer from
Toronto."

"Welcome to our home," the great man said.

"Ms. McClintoch is interested in Charles Rennie Mackintosh. She's looking for a writing cabinet for a client."

"We know an antique dealer from Toronto," Maya said.
"Don't we?"

"I'm not sure whom you mean," Robert said. "We have
some Mackintosh upstairs. I hope you saw it: a couple of

supremely uncomfortable chairs and a bookcase in my office cum den."

"You know," she said. "That cute young man who came to see us."

"Maybe I wasn't here at the time," Robert said, putting his arm around his wife's shoulders. "There are always cute young men around my wife, I have to tell you."

"Not really," she said in my general direction.

"Have you seen upstairs?" Alexander said. "And the kitchen? The kitchen is Maya's domain. I think it's officially off-limits, but given you've come so far, we'll make an exception, won't we, darling?"

"Trevor somebody or other," Maya said. "He was admiring our stuff. He liked Mackintosh, too." She slurred her words very slightly and was leaning against her husband. It occurred to me that this party, like Blair's, came complete with a dipsomaniacal spouse. Like Leanna the Lush, Maya must have started into the champagne before the rest of us got there.

"Doesn't ring a bell," Robert said. "You, Lester?"

"Not to me," Lester said.

"You'll be making Lester jealous, darling. He'll think we're fickle, dealing with other antiquarians."

"Heaven forbid," Lester said.

"I must say this one is much better looking than you, Lester," Robert said. "Toronto, did you say? Do you have a card, Ms. . . ."

"McClintoch," I said. "And yes, I do."

"You traitor," Lester said, but I could tell he was kidding.

"Wylie," Maya said. "Trevor Wylie. Do you know him?"

"Actually, I do. At least I did."

"Did?" Maya said vaguely.

"Unfortunately he's dead."

"Oh, no," she said. "Wasn't he awfully young? He can't have been much more than forty, could he?"

"An accident, I expect," Lester said.

"Mmm," I said.

"I don't recall the name at all," Robert said. "Would you like some more champagne?"

"I thought he was really cute," Maya said. "What happened to him?"

"Aren't you being a little ghoulish, darling?" Robert said.

"Um, he was murdered," I said.

"No!" Maya gasped. "That can't be possible. How? Was he shot?"

"My word!" her husband said.

"He was, er, sort of stabbed," I said.

"I had no idea Toronto was such a dangerous place," Lester said.

"Did they catch the person who did it?" Maya said.

"They have charged someone, yes. How do you know Trevor?"

"I can't really recall, but I'm sure he was here."

"Perhaps he's an old boyfriend," Robert said. "Maya and I are still in the honeymoon phase of our life together. I'm afraid there were other men before me, Ms. McClintoch."

"I'm certain we met him together," she said. "Didn't we? I suppose I'm a little under the weather right now."

"These evenings are so difficult for my wife. She really prefers to just putter in the garden. Come, darling, we must say our good-byes. The buses are scheduled to arrive about now to take everyone back into the city. Lovely to meet you,

Ms. McClintoch. If we're ever in Toronto, we'll look you up, and do give us a call if you're back in Glasgow."

"Or maybe he came to our place in Orkney," she said, as her husband lead her away.

"The buses are here," someone called out in the next room.

"Yes, I'm sure that's it. Orkney. We have a place there," she called over her shoulder. "We'll be there this weekend. Come and visit, and you can tell me about Trevor."

"Really, darling," Robert said. "I believe you are making this up."

"If you ever consider selling the Mackintosh, I hope you'll think of me," I said. "I'm interested in anything by Mackintosh, but I'm particularly keen on locating one of his writing cabinets."

"Most certainly," Robert said, "if Lester doesn't object."

"You can have it only if I don't want it," Lester said, laughing. "I suppose you've noticed she drinks a bit," he added when they were gone. "But really she's terrific when she's sober, and as you can see, he adores her. If you get a chance, you really should take her up on her offer to visit in Orkney. They own an equally fabulous place there. No weekend cottage, you understand. It's practically a palace. It's on Hoxa."

"Hoxa?"

"Near St. Margaret's Hope. Lovely little town."

This was just too good to be true. I was zeroing in on a revelation of great proportions, I was certain of it. "So have you ever heard of Trevor Wylie, an antique dealer from Toronto? He's originally from Scotland."

"I don't think so. Wait, he wasn't the one killed with an axe, was he? You said stabbed. Were you trying to be delicate? I read about it in the paper."

"One and the same."

"My, my! Hard to think Maya Alexander would know someone who ended up like that. It was over a piece of furniture or something, wasn't it?"

"Something like that."

"Come to think of it, I'm sure that explains all. She read it in the paper, just as I did, and in her present state, by which I mean a little tipsy, recalled the name, and decided she must have met him. The name obviously means nothing to Robert."

"I'm sure you're right," I said, but I really didn't think so. My heart soared. Maybe at last I was on the right track. Maybe this whole obsession of mine was not just me being silly. Forget that ridiculous conversation with Percy. Percy didn't matter. Who cared if he was looking for the same writing cabinet I was? Surely this could be win/win for both of us. So I hadn't been able to find an antique dealer by the name of Macdonald. That was too bad, but it was no longer a real problem. What mattered was that I had found a connection with Trevor Wylie in both Glasgow and Orkney, a connection, furthermore, which owned some Mackintosh furniture. Real Mackintosh! The following day I would be on a plane heading for Orkney. I decided I just might take Maya Alexander up on her lovely offer.

Chapter 5

And so Bjarni sailed for the Hebrides, or what he would have
known as Suðreyar, the Southern Isles. There was always loot to be
had there, especially in the churches and monasteries, and being a
pagan, Bjarni had no qualms about helping himself to what he
could find. To reach the Hebrides from Orkney and indeed Caithness,
however, required rounding the aptly named Cape Wrath, something
the Vikings did only when good weather permitted. But Bjarni did
not have the luxury of waiting for that, and confident in his abili-
ties as a sailor, he set sail. It was then that Bjarni's troubles began.

It has to be said that neither Bjarni nor Oddi, who was captain
of the second ship, lacked confidence in their skills as seamen. In
Bjarni's case that confidence was not misplaced, but in Oddi's, perhaps it was. They hoped to outrun a storm that was brewing over
the Atlantic, dark ominous clouds low on the horizon, but they
didn't make it. Bjarni made landfall, but Oddi didn't, and his
ship was thrown up on to the rocks near Cape Wrath. Several of
Oddi's men perished, but Oddi himself was saved.

There were many Norsemen in northern Scotland, although never as numerous as the Picts and Scots, but Oddi was fortunate at least that he was found on the shore by fellow Norsemen, who took him in. It took several days, but Bjarni and Oddi were at last re-united. Chastened by the storm and the loss of some of their comrades, several of the men opted to stay where they were, and take their chances with Einar, but Bjarni and Oddi sailed on. Now with only one ship, Bjarni and Oddi sailed for the Hebrides.

The Hebrides were well known to the Vikings. Some say the Viking Age began in 793 with the raid of the monastery on the English island of Lindesfarne. But it was at Iona in the Hebrides in 795 that the Vikings and the Scots first made contact, with the terrible sacking of the Irish monastery there. Many have written of it since, the ferociousness of the attack, the heartlessness of the marauders, the fear that struck every Scottish heart. It was on the crucible of Lindesfarne and Iona that the reputation of the Vikings as terrifying and destructive heathens was forged. And those raids were just the beginning. The monastery at Iona was sacked four times by Vikings between 795 and 826 alone, and it would continue to be a target for three centuries more. Even though a few years before Bjarni arrived, Olaf Sihtricsson, the Norse King of Dublin, had retired there as a penitent after his defeat at Tara in Ireland, the raids continued. For some, old traditions die hard. So Bjarni did what he had always done: alone under cover of darkness he slipped ashore. But this time the monks were waiting for him, and he barely escaped with his life.

His reception in Ireland wasn't any better. Sigurd had been defeated at Clontarf by the Irish King Brian Boru. The King died when Sigurd did, but there was no haven for Bjarni's type of Viking anymore. Bjarni, of course, had no idea that the Vikings in England would be defeated by their cousins the Normans within a few years, that essentially their glory days were over. It is interest-

ing to speculate whether he felt the occasional twinge of awareness that things were not as he would have them. He would surely be surprised to find that Vikings and Celts were living peaceably together in what he considered to be Viking Dublin. So Bjarni and his remaining men kept going, and from here on it was, at least for Bjarni, uncharted territory.

IN THE COLD hard light of dawn, my optimism evaporated. Gone was the lovely buzz of the champagne, the good cheer generated by pleasant company and exceptional surroundings. Gone, too, was the pale sunshine of the day before, to be replaced by a dismal drizzle. I was back to replaying my conversation with Percy. What had that conversation with Percy actually meant? I kept trying to recall his exact words and the possible interpretation of them. He could have been lying about his knowledge or the lack thereof of the writing cabinet's value, but he'd have to be a pretty good actor to look as surprised as he had. This did not bode well for this ridiculous trip to Orkney.

Then there was the small matter of John A. Macdonald Antiques. It didn't exist. I was sure there was something hugely important in this, beyond the obvious fact that it put the actual transaction into grave doubt. But this bogus transaction had to be part of something much bigger, something involving not one but two writing cabinets. I just could not fathom what this big something might be. After all, Trevor could have imported two writing cabinets from two different places with perfectly genuine paperwork for each piece. Did that mean that he'd stolen one of them? I'd checked all international databases that listed stolen items such as this, Interpol, for example, before I left. If it had turned up, then the fake invoice made sense. But it hadn't, so I was right back where I started.

These ruminations made me exceptionally irritable, and I stayed that way when the rain stopped somewhere between Glasgow and Inverness and even when the sun came out just as the aircraft crossed the coastline. Below were lines of oil rigs, a blight on the landscape, but interesting nonetheless, and farther out, visible through wisps of white clouds, a chain of the greenest islands I had ever seen. Given our flying time, I could only assume those islands were my destination.

The truth of the matter was that if it hadn't been for my rather quixotic quest, to use Percy's word, for a second writing cabinet, I wouldn't know where Orkney was. Oh, I knew what we call the Orkney Islands, and Rendall the publican called Orkney, were somewhere off the coast of Scotland, but where, exactly, I wasn't sure, and until now I hadn't had cause to ask. There were all those islands, some of them apparently quite beautiful, the Hebrides, Skye, the Shetlands, the Isles of Man and Arran, different, or at least I thought so, from the Irish Aran Islands where I'd actually been. Really, I didn't have a clue which was which. I think I had labored under the illusion that I would go to Glasgow, civilized place that it was, would find the antique dealer, and all would be made right. Instead I was reduced to consulting the route map in the magazine in the seat pocket in front of me, to find out that Orkney lay north and east of Scotland. Even with that, I still had no idea what the climate was like, had not booked a hotel, and just hoped that transportation would be available, whatever transportation, that is, that was required. From the air, I could see there were several islands, and I could only hope and pray that my destination was the one with the airport.

This is an embarrassing admission for someone who plans her buying trips with military precision, and who makes a point of knowing as much as possible about her destination before she arrives, but there you are. I was entering uncharted territory, and this fact alone left me feeling anxious and out of sorts.

The trouble was, all efforts to the contrary, I couldn't hold on to my vile mood. The airport was a dear little thing, and I had my suitcase within five minutes of entering it. Or maybe it was only three minutes. I was so nonplussed by this unseemly haste in unloading the baggage from the aircraft and getting it into the passengers' hands that I was about to say to the staff person who called out to ask if this was my luggage, now spinning all by itself on a miniature carousel, that it might look like mine but it couldn't possibly be mine, given I'd only just arrived. I hadn't even bothered to go look for it right away. I figured I had at least a half hour before the luggage carousel beeped loudly and turned on, only to circle empty for an eternity, and had gone to the gift shop to buy a map.

Ten minutes after that shock to my system, I had a car. The car rental agency was a counter in what would be a closet at home. The woman staffing it took my credit card imprint, and then, stuffing it into a drawer, told me it was a bank holiday of some sort, and she wouldn't be putting the charges through on my credit card for a couple of days or three. She didn't have one of those machines that charge you in a nanosecond, nor did she phone the credit card company to verify that I could actually pay for this vehicle of hers. She just handed me the keys, told me to enjoy my stay, and advised that if she wasn't there when I departed, I could just throw the keys in a box.

I eyed her suspiciously. In those three days, was she going on a buying spree with my credit card documentation, or even, heaven forbid, stealing my identity? Even if she had no such plans, was there sufficient security on this closet of hers, that my credit card documents wouldn't be stolen in the night? Those of us who live in big cities, especially those of us in a place of business that has recently suffered not one but two robberies in short order, know we have to be eternally vigilant. I decided I was just going to have to risk it. I asked for directions for St. Margaret's Hope, and rather than whipping some unreadable map off a desk pad, she painstakingly wrote out the directions by hand, explaining everything carefully as she did so.

But that was not the end of the startling events. Even more disconcerting, if not downright alarming, was the fact that actually getting to the rental car did not require a bus or train to transport me to the real car rental office a hundred miles or so from the airport. Indeed it was only a few steps from the terminal door to my car.

I was transfixed. I felt as if I had fallen off the edge of the civilized world, or more accurately, that I had fallen off the edge of an uncivilized world into paradise. There was one small problem in paradise ahead of me, though, and that was the right-hand drive, and the consequent necessity to shift gears with my left hand. I was a tiny bit apprehensive about pulling my little gray Ford into traffic, so I decided to circle the airport parking lot once before I headed out, just to get the feel of the car. That took approximately twenty seconds, thirty if you count the time it took me to find reverse and back out of the parking place. I crept up to the road in first gear, foot resting on the clutch the whole way so I'd be ready for anything, then stopped and carefully looked both ways. You have to do that when you start to drive on the left. It's hard to know until you get used to it, from which direction they'll be coming at you. Astonishingly, there was no car in sight, in either direction. "Good grief, where am I?" I said to the windshield, as I pulled out on to what my map said was a numbered highway. In what outpost, far from the aggravations of life as I knew it, was I exactly?

I had a rather jolly time of it, coasting along in third gear, no other vehicles in sight, and admiring the scenery, heading, at least I hoped that was what I was doing, for St. Margaret's Hope, home to one of the writing cabinets, if Trevor's documentation could be believed, which obviously it couldn't, given the business about John A. Macdonald Antiques. Somehow, despite the directions, I made the wrong turn, and found myself heading, not for St. Margaret's Hope, but rather into the capital city of Kirkwall. By and large I try to avoid driving in foreign capitals, especially on my first visit. They are large, aggressive, and scary if you don't know your way about. I can even get lost in Washington, or rather not lost exactly: I know where I am. I'm just always in the wrong lane for where I want to go. I've driven in London, Rome, and Paris and therefore don't think I need to prove anything anymore. So Kirkwall was to be avoided.

In a few minutes, however, the highway—I use the term reluctantly—turned into a street lined with houses, a handful of cars appeared to share the road with me, and shortly after that I found myself on a very narrow street, what I'd call a lane at home, with a tree in the middle of it, a tree that required some maneuvering to get around, I might add. Just ahead was a soaring cathedral in rather beautiful red stone that dominated the entire town. *Kirk*, "church," I thought. This really is Kirkwall. It was, well, small. It was also a bit complicated, at least for me. In my efforts to get out of town again, I did the unforgivable: I turned on to a one-way street from the wrong direction right in front of a policeman. Needless to say I was pulled over.

"I am so sorry," I said, putting on my very best contrite face. "I'm terribly lost. I was trying to get to St. Margaret's Hope."

"I'm afraid you're a long way from there," the policeman said. "I'm sorry about our street signage. We all know where we're going, you see, and sometimes the street signs are not as clear as they might be. You'll find that, especially outside of Kirkwall. You'll be following signs for places and then all of a sudden they'll disappear."

A couple of pedestrians came up at this point. "She's trying to get to St. Margaret's Hope," the policeman told them.

"That's a peedie bit of a drive," one of the women said.

"Aye. At least twenty minutes, maybe more," the other added. I didn't ask what peedie meant, although I was to later learn it meant small. Apparently they intended the opposite at that moment. I declined to mention that I have a twenty-minute drive to my local dry cleaners.

"I know I made an illegal turn," I said. "And I'm going the wrong way."

"Sorry. It's not easy to find your way here," the other woman said. What followed was a polite disagreement on the subject of whose fault it was I found myself in this particular spot. I couldn't believe my ears, and I'm a Canadian: step on my toe and I'll apologize to you. These people were arguing it was their fault I was going the wrong way on a one-way street. Not only that, when they'd given me new directions, the policeman made two drivers who had the legal right of way back out of the street so I could proceed! In some places in the world, I'd have been in handcuffs by then. There was something seriously the matter with these people.

In about two minutes, I was out of the bustling metropolis of Kirkwall, and on my way again. So unnerved was I by the display of the milk of human kindness I had just witnessed, however, that even with the new set of directions, I got lost a second time, and found myself on a road signed not for St. Margaret's Hope, but for Ophir. For some reason, I didn't care anymore. I rather liked the sound of someplace called Ophir; it had a rather exotic ring to it. Exotic it wasn't, although it was very pleasant, just a few houses on the side of the road. I barely had time to gear down before it was time to pick up the pace again.

Just outside of Ophir, there was a sign for something called a Bu, and the Orkneyinga Saga Centre, and having no idea what either might be, but curious, I turned off and had a look. I found the ruins of an old church and dining hall, called the Earl's Bu, once the haunt of Vikings and the site of a rather gruesome murder, if the film in an empty visitor center was anything to go by. In the film, which obviously was linked to some kind of motion detector because I didn't see another soul anywhere and it turned itself on the minute I sat down, they told some of the stories in something called the Orkneyinga Saga, the history of the Viking earls of Orkney. These Viking earls lived in what were obviously rather violent times. Still, I thought it was all very nice, except for the murder part, particularly alarming given axes were a weapon of choice. I was, however, surprised to learn that Orkney had been an important part of the Viking world, and indeed remained more Scandinavian than Scottish for a very long time. I gathered that the people here were rather proud of their Scandinavian heritage. I'm not sure what entitled me to be surprised, given that until a few hours ago I had had no clear idea of Orkney at all, but I was.

Soon, much better informed, I was back on the road. The sea was to my left, beautiful, really, and to my right, some hills. Across the water even higher hills were shrouded in mist. It was spectacularly beautiful, really, in a sedate, well-managed sort of way. But still, no people. I was beginning to wonder if this particular bank holiday was one in which everyone left the island, or indeed, if the world had come to end since I'd left Kirkwall and somehow I'd missed it. One car overtook and passed me, but that was all. Then I found myself heading downhill in the direction of a little town, its name, according to the sign, Stromness.

Stromness is built on a steep hill sloping down to a harbor. There is a ferry terminal, and indeed a large white ferry was just pulling away. The houses are mostly stone, and the streets the same, even narrower, if anything, than Kirkwall. I edged my way through the town in first gear. I had to keep my eye on the road ahead, as in several places the main street went down to one lane because of the corners of buildings that jutted out into the road. At the far edge of town I decided I had enough driving for one day, and was going to stay in Stromness, to regroup and get my bearings, but also to see if it really was as nice as it looked. After all, what was the rush?

I abandoned my car in a parking area that appeared to be free, as unlikely as that might be. I couldn't find any way to pay, but perhaps this was what they did to foreigners: they hid the meters and then towed our cars. After several passes up and down the main street on foot, admiring the lovely gray stone houses, the cobbled streets, and charming steep laneways with amusing names like Khyber Pass, and the last flowers of the season still blooming in window boxes, and actually having been smiled at by several people, I chose a bed-and-breakfast run by one Mrs. Olive Brown. She wasn't much for conversation, our Mrs. Brown, but she was pleasant enough and the place was spotless. She even had a place for my car, although the place I'd left my car was okay, too, and no, of course I didn't have to pay to park there. I told her I'd be staying a day or two. She didn't ask for a deposit, but I insisted on paying for two nights on the spot. I mean, certain people must be protected from themselves, and Mrs. Brown was one of them.

I went out again late in the afternoon. There was a very fine little art gallery in a converted warehouse or two down on the pier, with some rather splendid twentieth-century British artists, Barbara Hepworth and Ben Nicholson, for example. I also found a pleasant bistro down by the ferry docks for dinner, and stuffed my face with local seafood. As I climbed up to the third floor to my little attic room overlooking the harbor, I decided Orkney couldn't be the cultural backwater that Trevor had always implied his birthplace was, not with art and food like that. I thought the place was splendid. Even my little room was lovely, in pink and purple and white, and best of all, I had a rather fine view. I could see the street, the harbor, the ferry docks and the sky, clear now and filled with stars. I curled up on the window seat in my bathrobe, the shot of lovely single malt scotch Mrs. Brown had offered in hand, and watched as a ferry sailed in. The street was almost deserted except for the odd person or two, probably leaving the pub down the street.

For a while I sat and thought about Blair and the Mackintosh, and all concrete evidence to the contrary, I decided once again that everything was going to be all right. I suppose it was the place that made me feel this way, Mrs. Brown's quiet hospitality, the view, the sheer beauty that lay before me. It was one of the nicest places I had ever been, and therefore I was going to find the source of the writing cabinet, my reputation would be restored, to say nothing of my sense of personal worth, and somehow I was going to get Blair Bazillionaire, who really was a nice guy despite his temper, out of jail. I could almost hear him apologize for yelling at me both at his home and the police station.

I spread out the map I'd purchased at the airport and found St. Margaret's Hope. It was a town on an island called South Ronaldsay, but it looked to me as if I didn't need to sail or swim to get there. It was attached to the island on which I found myself, called rather quaintly the Mainland, by a series of causeways called the Churchill Barriers. The town itself was much smaller than Stromness and therefore entirely manageable. I also found Hoxa where the Alexanders holidayed. I would go there in the morning, visit any antique dealers there might be, inquire if need be in the local pub for a furniture maker, and presto I would find the source of the fake Mackintosh. Either that or I would make inquiries and find the former owner of the real Mackintosh. Doubtless either or both of these people would, like everyone else here, be terribly polite, honest as the day is long, and even possibly glad to see me in their quiet, reserved way.

It was once again, I'm afraid, a feeling I was unable to maintain for long, because as I sat there feeling positively mellow, passengers began to disembark from a ferry and make their way toward the town. One moment the spot under a streetlight between me and the ferry docks was empty. The next moment, a woman I could have sworn was Willow stood there. She was wearing jeans and a leather jacket, almost identical to what she'd been wearing when I had found her snooping about Trevor's store. I did not know what Willow would be doing standing under that particular light in that particular place. I'd told her I would go to Glasgow and if necessary on to Orkney, and she had seemed content with that. I had been completely open about my plans. If this really was Willow, she had not shared my candor.

I pulled on my jeans and a sweater, intent on getting a closer view and to berate her if it indeed was Willow. I made it down to the street just in time to see a motorcycle ridden by a man in snappy red and blue gear and helmet pull up beside her and the two of them speed off. I was to spend the next forty-eight hours trying to convince myself I was mistaken, that it wasn't Willow. If it wasn't she, though, then Willow had a double in Scotland.

I had no such doubts about the second sighting. As I stood there completely frustrated, someone else came off the ferry. This time I knew who I was looking at. It was Percy Bicycle Clips. He was walking his bike toward the street when I intercepted him.

"You!" he said. "Stop following me."

"I've been here for several hours, Percy," I said. "You just got off the boat. That means you are following me!"

"I live here," he said.

"Does your grandmother live here, too, because I'd really like to talk to her. What is your name, anyway?"

"Go away!" he said, leaping on to his bicycle. I tried to stop him, but he eluded me and before I knew it was pedaling furiously away from me. It was a scenario that was becoming a tad repetitious, because once again the outcome was the same. I chased after him for a minute or so, but I knew I wouldn't catch him. I watched his back disappear over the top of the hill from whence I'd entered the town. He appeared to know his way around the place rather better than I did. I still didn't know his name.

As I mounted the stairs to my dear little attic room, it occurred to me that while twenty-four hours ago I barely knew where Orkney was, I was acquainted with a lot more people on this island than I would ever have dreamed. Orkney was getting just a little crowded for my taste.

The next morning it was kind of hard to know where to begin. Should I look for Willow, ask her why she'd come to Orkney without telling me? Should I try to find Percy and shake him until he told me who he was and what he was doing? Should I go to this town with the lovely name of St. Margaret's Hope (what did St. Margaret hope for, I wondered) and try to locate the dealer who sold Trevor the other cabinet, or should I seek out Hoxa and the Alexanders' palace?

What I really wanted to do was wander the lovely streets of Stromness and gaze out at the water, and indeed I did permit myself a short walk along the pier. The morning was clear and the town was perfectly reflected in the absolutely still waters of the harbor. I could have stood there forever, but finally I told myself to get moving. I made a half-hearted attempt to consult the local phone directory for Wylie, but there were a lot of them, and Willow had said Trevor had never mentioned any relatives, and he'd left Orkney a long time ago if one were inclined to believe what he said.

I decided to take a more direct route back to Kirkwall, reasoning that the capital city with its hotels and shops would be a likely place to find Willow and possibly Percy. It would also take me back to a place where I could pick up my missed route to St. Margaret's Hope. The highway, again loosely defined, was much busier than the Ophir road. I swear I saw at least five other cars. The island had a rather gentle typography, rolling farmland more than anything else, although I could see dark cliffs off in the distance. As I was whipping along at a stately forty miles per hour, I noticed, at the side of the road, a rather pathetic-looking creature, thumb out, a decidedly damaged bicycle at his feet. It was my pal Percy again. I pulled over and got out.

He was a mess, shirt sleeve badly torn, hair definitely askew, his hands cut up, and his pants were covered in mud. I don't think he recognized me at first, because he was trying to keep broken glasses on his nose and not particularly successfully. When he did realize who it was, though, he did the predictable. "Go away," he said.

"Have you noticed how few cars there are on this road?" I asked. "I wouldn't be so hasty. What happened?"

"I fell," he replied sadly. "Straight into a ditch and then into a barbed wire fence."

"I'll give you a lift," I said. "If you'll tell me your real name."

"It's Percy," he replied. "Just Percy."

"Then why does Rendall Sinclair, the publican at the Stane, think that it's Arthur? I've never known Rendall to get a name wrong."

"Arthur Percival," he said after a long pause, as another car sped by. "Everybody calls me Percy."

"Put your bike in the back and get in," I said.

He hesitated. "How do I know you won't kill me? Maybe you killed that antique dealer."

"Do I look like an axe murderer to you?" I said.

"I don't know what an axe murderer looks like." I glared at him. "Perhaps not," he agreed.

"You could be the axe murderer," I said. "You were there when Trevor was showing the writing cabinet, and you were there again when I arrived the time that, well, you know, that unpleasant business with the axe."

"Do I look like an axe murderer to you?" he said, looking morosely down at his stained and rumpled pants and his torn shirt sleeve.

"Perhaps not," I said. "Anyway, we've had this conversation before. Put your bike in the back, and let's go." I watched him fumble around a bit peering at the back of the car for the latch, and realized he could hardly see a thing. I got my bag out and found a safety pin. "Here," I said. "Give me your glasses." I managed to attach the arm to the rest of the frame, and I cleaned them up a bit. "These will do until you get home." He put them on. If anything he looked more comical than ever, but I tried very hard not to laugh.

"Thank you," he said. "This is good."

"Where to?"

"Kirkwall, I suppose. I will have to try to find somebody who can fix my bicycle right away or maybe rent me one in the meantime. Just please don't ask me questions."

"I don't think that's fair. I've told you everything I know or suspect in this matter. In fact, I've poured out my heart to you, and you have told me nothing."

"I can't," he said. "For one thing you would think I'm crazy."

"Try me," I said, but he wouldn't.

"Your first trip to Orkney?" he asked in a conversational tone after a few minutes of silence.

"Yes. It's wonderful."

"It is. Have you seen that?" he said, pointing to a small hill a few hundred yards from the road.

"What is it?"

"Maze how," he said.

"Maze who?"

"M-A-E-S-H-O-W-E," he spelled. "Maeshowe. You don't know what it is, do you?"

"Obviously not," I said. "As we've already ascertained, I've never been to Orkney before."

"You still should know what it is," he replied.

"But I don't, so why don't you enlighten me? I can tell you're dying to."

"Pull over," he said pointing. "There, beside that building. You buy two tickets, and I'll go clean myself up a bit," he said. I did what I was told. Before I knew it we were across the highway and walking toward a hill. Percy definitely looked better with the blood washed off, and his hair slicked down. We were greeted by a perky tour guide at the entrance of what looked to be a big hill of grass.

"Welcome to Maeshowe," she said. "One of the world's greatest Neolithic chamber tombs."

"Wow," I said. Percy looked smug.

"You are in what UNESCO calls Orkney's Neolithic Heartland," she went on. "It's a World Heritage Site, actually a combination of sites, most of a ceremonial nature. Over there in the distance you can see the Ring of Brodgar, and the Standing Stones of Stenness, and, of course, farther north, you can visit the ancient town of Skara Brae."

"You mean a ring like Stonehenge?" I said peering off into the distance in the direction of the guide's pointing finger. Percy gave me a "Don't you know anything?" look.

"Not identical, but yes, a henge ring of standing stones," she said.

"Why didn't I know about this?" I said to Percy. "I love this kind of thing."

"Shush," he said, so I did. I soon found myself bent over and entering a long passageway, the walls of which were made out of the most amazingly large stone slabs, and thence standing in a large, somewhat beehive-shaped stone chamber. It was extraordinary, very sophisticated in design and construction, and dating apparently to almost five thousand years ago! It must have been one of the greatest architectural achievements of those times. First Vikings and now this! Who knew?

Maeshowe might date to Neolithic times, the most important but not the only chamber tomb to dot these islands, but apparently it had been reused by Vikings, possibly as the tomb of some important person in the ninth century, then looted three centuries later. There were inscriptions on the walls, Viking runes that had been translated, and if you judged the Vikings by these runes, they were a lusty lot. There seemed to be several claims to sexual exploits. There was also a reference to well-hidden treasure, but apparently none had been found there.

"You mean to tell me that Orkney is just covered with Neolithic tombs?" I said to Percy when we'd finished our tour.

"There are lots of them," he said. "They're still finding them on a reasonably regular basis. They just look like hills or mounds of earth, and they're often found by accident. Mine Howe in Tankerness, for example, was found because a cow fell through the roof of it. Others are found when somebody's sitting out admiring the scenery and the leg of the

stool breaks through or something like that. There are lots
here as yet undiscovered, I'm convinced of it."

"And you want to find one?"

"Yes, I wouldn't mind that at all."

"I got the impression you knew how to read those runic
inscriptions."

"Sort of. I can't do it without a textbook in front of me,
but yes, with some effort I can."

"That's amazing. Can we go see these standing stones,
seeing as we're in the neighborhood?"

"I guess," Percy said. He sounded a bit resigned, but
when we got there he proved to be an able and enthusiastic
tour guide.

The Ring of Brodgar is simply astonishing, a perfect circle of megaliths or stone slabs that measures something over
three hundred feet in diameter, the slabs themselves up to
about fourteen feet high. It is surrounded by a ditch, and
has as its backdrop the lovely water of a loch. Purple heather
blooms in and around it. There are thirty-six stones now,
but apparently there were sixty, and this monument, too,
dates back to the Neolithic Age. The Stones of Stenness,
part of another stone circle that was in use beginning about
five thousand years ago, are very tall stone slabs, a little under twenty feet. Sheep graze amongst the stones, the circle
empty except for them and Percy and me. I was absolutely
enchanted. What ancient ceremonies would have taken
place there? What deities did these people believe in?
When had the Vikings arrived? I wanted to know.

Percy insisted we drive farther north to a place on the
coast called Skara Brae, site of a Neolithic village. It was an
extraordinary place. You could actually see how people lived
thousands of years ago, with their built-in box beds and

their hearths. There were several layers of homes built over time, covering many, many centuries of habitation. I had thought, I suppose, that Stone Age peoples lived in ghastly huts, and was surprised by how sophisticated these houses were. Skara Brae was another of those serendipitous finds, having been revealed in 1850 when a terrible storm stripped the surface away.

Percy eventually tired of my endless questions and exclamations of delight, and he was limping more obviously the farther afield we went. "Kirkwall," I said, taking pity on him. "I'll come back and see these again later. Thank you for showing them to me."

"That's okay," he said.

"I don't suppose you would tell me why you were in Glasgow," I said.

"Same reason you were, I expect," he said.

"And what would you say that was?"

"I don't know. The startling revelation, perhaps. The easy solution."

"I didn't find either of those."

"Nor I. Wishful thinking, then," he said. "For both of us."

"We could join forces. To find the source of the second writing cabinet."

"I don't think so."

"Why not?"

"Fundamentally we're looking for different things," he said. "Yes, we are both looking for a piece of furniture on one level, but you are really seeking vindication."

"When you put it like that, I suppose you're right, but I am also looking for justice, and I remain unconvinced that justice is being served in the arrest and trial of Blair Baldwin."

"Okay, justice, too," he said. "I suppose."

"Thank you for that concession." He almost smiled. "And what is it you are looking for?"

He paused for a moment. "I'm not sure. Salvation, maybe?"

"And what form will this salvation take?"

"The Wasteland," he said. "Since you won't stop asking until I tell you."

"I see. Are we talking a wasteland, or *The Wasteland* with capital *T*, capital *W*?"

"So many questions. *The Wasteland*," he said, with the emphasis on 'the.' "The Wasteland, the maze, the wounded king." He laughed then, but it was a humorless sound, more bark than anything else.

"The Wasteland," I repeated. "As in T. S. Eliot. It doesn't look very wastelandish here. In fact, it's one of the greenest places I've ever been."

"I'll find it," he said. "I hope we will both find what we're looking for."

"But we can't do this together?"

"No, I don't think so. It is a solitary quest, after all. We have to choose our own paths. It is simply a matter of asking the right question, and each of us in our own way will have to do that."

Great, I thought. *It's possible I'm in a car on a relatively untraveled road with a delusional and possibly seriously disturbed person.* I wanted to ask more, to tell him to stop being so obscure, but in the end I didn't press him. Perhaps the native niceness was wearing off on me, or maybe I wasn't in the mood for riddles. I could tell his injuries were really starting to hurt him now, and he looked very discouraged. I parked on the edge of town where he directed me, and I watched him limp away, his bent and twisted bicycle in his arms. As he reached the first corner he turned back for a moment, and I had the impression he was coming back, that there was something more he wanted to say. But he only inclined his head toward me. At the time I took that to be a silent thank-you, but since I've wondered if it was an acknowledgment that we were two of kind, kindred spirits, both of us unable to rest until our questions, both temporal and spiritual in the broadest sense of the word, had been answered. It is a picture of him that will stay with me a very long time.

Chapter 6

Bjarni and Oddi would endure tremendous hardship before they would reach landfall again. Buffeted by waves in the Channel and then fierce storms in the Bay of Biscay, they finally ran aground in Galicia in what is northern Spain. At the turn of the last millennium, Galicia was something of an anomaly, a rather isolated place, surrounded by sea to the north and west, cut off from the rest of Europe by mountains to the east and the armies of Muslim Spain to the south. The cape that juts out into the sea in Galicia is not called Finisterre, the end of the world, for nothing.

Exhausted and hungry, Bjarni and his men tried to steal food, but once again their plans went awry. Galicia had been raided for years by Vikings, and by Saracen pirates from the south, and the landowners were ready for them. Ever the opportunists, however, the Vikings abducted the younger daughter of the landowner whose larder they'd unsuccessfully tried to rob and demanded a great ransom for her safe release. It was a heinous crime, of course, the act of desperate men, and it had unexpected consequences.

While Bjarni was negotiating his price for the return of the young woman, whose name was Goisvintha, Oddi was put in charge of guarding her, which put the two of them, strapping Viking and comely young woman, in constant contact. I suppose the inevitable ensued, first pleas for freedom on her part, words of sympathy on his, then jest, and eventually passion: Oddi and Goisvintha fell in love or at least in lust, and Oddi was not for sending her back to her father, one Theodoric by name, no matter the price, nor was she for returning. Oddi sent his brother back to negotiate a marriage rather than a ransom, and Theodoric reacted as one might expect. No daughter of Theodoric's was going to marry a Viking pagan. Bjarni told a disappointed Goisvintha and Oddi of her father's intractability on that subject.

"I've come up with a plan," Oddi told his brother. "We'll dress one of the thralls in Goisvintha's clothing, and you'll exchange him for the money." Thralls were servants or slaves really and didn't have much to say about what happened to them. "In the dark, Theodoric won't notice until it's too late. The rest of us will wait for you at the boat, and we'll all be on our way, including Goisvintha, as soon as you and the money arrive."

What Bjarni thought of this plan, we'll never know, but apparently he agreed to it. Theodoric, perhaps knowing his daughter's nature very well, or being at least as crafty as Oddi, was not fooled at all, and what Bjarni got for the thrall in woman's clothing was a sack of sand. Bjarni made a run for the boat, Theodoric and his fellow landowners hot on his trail. What ensued was a rout, one in which Bjarni's only boat was destroyed and the other Vikings killed. Only Bjarni, Oddi, and his Goisvintha, and the poet Svein were able to escape into the night. But they were not free for long.

* * *

MAYA ALEXANDER WAS on her knees weeding in her garden when I found her, her long ash blond hair tied in a ponytail, in jeans and a sweatshirt. She was being helped by a rather muscular man in army fatigues, with short-cropped hair and dark eyes, the kind of man you notice partly because he's good-looking, but also because he's a bit intimidating. It had been quite easy to find her. I just followed the road across the Churchill Barriers, causeways that linked a small chain of islands, and then turned on to the road to Hoxa. Then I simply stopped at the largest house I'd seen since I'd arrived.

Maya looked genuinely pleased to see me, even if my name eluded her. "It's . . . I'm sorry, I'm just so bad with names. You're the antique dealer from Toronto and your name is?"

"Lara McClintoch," I said. "This is very presumptuous of me to just show up, but Lester described your home very well, and I knew it had to be yours the minute I saw it. It is as spectacular as he said it is. I won't stay. I just wanted to say hello." Lester had likened the Alexanders' Orkney residence to a palace, but it wasn't really. It was, however, a very fine three-story stone house with acres of land around it, a tree-lined drive, and a wonderful view across Hoxa to the sea.

"But I invited you," she said. "I may have had too much champagne that evening, but I remember that very well. Please come in. I'll just wash my hands. Drever, this is Lara McClintoch. Lara, this is Drever Clark, who looks after the place for us. Drever, you'll have to carry on without me." Drever nodded in my general direction and then went back to his work.

Soon we were comfortably ensconced in a sunroom, filled with plants and flowers, and white wicker furniture. The

view from this side of the house was also fine, but marred by
a rather decrepit-looking structure, this one a real castlé of
sorts, but terribly run down, with a garden that hadn't been
tended in years. There was some kind of hedge that was
completely out of control, and weeds everywhere, and a barn
way out back that looked about to fall down. Maya found
me looking at it as she brought in a tray of tea and short-
breads. She'd changed into a cashmere sweater and leggings.
"Awful, isn't it?" she said. "I don't know what to do. I cannot understand why anyone would take so little care of a
place like that. I want to run out and fix up that garden
every time I look at it. The worst part of it is the dogs. I
don't know if the neighbors were breeding them or what,
but they were big and vicious, at least I think so, and they
kept running all over our property, and there's this man who
lives there who just hangs around. There's something the
matter with him. He's not quite right, if you see what I'm
saying. The concept of private property seems to be mean-
ingless to him. He just wanders over here whenever he feels
like it.

"Robert tells me to relax, to live and let live, you know,
be an accommodating neighbor. He says he'll buy the property at some point, and tear that ghastly medieval thing
down. The owner won't sell right now, but Robert says he's
elderly, his wife died very recently, and he has been unwell
himself for years, some World War Two injury apparently.
He will have to leave eventually, one way or the other. I just
grit my teeth and pretend it's not there. Heaven knows
what it's doing to the value of our property, but I guess we
don't want to sell. I don't anyway."

"Everything around here is so pretty," I said. "It does

rather stand out. Most of the houses are beautifully kept up. Orkney seems to be such a nice, orderly place, with really pleasant people." As I spoke a cyclist hove into view and just as quickly disappeared. I was reasonably sure it was Percy, but there was nothing I could do about that at this very moment.

"It is pretty, and everyone is genuinely nice. I love it here. I wish I had friends, that's all. People are very pleasant, but they don't really warm to outsiders. I tried throwing a party when we first came here, but the only people who would come were tourists like me."

"Maybe they were afraid they'd have to reciprocate. Your home is a little overwhelming, you have to admit."

"Maybe," she said. "I remain convinced they'll get used to me eventually. But you're here now and I'm so glad."

The property itself was beautifully landscaped, taking real advantage of the rolling terrain. "Is that a golf course I'm looking at?" I said pointing out the side window.

"Sort of. It's a driving range, and there's a putting green down by the water. Robert is nuts about golf. I complained about being a golf widow, so he put this in so he could play here part of the time. Ridiculous I know. Drever spends more than half his time working on it, I swear. I don't know what Robert was thinking."

I laughed. "If he can afford it, why not?"

"He can afford it," she said. "I can also tell you he loses most of his balls in the sea."

We talked for a while, small talk really. Maya struck me as a little bit sad in some way, as if life hadn't quite turned out the way she wanted it to. Most of us would kill to have a beautiful home in Orkney, another in Glasgow, and, ap-

parently, a condo in Spain. This place in Orkney was her favorite she said. She'd stay all year long if she could, but her
husband's business dealings prohibited that.

Maya kept bringing the conversation back to my antique
shop, which was fine with me. I knew she was working her
way around to asking me about Trevor, just as I was interested in finding out where she and her husband acquired
their furniture and if Trevor had played a role. That opportunity came for both of us when she gave me a tour of her
house. We were in the master bedroom, which was completely white, or rather ivory, not what I would have chosen
in this northern climate which seemed to me to cry out for
something warmer, but striking just the same. I knew what
it had been modeled on, right down to the last detail: the
bedroom Charles Rennie Mackintosh had designed at 78
Southpark Avenue, now reassembled and part of the
Hunterian Art Gallery of the University of Glasgow. I knew
that because I'd seen it.

"Lovely Mackintosh reproduction," I said. "Fabulous
workmanship. Where did you get this made?"

"Isn't it real?"

"Some of it is, but the bed is a reproduction for sure. It's
a queen for one thing. The real bed was smaller."

"I wish I knew more about it," she said. "I should, I
know, because Robert is so keen on it. This was Robert's
home long before I moved in. He and his first wife lived
here. You would have to ask him. I would have liked to
change it, not because it isn't attractive, but you know,
when you follow another woman into a home you'd prefer
to, um, erase all traces of the previous relationship. But I
can't. I have been able to change a lot, but not the bedroom,
wouldn't you know, nor Robert's dressing room and study

next door. He's not here, so we can take a peek at that, too, if you like."

"I would," I said. We went down a short corridor, and into a rather dark room, its large window covered with heavy drapes. It was filled with dark furniture, pleasantly masculine, and lined with photos of Robert at important moments of his life. In one or two he was in military uniform, not surprising given his comments about his past as an army captain at the fund-raiser, in others he was with various important people including a couple of British prime ministers, a wedding photo in which both he and Maya looked very fetching, and a photograph of a woman I didn't know. I noticed Maya's eyes were fixed on that photo.

"Was your husband in the military for long?" I asked, trying to get her to stop looking at the photo.

"Several years," she said. "I think he was planning to be a career soldier, but he got interested in business, and certainly he has been very successful. I don't think he has any regrets about leaving the military, although he does talk about it a great deal. He was in a lot of the hotspots, Croatia and places like that, so I guess there was a lot of male bonding. Some of his men still drop by to see him from time to time. That's how we found Drever. Drever served in the army and was posted with peacekeepers in Afghanistan. He left the forces when he came back, did odd jobs for a while before Robert offered him the job here. He is not what you would call a natural at gardening or anything, but he's willing, and it's good to have someone here all the time. There's a very nice little apartment in the house and he lives there. He tends to the place when we're in Glasgow. I guess what I'm saying is that while Robert's army career is over, it's still very much a part of him."

"What business is Robert in?" I said.

"Lots of things," she said. "He invested in a few businesses with a couple of his army buddies, light manufacturing, textiles and so on, and now I guess he makes most of his money on his investments. I don't really know, to tell you the truth."

"It's a very attractive man's room, but I like your white wicker in the sunroom better," I said.

"Me, too," she said. "That room I got to decorate exactly the way I like it."

"I think the pieces in this room are genuine, unlike the bedroom," I said. "Did you know that Trevor Wylie was killed over a piece of reproduction furniture?"

"Trevor Wylie," she said. "You know I thought that name was familiar when you mentioned it in Glasgow, but I can't recall who he is, or was. I must have confused him with someone else. Or maybe I did meet him somewhere else. You did mention he was killed, I recall."

"I'm afraid so. He was a Toronto antique dealer, but born here in Orkney, I understand."

"Really? Maybe that's why the name is familiar. My husband can't recall the name at all, so if we did meet, it can't have made much of an impression. I expect I'm just confused. I'm having trouble with names these days. I believe it's common with women my age."

"It does seem to be," I said, and we both laughed.

"Robert thinks I must have read about him, about the murder, and just assumed I knew him. Do I recall your saying he was killed over a reproduction?"

"Yes. Apparently he sold a fake Mackintosh writing cabinet to the wrong guy. That man has been charged with Trevor's murder. I guess he figured it out and wasn't happy."

She thought about that for a minute. "Did you not say you were looking for a Mackintosh writing cabinet?"

"I am."

"Why?"

"Because I have a client who wants one." I justified the lie by telling myself that if I found one I could almost certainly sell it. "I'd prefer it to be the real thing, but now that I see the reproductions here, I have to say I'm impressed. No wonder Trevor could pass one off as real if there is workmanship as good as this around here. At least I assume it's around here, given you have several pieces."

"I really don't know. It was here when I got here. Robert hasn't let me change a thing in this room either. I think he wants it to remain exactly the same forever."

Actually, I didn't think that was true. Indentations in the carpet of Robert's room indicated to me that the furniture had been rearranged at some point in the not too distant past. Maybe Maya knew that, and maybe she didn't. Maybe she didn't get into this inner sanctum often, a wild guess on my part that was confirmed when Maya looked out the window and quickly led me from the room. A minute or two later, we heard the front door open. "I'm back, darling," Robert called out.

"I'm upstairs," Maya replied. "With a guest." By the time Robert found us we were sitting in Maya's dressing room cum den looking at photographs of their condo in Spain.

"You remember Lara McClintoch," Maya said. "I invited her to visit and here she is. She was just driving down the road and she saw me working in the garden."

"Wonderful! I saw a mystery car in the driveway, and wondered who was visiting. Will you stay for dinner? Maya

would love to have company here, as would I." He was
speaking to me but he was looking at Maya.

"Please do," Maya said.

"I'd love to, but I am meeting a friend for dinner."
What I meant was that I was planning to do what I'd done
unsuccessfully the previous evening after dropping Percy
off, which is to say to comb the restaurants of Kirkwall
looking for Willow. She was a tourist. She had to eat somewhere.

"Some other time, then," Robert said.

"Lara is wondering where you got the reproductions in
the bedroom," Maya said. "I couldn't help her." Robert
turned his full attention to me.

"I think I told you I was looking for a Mackintosh writing cabinet for a customer," I said. "Which I am, so if you
hear of one, and you don't want it for yourself, of course, I'd
love to know about it. But I was just blown away by the reproductions in the master bedroom. It is such a gorgeous
room. I do carry some reproductions, plainly marked as
such, of course, and given most people can't afford their own
Mackintosh and he's so popular now, I thought that might
be a good line for our shop. Can you tell me who made it for
you? It must have been custom work."

"It was, but I don't think I can recall, if indeed I ever
knew," Robert said. "I've had it for at least fifteen years, got
it when I first bought this place. We, I, hired a designer who
found it for us." Maya winced slightly at the "us" and "we"
that didn't include her.

"Local?"

"The designer? No. Edinburgh, I think. It was Bev, that
is to say my first wife, who arranged it all." He took a deep
breath. "Sorry, darling."

"Please, Robert, it's quite all right. I'm not at all upset about it." She was, of course, lying.

"I'm sorry," I said. "I'm the one who is upsetting everyone. I've obviously said something quite inappropriate."

"Please! How could you know?" Robert said. "My first wife died. Drugs. It's why we support the drop-in center in Glasgow. Maya has been very understanding. I'm sure she has charities she'd like to support, too, but really, I feel responsible in a way for what happened. I didn't see, I didn't comprehend what was happening to her. I should have known, but I didn't and she died of a massive overdose of cocaine. Bev was a wonderful person until she was caught in the grips of that monster. I'm fortunate to have been able to rebuild my life, thanks to Maya. Maya and Bev were friends, and Maya was a rock when Bev died. I don't know what I would have done without her." The understanding Maya rested her hand on her husband's forearm and gave me a beseeching glance. I didn't know what she was pleading for: my understanding, my sympathy, my hasty exit?

"I'd like to help you, I really would," Robert said. "We share a passion for Mackintosh, after all. But I can't recall much about it, I'm afraid. We, I, did bring in a lot of furniture from our home just outside of London, and we purchased furnishings in both England and Glasgow, and presumably here, too. But sorry, I just can't recall if the craftsman was here or somewhere else. It just wasn't my bailiwick, you understand, the decorating. I just paid the bills. Now really, can we persuade you to stay for dinner?"

"I'm afraid not," I said, feeling like a complete jerk. I had lots more questions, like was there any chance the furniture had been made locally, but even I, compulsive seeker for information that would justify my petty existence, could not bring myself to ask them. I could hardly wait to drag my hopelessly shallow self out of their lives. "I must be going. Thank you, though, and thank you for tea, Maya. It was a real pleasure talking to you."

"It was for me, too. I hope you'll come again," she said, and I think she meant it. She stood at the door waving to me as I left, a woman with a ghost looking over her shoulder, a woman who slept with her husband in a bed chosen by her predecessor. My Rob had been a widower when I met him, but he'd been that way for quite a long time. I knew he'd married his high school sweetheart over their parents' objections, he being Catholic, she a Baptist, and I knew she had died long before the bloom was off the rose where their relationship was concerned. Still, while I might have worried about his ex-girlfriends, particularly one young and perky paragon of virtue by the name of Barbara who immediately preceded me, and I might fret about being a suitable stepmother to Rob's daughter, Jennifer, I didn't think for a minute I was sleeping with a ghost. For that I was suddenly exceptionally grateful. I resolved to call Rob that very night to tell him so.

But first I was going back to Kirkwall. Even then I took a little detour, to look at the house I'd seen from the sunroom windows. It was an interesting contrast to that of the Alexanders. Both were that typical gray stone, very large and imposing. There the similarity ended. Where one was in remarkably good nick, to use the British expression, with manicured lawns and exquisitely designed gardens, including the putting green, fresh paint on every wood surface, not a twig out of place, the other, while possibly even grander at one time, almost castlelike with a tower on one end, was a mess. What might once have been a kitchen garden was now all weeds and plants gone to seed. The gate was hanging by a thread, the front porch used for storage, and there was a dry and cracked fountain that would have been at the center of what might have been a geometric garden of some sort. Out back, visible in the distance was a rather dilapidated barn.

As I watched, fortunately from some distance, a van pulled into the driveway, and a man got out. He went around to the back, and pulled something out, which it took me a minute at this distance to realize was a wheelchair. An older man was assisted into it and rolled up the driveway to the house. After a few minutes, the first man headed toward the barn, which like the house was in serious disrepair. I looked back at the Alexander house, and noticed that Drever was watching the place, too. The whole scene rather depressed me.

Where the Alexanders' home looked across a splendid vista of rolling hills and beautifully tilled fields to the blue waters of Scapa Flow, this one looked across windswept terrain to what appeared to me, as I got closer, to be huge chunks of broken concrete on the shore. I drove along to see what this would be, and after parking my little car and walking along a road found myself on a cliff top overlooking the water. I wandered for a while among these concrete structures before I realized I was looking at bunkers. This could only have been a lookout point during two World Wars. It was desolate, attractive only to a military buff, and somehow very sad. I went down the steps into one of the bunkers and looked across the water. Men must have spent hours, days, months watching for German ships and submarines eager to destroy the British fleet in Scapa Flow from this cold, unpleasant spot. I saw no sign of Percy.

Almost equally depressing was the time I spent roaming the streets of Kirkwall for an hour or so. No Willow, and no Percy either, but at least I had another fine seafood dinner. It capped off a spectacularly unsuccessful day.

I'd wandered the streets of St. Margaret's Hope, a pictur-esque little village to be sure, and it was soon clear to me that neither the dealer who sold the real writing cabinet, and the craftsman who made the fake one, were in St. Margaret's Hope. I'd stopped in at the antique store, and had asked at the artists' cooperative in the harbor area, and while there was some very beautiful work on display, silver jewelry, fabulous knits and pottery, for me there was no joy. I was rapidly coming to the conclusion there had been not one but two fake invoices, one for an antique dealer in Glasgow who didn't exist, and another for a dealer in St. Margaret's Hope who didn't either. I wasn't sure what that meant exactly, but maybe in some way it was good news. It could mean that this was one enormous scam involving two writing cabinets, which of course was exactly what I wanted to hear.

Finally I went back to Stromness and my lovely little attic room and called Rob. I caught him just as he was leaving for the restaurant where I suppose he saw to it that the Chicken Kiev was placed promptly in front of the Ukrainian gang-sters who were counting on him to launder their funds, while Rob and his fellow law enforcement pals were trying to fig-ure out from which revolting activity these funds had come.

"How's it going?" I asked. "The restaurant business and all?"

"Oh, all right, I guess," he said. "The joke around here is how good I am at money laundering. I'm making a fortune for the taxpayers. As one of them, you should be grateful."

"I am. I'd like you to get out of this, though."

"Not until I reel in the big fish. It's drugs, you know, that and people smuggling. The substantive crime, that is, the one that is generating all this money they need me to take care of for them. I'd like this to be over, too. I am ceasing to enjoy being a restaurateur. Once this is over, I may never cook again, and I'm sure not doing dishes."

"I hope you're not counting on me to do all the cooking and the cleanup, because it's not going to happen," I said.

He laughed. "We'll have to order in and eat off paper plates."

"Any developments in Blair Bazillionaire's case?"

"It's working its way through the system. The big news is that he fired his lawyer."

"Don't tell me he's going to try to defend himself! I know he thinks he's the best lawyer there is anywhere on the planet, but what is it they say about lawyers who defend themselves?"

"They have fools for clients. Baldwin isn't a fool whatever else you might say about him. No, he's retained Desmond Crane."

"I thought they disliked each other. No, stronger than that, I thought they loathed each other."

"Maybe some of that was for show in court, part of the performance. Really, though, isn't that exactly the kind of person you want to have in your corner, the opposing lawyer who gave you the most trouble? I think it's smart of him. It's bought him some time, too, which may also have something to do with it. Crane has petitioned the court for more time so he can prepare the case. As a result, you will have a longer wait before you're called as a witness."

"What would he want to buy time for, given he's going

to spend it in jail? I could understand it if he were still free and wanted to prolong that. I wish I were completely convinced he did it, given I'll have to testify about both finding the body and the little dustup at his party. On a happier subject, at least I think it is, have I ever mentioned how happy I am not to be sleeping with a ghost?" I told him briefly about the fund-raiser at the Alexanders, and my visit to their home in Hoxa.

He chuckled. "No, you haven't mentioned it, and I suppose this is where I'm supposed to confess that I've had a few bad moments about your still being in business with your ex. I'm getting over it, though, and I never figured I was sleeping with him."

"Good," I said.

"Where are you and these people you've met exactly?"

"Orkney. It's the most wonderful place. I'm quite infatuated. I want us to come here for a real holiday next spring. It has all these Neolithic sites to visit, tombs and houses, and there were Vikings here, too. It's beautiful, and the people are really, really nice."

"But where is it?"

"Islands off the northeast coast of Scotland."

"Scotland! This isn't about the Neolithic, is it? It's about Mackintosh writing cabinets. Get over it, Lara! Everybody makes a mistake from time to time."

"I'm trying. I know it wasn't the first mistake I've ever made, nor will it be the last. I'm not naïve. I know forgers are getting to be awfully good at their trade, and unfortunately science and technology is helping them. But usually my mistakes do not involve murders for which my client is charged."

"This isn't about you, Lara. It's about a conman by the

name of Trevor Wylie who gambled big and lost. And it's about someone else with a terrible temper, a wife-beater after all, who consorted with violent criminals. Maybe some of it wore off on him."

"You consort with violent criminals. It hasn't worn off on you as far as I can tell."

"Maybe that's because of you, you and Jennifer. Maybe Blair drove away the person who kept him grounded when he scared away his wife. And by the way, promise me if it ever does start to rub off on me, you'll smother me in my sleep."

"Count on it," I said, and we both laughed.

"Come home," he said. "I miss you."

"I think I will," I replied.

That night I dreamed about a windswept hill and a derelict castle in which lived an old, frail, ill man who sat in his wheelchair near a window, watched over by the ghost of a woman. He sat looking at a cracked and dry fountain that I was trying to reach, but I kept getting lost in the trees which sprang up along the paths created in the geometric garden. Across the burned countryside there was a desolate shore where human skeletons with guns and binoculars sat watching the sea. As I awoke a thought sprang unbidden: The Wasteland, the maze, the wounded king. I'd have to tell Percy about that place next time I saw him. It was difficult to believe salvation lurked in such a pathetic spot, but I suppose one never knew.

I couldn't get a seat on the plane for Glasgow the next day, so I decided to give my mission just one more try. I was on my way back across the Churchill Barriers to widen my search out from St. Margaret's Hope when a motorcycle overtook and passed me on one of the causeways. I don't know motorcycles, so couldn't swear it was the same one I'd seen in Stromness. However, there were two people on it, the passenger a woman with long dark hair blowing out from under her helmet, and the rider wore what looked to be the same skintight red and blue leather gear. I stayed with them across two more causeways, and the islands in between, and then as they swept past the turnoff for St. Margaret's Hope. They were going faster than I was actually comfortable driving on these roads, but I tried to keep up with them with some success until I got trapped behind a farm vehicle. With so little traffic, this would have to happen right then! I saw them turn off the road to the left some distance ahead of me, at least I thought I did, and when I came to a road that I thought was more or less in the right place, I turned, too.

I followed a country road signed for something called The Tomb of the Eagles, slowing to look down side roads for any trace of the motorcycle. There was none. When I reached this Tomb of the Eagles, it turned out to be another five-thousand-year-old Neolithic tomb, this one managed by the farmer on whose property it had been found. There was a parking lot with a couple of cars, and a rather jolly exhibit center where family members explained what there was to be seen, but there was no Willow. I listened to the presentation anyway, hearing all about the tomb and how it was named for the eagle bones and talons that had been found in it along with the bones of more than three hundred people, and then walked with three fellow tourists some distance across fields to actually see it. The tomb was another grassy mound, but much smaller than Maeshowe, perched high above the sea. I could see how these tombs were still being found, as Percy had told me, given that they looked like an ordinary part of the natural landscape, a grassy knoll, a pile of earth long since covered over. They would be easy to overlook.

A motorbike with two riders shouldn't have been easy to either overlook or lose, but I could see no sign of them, and even lay on my back on a dolly and pulled myself into the tomb with the rope provided to make sure they weren't in there. They weren't. The others did not recall seeing a motorcycle on their way in. Discouraged, although I'd enjoyed the place, I made my way back to St. Margaret's Hope and continued my still unsuccessful search for the craftsman who made the reproductions at the Alexanders. Everybody knew the Alexanders' place, but not much about them. It seemed they kept to themselves.

I had decided it was time to let this ridiculous notion of mine go, a feeling I thought might be quite liberating if I could manage it, and head back to Stromness to pack up my bags so I'd be ready to head home. It was then that once again a motorcycle with two riders roared past me. By the time I had reached my car, it had disappeared down the road that led to Hoxa and the Alexanders' home. I took the road right to the end, but Willow, if indeed it had been Willow, was long gone. Still, the sun was going down and the sky looked absolutely wonderful, the pink just starting, shot through with brilliant azure and clouds with a touch of purple. I decided to park where I had before and hike up the road to the cliffs above the sea.

I was just standing there breathing in the fresh air, and trying to imprint this view on my memory, when I heard something, I wasn't sure what, a groan, perhaps. It seemed to be coming from the concrete bunker just a few yards away.

"Hello?" I said. For a moment there was nothing, just the wind, but then I heard it again. It might have been an animal, injured perhaps. I decided I couldn't just walk away, so I went down the steps leading into the bunker and stepped in. It was damp and cold and rather musty, and it took me a minute or two to adjust to the light. When I did, I saw Percy framed against the opening out to the sea. He was lying on one of the slabs and wasn't moving. I hurried toward him, stumbling on something, his bicycle, as I went. There was blood everywhere, all of it gushing from a wound in his side. "Percy!" I said. "Can you hear me?" His eyelids fluttered slightly, then opened, but I wasn't sure he could really see anything. "It's Lara. I'm going for help."

"Lara," he gasped.

I cursed when I realized my cell phone was dead, not that I would know whom to call. "Hold on, Percy," I said. "I'll be back very soon."

As I turned to go he grabbed my arm with astonishing strength and pulled me down toward him. He tried to speak but I could hear nothing and I tried to pull away. "Let me go, Percy. You can tell me later. I'm going to find a doctor." He was going to bleed to death very soon if I didn't get help very fast.

"Before he went mad," Percy said in a kind of gasp, holding my arm in a vicelike grip.

"What did you say?"

"Before he went mad," Percy repeated, but then his eyes shut. I tried to pull away again, but as I did so more blood, and maybe some of his insides, poured out of the wound. In vain I tried to pry his fingers off my arm.

"Bjarni the Wanderer," he gasped. There was this kind of gurgling sound in his chest.

"Bjarni the Wanderer? Is that what you said?"

"Hid the chalice . . ."

"The what?"

"In the tomb of the orcs," he said, and then Percy died. Or rather, Magnus Budge did.

Chapter 7

Our hardy band of travelers, now reduced to four, and pursued re-
lentlessly by Goisvintha's father, Theodoric, fled south, the path of
least resistance, I suppose, but one that led straight into the territory
of the caliph of Muslim Spain. Desperate for provisions, Bjarni
and Oddi attacked a merchant's retinue in the dead of night. Taken
by surprise, some fled, and some were killed by the three Vikings.
One, obviously the leader, fought Bjarni for some time and would
not yield. Finally Bjarni gained the upper hand, and the man fell
to the ground. Bjarni raised his axe, intending to deliver the final
blow. The man said nothing. He did not beg for mercy. He did not
cry out in fear.

Bjarni lowered his weapon. "You are a worthy opponent," he
said to the man. "I will not take your life, and I would appreciate
it if you would extend me the same courtesy. I will take only what
we need from this wagon of yours, and be on my way." With that he
turned his back on the man, a gesture that some would say was fool-
hardy, but in a short time Bjarni, Oddi, Goisvintha, and Svein

the Wiry disappeared into the darkness, unfortunately straight into a military encampment. Soon after that they were on a forced march toward Cordoba.

It would be fair to say that Bjarni, Oddi, and Svein, and even possibly Goisvintha would have been amazed by what they saw as they made their way across the countryside. By the early days of the eleventh century, Spain was surely the most sophisticated place in Europe. Aqueducts crisscrossed the country, the remarkable irrigation systems ensuring orchards and grain fields aplenty. The towns would have been simply extraordinary. Cordoba, the seat of the caliph, was certainly a most impressive place. There were fabulous mosques, gardens, fountains, hospitals, great libraries, magnificent palaces, public baths. Houses were well-kept and flowers, trees, and shrubs bloomed everywhere, most of which Bjarni would never have seen before. And wonder of wonders, the streets were not only paved, but lit and patrolled. Remember, the streets of Paris were not paved until the thirteenth century, those of London, the fourteenth. To Vikings accustomed to the stone houses of Orkney, and the muddy, dangerous roads of the territories they knew so well, Cordoba must surely have been astonishing.

Bjarni and the others were brought before someone he knew must be important, and he thought they all would die. Now Vikings were well known in Spain. They were a nuisance most of the time, and a great deal of trouble some of the time, and indeed were called madjus or "heathen wizards." Vikings had sacked Lisbon, Cadiz, and even Seville in the ninth century, until eventually repulsed by the highly organized army and navy. Muslim Spain had never really been good hunting for the Vikings, but they would still have been considered a threat. There would be none feeling too kindly toward Bjarni and his friends.

But then a voice was heard from the back of the room. There was much consternation in the group at the words. "This captive may

not be a man of the book," the voice said, by which he meant a Mus-
lim, a Christian, or a Jew, "but he is a man of honor. He spared my
life, and I would ask that his life and that of his companions be
spared in turn." Bjarni must have looked in surprise at the man he
had almost killed, now resplendent in silk.

So Bjarni and his tiny retinue were set free. But Bjarni would
have to carry on alone.

WHO WOULD KILL a poor sod, a harmless dreamer like
Percy Bicycle Clips? Or Magnus Budge, or whoever he was?
He'd always be Percy to me, an unusual little man pedaling
furiously toward what he hoped would be salvation. And
not just kill him, but stab him over and over again, then
leave him to bleed to death, his eyes to cloud over, his
breath to come in gasps, as the last of his life oozed from
him, alone on a cold concrete slab.

Trevor Wylie I could almost understand. I wouldn't go so
far as to say he deserved it or anything, but he did, I suppose, make a credible murder victim if one might be permitted to put it that way. But not Percy Bicycle Clips.

I was very glad I hadn't mentioned a name when I
pounded on the door of the nearest house I could find to get
help for Percy, help that even then I knew was too late. That
meant that when I was interviewed by the Northern Constabulary both in their squad car and later that evening in
Kirkwall, I had not had to explain the name Arthur Percival
when in fact all of the corpse's identification proclaimed
him to be Magnus Budge. No doubt they would have found
that a little odd. Even I found it so. As it was, I was just a
tourist who had happened upon a grisly sight while hiking
around the World War Two bunkers on Hoxa Head. Every-

one was terribly apologetic that such a dreadful thing had happened to a visitor. They kept telling me that violent crime was very rare.

I believed them, not that it helped much. Somehow, despite the fact he'd lied about his name, and had not been very forthcoming on any subject of interest to me, I'd come to regard him as, if not a friend exactly, someone I was fond of in a rather peculiar way. It's not everybody who can make a tour of the Neolithic interesting, even for somebody like me, who is inclined to like just about anything about the ancient past. When I'd seen the old house with the man in the wheelchair, I'd really hoped I would find Percy before I left so I could tell him about it. I wasn't sure what he meant by The Wasteland, the maze, the wounded king, but if he thought salvation lay there, then I wanted to make sure he'd seen what I had.

Everyone was, of course, exceptionally nice to me. My jacket had been splattered with blood, and carried the bloody imprint of Percy's fingers on the sleeve. The soles of my shoes were caked in both mud and blood. I kept telling everyone I was fine, but I couldn't stop shivering. I could not understand why they kept the station so cold. They plied me with enough sweet tea to float an ocean liner, but it didn't help much. They even sent a squad car to Mrs. Brown's guest house to pick up some clean clothes to replace the ones they had to take as evidence. I have no idea what Mrs. Brown thought of this at the time, but she was more than solicitous later. The police told me I might get my clothes back but it wouldn't be for a while. I said I never wanted to see them again.

I was asked to tell my story of how I'd found him over and over again. I did the best I could. I told them he'd been alive when I got there, and that when I'd gone over to try to help him, he'd grabbed my arm. They asked me if he'd said anything, and I said he had, but for the life of me I couldn't remember what it was. They asked me if I thought he'd named his killer. I said I didn't think so, that while I couldn't recall what he'd said, I did remember that I'd thought it was gibberish at the time. They told me to take my time, that it might come back to me, and if and when it did, I was to call.

Various people came and went while I sat there, sipping tea. The couple who had answered their door came in to give and sign a statement. Other than this strange woman splattered with blood yelling and pounding on their door, they had seen and heard nothing. Nobody, when it came right down to it, had seen or heard anything.

They asked me if I knew the victim. I had told them I'd given him a lift a couple of days before when we'd both been visiting Historic Scotland sites, when he'd fallen off his bike and damaged it. I tried to be as honest as possible. I am, after all, virtually living with a policeman. I told them that while we'd spent some time together, I hadn't known his name. The last part, clearly, was true. I somewhat reluctantly told them that he'd said his nickname was Percy, a little editorializing there on my part, as the word nickname had never come into it, and they solemnly wrote that down. When they asked me why I'd stopped to offer him a lift, I said he looked familiar to me, like someone I knew from home. He wasn't from home, however. He lived with his mother in an old house in Kirkwall, I was to learn soon enough. They told me they would have to keep my rental car.

While I waited, a never-empty mug of tea in hand, a

rather plain woman, sixtyish, in a drab and rather worn brown coat and matching hat, came in. She looked just like Percy, only about twenty-five years older. She had to be his mother. She had a handkerchief balled up in one hand and kept dabbing her eyes with it. She had a runny nose and didn't seem to notice. For a while we sat in the same room, under the watchful eye of a rather stern policewoman.

"My boy has had an accident," she said after a few minutes of rummaging about in her handbag for another handkerchief.

"I'm so sorry," I replied.

"He must have fallen off his bicycle and hit his head. I'm sure he'll be feeling better in the morning." I believe I winced slightly because the policewoman coughed and then almost imperceptibly shook her head.

"The police have some other idea entirely about what happened to him, but they can't be right. There has been some mistake. He was always off riding his bicycle. He quit his job, you know. I don't know why. He was a dreamer, my boy was. Some woman found him."

I said nothing for a moment. Was it a good idea to tell her I was the one who found him?

"I hope he didn't suffer," she said, sniffing. "I hate to think he was in pain."

I took a deep breath. "I am the person who found him. He didn't suffer at all." She got out of her chair and rushed over to grab my arm. Her grip reminded me all too well of Percy's dying grasp. "Promise me he wasn't in pain," she said. "Please."

"I promise," I said.

"Did he say anything?"

"I'm sorry I can't remember."

"He was a good boy. Odd, but good."

"That's exactly the way I think of him," I said, as the policewoman gently pulled her away from me, and actually gave me a wan smile. She was much nicer looking when she smiled. I found myself thinking of Percy after this exchange with his mother, how he'd tripped over the merchandise in Trevor's store, the way he always seemed to use bicycle clips whether he needed them or not, and his glasses askew. I thought about how enthused he was about the ancient sites we were visiting together, actually showing some personality as he pointed everything out, despite looking rather rumpled and dirty from his bike accident. Most of all I thought of his salute as he left me in Kirkwall, broken bicycle in his arms, his sleeve torn, his glasses, now held with one of my safety pins, even more crooked than before.

"Glasses," I said aloud. "We have to find his glasses." The policewoman now came over to sit with me, obviously thinking I was in as bad shape as Percy's mother, which in retrospect maybe I was. Not as bad as a mother perhaps, but certainly right up there in the out-of-it category. "He'd lost his glasses."

"Glasses?" she said.

"Spectacles," I said. "Whatever you call them here. He wasn't wearing his glasses when I found him. I lent him a safety pin to hold them together."

"I'm sure he appreciated it," she said, patting my hand.

I thought about that, slowly and carefully through the fog in my brain, and realized finally that she thought when I found him dying I'd fixed his glasses. "I mean when he fell off his bike the other day. He broke the arm of his glasses. He couldn't see without them. I gave him a safety pin to hold them together until he got home."

She looked at me for a minute, then went into the other room. I hoped it was to tell them about the glasses, because I had this idea that when I was feeling better, I would think this was significant, the fact they weren't there, that is. A couple of minutes later, she came out, sat down with Percy's mum and asked her if her son wore glasses.

"Oh, yes," she said. "I hope he hasn't lost those. He's always breaking them. I think we have a spare pair at home, though, that he can wear until his good ones turn up." The policewoman patted her hand, gave me a significant look, a nod, really, as if to acknowledge she now understood what I was saying, and went back to standing at her post. At this point a clergyman arrived, and immediately went to sit with Percy's mum. She seemed to alternate between knowing her son was dead, and thinking he'd be fine soon, but I think reality was starting to sink in. She cried and cried, and the clergyman patted her arm and murmured comforting thoughts, I'm sure, although I couldn't hear them. A few minutes later he came over to talk to me. He took my hand in his. "Your hands are like ice," he said.

"Yes, I don't know why they don't put the heat on here," I said. "At the guest house I'm staying in, it's always nice and warm."

"You are very pale," he added. *Of course I'm pale. I'm always pale. That's the way I was born.* I know that when I'm not feeling well, which would be now, and when I don't have any makeup on, which was also probably now, given the rather rudimentary dusting I'd given myself that morning, I scare people. I have always considered that to be their problem, not mine. However, I was sure if they turned on some heat, I'd look and feel better. Instead they called a doctor. He recommended more hot tea with lots of sugar. No alcohol. That was too bad, because I was looking forward to some of Mrs. Brown's scotch.

The policewoman came over to ask me to go back to talk to the policeman in charge of the investigation. I believe she said his name was Cusiter, although she made it sound as if it had an extra *r* in it, after the *u*. I was having trouble concentrating. As I left I heard the clergyman ask Percy's mum if there was someone who could come and stay with her that night. "I'll be all right," she replied. "My boy will be home soon."

"Perhaps someone else," the man said patiently.

"Perhaps my neighbors in St. Margaret's Hope," she said. "The Millers."

"You remember now, Emily, that you moved to Kirkwall when your husband died ten years ago."

There was a pause. "Yes," she said. "That's right. Magnus and I moved to Kirkwall. Magnus will come and get me." I thought if I could feel anything at all, other than cold, I would find this very sad.

The police may have been very courteous, but they weren't for letting me take the flight out of Orkney I was booked on. I was asked to remain there until the forensics team arrived from Aberdeen, headquarters of the Northern Constabulary, and had had a chance to do whatever they do. Such expertise, it was explained to me, would have to come outwith Orkney. "Outwith" was not a word I was familiar with, but it sounded rather nice. I told them about Rob, which softened them up considerably, and that I knew that staying as long as necessary was the right thing to do.

Percy's mum was leaving just about the time I was told someone would drive me to Stromness. A neighbor from Kirkwall had come to take her home. I didn't ask her about

Percy's granny and her furniture, because I didn't think of it, and even if I had her grip on reality still seemed a little tenuous, and furthermore it would hardly have been the appropriate time. I've wondered since, though, whether it would have made a difference. I suppose had Percy been alive he would have told me it was one of the questions I was supposed to ask.

Detective Cusiter, if that was what his name was, had been good enough to have someone phone the car rental company to explain my situation, and they in turn were nice enough to deliver another car to Mrs. Brown's place in Stromness shortly after I got there. The man who delivered the car apologized profusely for my inconvenience, which was an unusual word under the circumstances. "Please be assured that you will not be charged for the second car. We are terribly sorry for your loss." My loss? Loss of the car? Loss of a friend? Loss of my seat on the plane? I told him that was exceptionally decent of the rental agency, and really it was. Everybody was so nice here.

The other residents of the B&B were equally aghast and sympathetic. "Travelers," one man opined. "No one from Orkney would do such a thing. In the good weather, they come in on the ferry, do their nefarious business, and then take off on the next boat. They'll never find them."

"Travelers?" I said.

"You know, gypsies, other criminal elements."

I thought that was rather unfair, but what did I know? I needed a scotch, and I didn't care what that doctor said. What I also wanted was for everyone to stop being so nice. I wanted them to take to the streets to protest what had happened to Percy. I wanted them to unleash that Viking blood they kept telling me flowed in their veins, to hunt down the killer, take justice into their own hands, and tear this terrible person to pieces. That's what I wanted them to do, because I myself was too tired and too cold to do it. I had a large scotch, despite doctor's orders, left a voice mail for Rob telling him I wouldn't be home immediately and why, then went straight to bed, and enjoyed a dreamless sleep that left me even more tired than I'd been when I lay down. I still couldn't remember what Percy had said to me.

The next day, after Mrs. Brown plied me with bacon and eggs and some rather lovely brown bread in the notion that it would help, which indeed it did, I undertook a self-guided tour of the Neolithic in Percy's honor. I really just wanted to stay in bed, but I had a feeling that if I did so, I'd never get up again. I crawled on all fours or slithered into every chamber cairn I could find. I climbed up Wideford Hill, and down into Wideford Cairn, then Unstan, Cuween, Grain, Mine Howe; any tomb or earth house or whatever I came across, I entered. They were all rather interesting, from the outside just grassy mounds, but with stone entrances, and inside stone chambers, often more than one. I could almost hear Percy telling me about them. I hoped I'd done him proud. I went to a place called the Brough of Birsay which held the remains of a Viking church and homes. It wasn't old enough for Percy to have recommended it, but the sun was shining as I walked across the causeway usable only at low tide to see the place, and from the vantage point of lighthouse high atop the hill, I looked down a coast of spectacular cliffs disappearing into the mist, and across water that would have stretched without interruption back to my home country. I decided Orkney might have the biggest sky I had seen in a very long time, bigger perhaps than the prairies of home. It was very, very beautiful, breathtakingly so.

Then I went back to the Stones of Stenness and walked around the Ring of Brodgar. The pastoral view was truly lovely, and I wished Percy were there to share it. After that I just drove around the island, I don't know why, maybe searching for someone who looked as if he'd killed my strange friend, Percy. Occasionally I stopped to eat. Stuffing food down my throat seemed to be the only thing that kept me from doing something else, although what that something else was I didn't know. I did know I didn't feel like crying.

It was thus that I found Willow in the Quoyburray Inn in Tankerness a couple of days later, but by then I didn't care. She was sitting alone at a table in the corner of the bar with a plate of fish and chips in front of her, and, in a choice of questionable taste given the recent demise of her boyfriend and the means of his dispatch, a bottle of Skull-splitter beer. With Percy's death, my interest in Blair and Trevor, the furniture, and therefore Willow had evaporated.

Willow, and I've thought about this a lot since, seemed very surprised to see me. I didn't care about that either. In fact, I didn't give a fig about anything, although a small part of my brain was trying to tell me I should. Willow dropped her fork, put her hand to her mouth, and said "Lara!" in a rather strange tone of voice. There was a pause, and then she said, "I've been looking for you everywhere."

Sure you have, I thought. *You have been roaring around Orkney on the back of a motorcycle piloted by a rather well-built young man in red and blue leather just hoping to see me standing by the side of the road.*

"What I mean is, I thought I'd missed you, that you would have gone home by now. I'm so glad you're here."

"I don't believe I knew you were coming to Orkney, Willow," I said, through clenched teeth. "Had I known, I would of course have told you where I was staying."

"I know that," she said. "I trust you." If I hadn't felt so awful, I probably would have laughed. She gestured to me to sit down and then leaned forward conspiratorially. "I found it," she whispered. "As soon as I found it, I called your shop, and a nice man told me you were taking a bit of a holiday in Britain. I knew that meant you'd headed for Orkney, so I flew out the very next day. I figured I'd just find you here somewhere. After all, it's not a very big island."

A nice man? Surely she didn't mean Clive. "You found what?" I asked in a normal speaking voice. "The money?"

"Shush," she said. "Not the money, but the closest thing to it."

"And what might that be?"

She leaned forward again. "The treasure map," she mouthed. *Oh, spare me*, I thought. "I see," I said. "That's exciting. I knew you were here, actually, Willow. I saw you get off the ferry and then again on South Ronaldsay, but I couldn't catch you because you were on a motorcycle with a rather fetching young man."

"That's Kenny. Isn't he cute as anything? All that leather! I met him on the ferry, and he's helping me find the you-know-what."

"That's nice," I said, but my tone betrayed me.

"You don't believe me, do you?" she said. "You think I'd cut you out of the deal. But I'm going to show you what I found, and when Kenny gets here, he'll confirm that I made it very clear to him that you are to be a part of this, that we'd split it three ways, and that our number one priority, well, maybe number two, has been to find you. We asked for you at all the hotels in Kirkwall and Stromness, believe me. Oh, there he is. Kenny, we're over here!"

Kenny was there all right, all six-foot-something of him, with dark curly hair and lovely deep blue eyes, and a physique that was indeed rather impressive in all that leather. He was, as Willow had already pointed out, cute as anything.

"Hello," he said to me, before leaning over to peck Willow on the cheek.

"This is Lara," Willow said, before he could say anything else.

"Lara!" he exclaimed. "Wow! Brilliant! Nice to meet you. I'm Kenny. How did you find each other?"

"She found me," Willow said, going on to explain in some detail that I'd seen them both and where. Alarms bells were ringing here. It might be that she really wanted Kenny to know all about it, or that she was trying to make sure he knew so he wouldn't say anything she didn't want me to hear.

"Brilliant!" he repeated. "Willow thought, she was afraid you know, you'd be headed back home by now."

Oh, please, I thought again.

"Actually, why aren't you heading back by now?" Willow said. I pointed to the newspaper sitting in front of her, tapping the article about Percy's demise.

She scanned it for a moment. "Lara! How awful!" She leapt up and threw her arms around me as Kenny grabbed the paper to see what we were talking about. "Omigod," she kept saying over and over. "I didn't even see your name until right this minute. This is just too horrible. First Trevor, and now this complete stranger. How unlucky can you get?"

That was a good question, even if Percy had hardly been a complete stranger, a fact I decided I was not going to mention. She would hardly put the name Magnus Budge and Percy together. Even I was having trouble with that.

"I guess that's why you didn't e-mail me that you were staying over," she said. I bit my tongue, and, instead of clawing her eyes out, just gave her a baleful glance. "Did you not get mine?" she said.

"Strangely enough I didn't, no."

"No wonder you're looking at me like that. Did you check your e-mails?"

"I did." I had, too, every day in Glasgow, at the airport before I left, and in the only Internet café I could find, in Kirkwall, when I took Percy back with his ruined bicycle. There had been no e-mail from Willow.

"Technology," she said. "Great when it works, and a real pain when it doesn't." I said nothing.

"This is a terrible tragedy," Kenny said solemnly, pointing to the newspaper. "But we've got something to take your mind off it. Now that you're here, we can turn all of our attention to our, um, project."

"He means finding the you-know-what," Willow said. She and Kenny exchanged glances.

"Exactly," he said.

"You two had better order something to eat, to keep up your strength," she said. "The fish and chips are excellent." She was right about that. I enjoyed my meal very much despite their tiresome attempts to persuade me that they'd spent their every waking moment looking for me. Soon I was driving down the highway behind the motorcycle, this time traveling at a pace I could match. I had no idea what

Willow wanted to show me, but what else did I have to do until the expertise that normally resided outwith Orkney did its thing?

Willow and Kenny were staying at a pleasant bed-and-breakfast place in Deerness. They had separate rooms, they assured me, as if I cared, but it seemed rather a technicality given they shared a bathroom in one of those arrangements where there is a door from each room into the bathroom. We gathered in Willow's room.

"Ready?" she exclaimed, placing in front of me a rather odd object. It was a long piece of cloth, rather scroll-like in appearance with a primitive but unusual drawing on it. There was a central panel on which was depicted, from the top, an animal, probably a camel, then a castle, a zigzag design, a head with mouth and eyes open, an image that made me feel a bit queasy, and, at the bottom, a bowl-shaped object of some kind. Down the sides were twiglike figures, and along the bottom some wavy lines in an irregular pattern.

"I found it hidden in the suitcase that Trevor had packed for his getaway," she said. "It was under the lining. I almost gave the bag and its contents all away to a charity, but there was this long thread that didn't look right in the lining, and I opened it up and there it was. Trevor couldn't sew to save his life." I thought that was maybe an unfortunate choice of phrase, but I suppose if she could drink Skullsplitter beer without a qualm, she was well over Trevor. I'm sure the delectable Kenny was helping with this transition a lot.

"I wasn't sure what I had, other than it looked like a map, but Trevor's ticket, the around-the-world ticket that I believe I have mentioned I paid for, had a first stop in Orkney. I am just guessing, of course, but I'm willing to bet he found this in that writing thing that you are so keen on finding. You did tell me that you thought the desk came from either Glasgow or Orkney, did you not? So I figure there is no money, but there is a treasure somewhere, and Trevor was heading off to find it. Or maybe, I suppose, it's possible he already did, but then where is it? I flew to Edinburgh, took the bus to Scrabster and then the ferry, hoping, assuming, I'd be able to find you here. Fortuitously, I met Kenny on the boat. He knows all about this kind of thing, don't you, Kenny?"

"A little," he said. "I'm studying Scottish history in Edinburgh. My thesis is on Viking Scotland with particular reference to Orkney. That's why I could decipher the runes around the side here. Stop me if you know all this, Lara, but Orkney was an important part of the Viking world. It was settled by the Norwegians, Norse in other words, probably some time in the ninth century. The Vikings *jarls* or "earls" were very powerful men, some of whom extended their territories into northern Scotland, Caithness, and Sutherland, and even beyond. We know about this period from archaeology, but also from something called the Orkneyinga Saga which is the story of the earls of Orkney. It is probably part history, part myth, but useful just the same. I think we're really on to something, that there is a real Viking treasure to be found. I don't know if you've been to Maeshowe, Lara, but if so you'll know there are many Viking runes there, which we can actually read. The alphabet is called *futhark* for its first six letters, *th* counting as one."

"Isn't the word *futhark* cute?" Willow said. "The things you learn."

"Some of the runes found in Maeshowe refer to well-hidden treasure in the tomb," Kenny said. Thanks to Percy,

I already knew that. "Treasure for the Vikings, I have to tell you, almost invariably means gold and silver. But Viking treasure wasn't found in Maeshowe. Maybe it's somewhere else. I'm thinking that these swirls along the bottom are actually a map of the shoreline where the treasure was buried."

I was suddenly very depressed. A treasure map, of all things, a map to buried Viking jewelry or something. I mean, how tiresome! Should I point out the obvious to them? I decided I would, even if it felt like too much of an effort. "What would a camel be doing in Orkney in Viking times?" I asked. "Or any other time for that matter?" If Orkney had a zoo I hadn't seen it yet.

"We were wondering about that, too," Willow said. "I don't think it's a camel, though. The artist wasn't exactly Rembrandt or anything. Unfortunately the rather poor talent for perspective here is not going to help us at all. It's probably a horse. They had horses, right, Kenny?"

"Right. Some have claimed the islands were once named for the horses, Hrossey, that is, and there is still a festival of the horse held on South Ronaldsay every summer. So yes, this is most likely a horse."

"It has a hump," I said. I was feeling disagreeable and it showed.

"I'm sure that was just a mistake," Willow replied. "It's a horse." She was obviously determined that there was treasure to be found. She hadn't managed to find the cash of Trevor's that she so desperately believed in. Now she'd transferred this desire to a treasure map. She saw what she wanted to, but I suffered under no such illusion, and it was very plainly a camel.

My friend Moira says I can be a spoilsport from time to time. A poop is what she calls me. Maybe she's right. "If these swirls are the coastline, would that have not perhaps changed over the intervening, say, one thousand years. You did say the Vikings came here in the ninth century and stayed for how long?"

"The era of the Viking earls ended in the thirteenth century," Kenny said. "I suppose it might have changed a bit since."

Good grief again. I posed my next disagreeable question. "How old would this scroll have to be?" Personally I made it nineteenth century at best, the day before yesterday at worst, and while I was no expert on the Vikings in any shape or form, and I would certainly get something like this tested, I could tell just looking at it that it wasn't a thousand years old.

"I know what you're thinking, that this isn't that old," Willow said, smart young woman that she is.

"It could be based on something much older though," Kenny said. "There is something about it." Could that something be called wishful thinking, do you suppose? "This hill might be a chamber tomb, like Maeshowe or the Tomb of the Eagles, perhaps one as yet uncovered. That would be amazing in and of itself. It would be even more so if it turned out to be a place where Vikings stashed their treasure."

Tomb of the Eagles, I thought. Was that the name? It didn't sound quite right to me, but why? But yes, it was called that. I'd been there. It was nice. Anyway, surely Kenny who was not only cute but obviously intelligent knew what the tomb thing was called, even if he wanted to believe this scroll was several centuries old. More to the point, why was this conversation upsetting me, other than the obvious, which is to say, the total futility of it? I could feel my heart pounding a little, my palms sweating, and I felt a little shaky, almost like a panic attack, or maybe as if I'd just gulped four quick espressos in a row. I just couldn't think of any reason to feel like this at this particular moment.

"I think this is a map, of sorts. See there's water, and a shoreline, a bay really, with a very distinctive shape. I think we need to find that piece of shoreline. There is a tower, too, a broch. So we're looking for a distinctive piece of shoreline where there was once a tower, with a hill, or rather an undiscovered tomb nearby. There are some other really interesting symbols here as well, that make me think that it's old. The disembodied head that speaks, for example, was a very important image in pagan times, as is the castle and the maze." Kenny gestured to the symbols down the side. The word "maze," of course, took me back to Percy, bleeding to death: The Wasteland, the maze, the wounded king. Even with that, though, I was not prepared for what was coming.

"Tell her what the runes say, Kenny," Willow said.

"Yes, don't keep me in suspense," I said, trying to keep profound cynicism out of my voice. There was a slight throbbing at my temples that indicated a headache was on its way, due perhaps to the strain of keeping myself from snapping at them.

"It says," Kenny replied, pointing at the sticklike figures down one side, " 'Before he went mad, Bjarni the Wanderer hid the cauldron in the tomb of the orcs.'" At the sound of these words, I dashed into the bathroom and threw up.

Chapter 8

Do I detect some skepticism on your part? I could hardly blame you for that. What are the chances, you are asking yourself, that a Viking from Orkney, of good lineage, but neither king nor earl, would be taken to the court of the caliph of Spain? In the highly unlikely event that he was, what language were they speaking? Did the caliph speak Old Norse? Was a translator provided? Did Goisvintha, descended from Goths of northern Spain, provide the necessary interpretation?

But surely that is always the issue with sagas of this type. How does one separate the wheat from the chaff, the true historical background from the ripping good yarn? How can you extract the nugget of truth in what is otherwise a fable? I'm not just talking about Bjarni's story here, you understand. The much-revered *Orkneyinga Saga*, the history of the earls of Orkney, believed to be the only medieval chronicle centered on Orkney, was not the work of someone in or from Orkney, despite what you might think. Rather it was written by an unknown Icelandic poet, probably about 1200, but based on ancient traditions and tales, stories told on the long winter nights, and set out in such a way that they would be recited by rout, and thus passed from generation to generation. Icelandic verse was extremely complex, with many strict rules governing it as to the number of syllables permissible in each line, the use of internal assonance and rhyme and so on. These rules served as an aide-memoir, really, the complexity ensuring that the story, which was passed along orally for possibly hundreds of years would survive intact.

In the same way, Bjarni's saga was not written down as it happened, indeed not until much, much later. Still, my family believes it to be an eyewitness account by Svein the poet, passed along orally through many, many generations before finally being given literary form. Perhaps it is. Perhaps it isn't.

Were there embellishments to it over the centuries? Of course there were. That does not, however, make the tale a lie. Was the story of Bjarni's sojourn in Spain added by one of my forbearers eager to establish a more important family pedigree? Was it an exaggeration or even a fiction told by Bjarni himself in a boastful way, something one is inclined to assume he was more than capable of, or perhaps instead to justify his rather extended absence from home and hearth? Or, unlikely as it might appear, did all this actually happen? Did Bjarni really visit the caliph of Spain? I have spent much of my life trying to decide what it is I believe.

I can tell you that the saga's description of the Spain of the Umayyad caliphate does not arouse much argument from those who study such things. As the saga says, it was an extraordinary place. In Cordoba, the streets were indeed paved, lit, and patrolled as the story relates. In Bjarni's day the caliphate was still in power, but it was soon to disintegrate amongst warring factions and then to fall to the Reconquista, the reestablishment of Catholic power, the beginning of which is often said to be the fall of Muslim Toledo in 1085.

I leave it up to you to decide how much or how little to believe. All I ask of you is an open mind. I can see you are tiring, or perhaps it is that you are impatient to find how this story ends. Let me pick up the thread and speed Bjarni on his way.

IT IS POSSIBLE that mine was not the reaction Willow and Kenny had been expecting when they told me what the runic inscription said, and it was certainly a waste of a very good meal. "I'm being just so thoughtless," Willow said. "Here you've found another body, and then I spring this treasure map on you. It's all too emotional, I can tell. Look, we're going to get you some hot tea, and then see that you get back to your B&B. You can have a good rest, and we'll come pick you up tomorrow morning. Can we use your car, given there are three of us?"

"I guess so," I said. "No tea, please. I really just want to go back to my B&B." Why did everybody here think hot tea would solve everything?

"You drive her car, Willow, and I'll follow on my bike," Kenny said.

"No, I'm okay," I said. I didn't really want them to know where I was staying until I'd had time to think this all through. Still I couldn't avoid giving them Mrs. Brown's name. It would have seemed rather peculiar not to, but now that I'd found her, I really just wanted to get away from Willow and her Kenny. Menace seemed to lurk everywhere, but it was a fuzzy everywhere, and I couldn't decide where the real danger might lie. All I knew is that I wanted to be very far from anyone associated with mad Bjarni the Wanderer, because people interested in this Bjarni person ended up dead. A means of evading Willow and Kenny was waiting for me back at Mrs. Brown's place, along with a nice shot of her single malt scotch. It was a letter from Maya Alexander, which read:

> *I heard about your terrible experience. You must have been terrified, and you simply must come and stay with us. We'll be here for two or three more days at least, and I can stay longer than that, if you need to stay. Both Robert and I insist you come. You can't stay all by yourself in that B&B after what has happened. Please call any time, day or night. Love, Maya.*

I called. They said they would come to get me immediately. I told them I would find my own way there the next day in time for dinner, not wishing to insult Mrs. Brown. I wondered how they found me. Maya told me Robert had got on the phone the minute they'd seen the article in the paper. I guess if you have enough money and influence you can do just about anything. At least I hope that explained it.

That night I alternated between nightmares, in which disembodied heads featured prominently, and fussing about what all this meant. It was just too much of a coincidence that both Percy and Willow were looking for the same thing. Both Percy and Willow, by way of Trevor, had an association with the writing cabinet. But neither was really interested in the writing cabinet, I now realized. I was the only person who really gave two hoots about the Mackintosh.

The two lines, Percy's dying words and Kenny's translation of the Viking runes, were not identical. I was sure that Percy had said Bjarni had hidden a "chalice," not a "cauldron," in the tomb of the orcs. His last words were now burned into my memory. Was that semantics, a slightly different translation of the same word, or was there something more significant, or sinister about it? And if there was such a thing in Orkney as the Tomb of the Eagles so-named for the eagle talons and bones found in it, and of course there was because I'd been in it, what, other than a creature in Tolkien, was an orc?

I was up very early the next morning. The good news was that in addition to the fish and chips, I seemed to have purged that cold, hard lump in my chest. Now instead of numb, I was mad as hell. In other words, I was feeling a whole lot better.

There are not that many hedges in Orkney, the terrain tending more to rolling farmland, dark hills, and high cliffs by the sea where the waves crashed in. Still, there was a hedge at Willow and Kenny's place, and early the next morning, I was in it. It did occur to me that I was spending rather too much time in hedges, an undignified activity if ever there was one, since Blair Bazillionaire's cocktail party. This time I wasn't looking for pathetic remnants of furniture. I was getting ready to follow Willow. At the crack of dawn I packed my bag, bade the lovely Mrs. Brown adieu, phoned the Northern Constabulary to tell them what Percy's last words were—I believe I heard a snort of disbelief when I told them—and where they could find me that evening. Then I headed out for Deerness and Willow and Kenny's B&B.

On the way, I called Willow from a phone booth, one of those lovely old red ones you don't see much anymore, in the corner of a field—seriously, there were cows in the field that looked as if they were lined up to use it—to tell her I still wasn't feeling very well, and they should carry on without me for the day. I'd promised to call the next morning, a promise I had no intention of keeping. Had I believed her question, delivered with wide-eyed innocence, about my not receiving her e-mail? I had not. Did I believe the "Wow, we've been looking for you everywhere," from Kenny? Not that, either, no matter how cute he was. Did I even believe they had just met on the ferry? No, again. I had no idea what was going on here, but I knew I didn't like it.

Willow, of course, had been terribly solicitous when I called. She said she understood completely, that I must rest after such an ordeal, and that they would let me know what progress they'd made when they saw me. She told me they had ordnance maps and were looking for a bay with the right shape, and that Kenny was going to try to do some research on the Internet to narrow their area of search down a little. I told them that was a good idea. Then I drove to Deerness, pulled my car off the road, and went and stood in the hedge.

It was not long before Willow and Kenny, arms around each other, emerged from the house. By the time they'd got the motorcycle out of the garage and put on their helmets, I was back in my car. My car looked very similar to most of the other cars on the road, so I wasn't too worried about their recognizing it. Soon however, they left the bike and headed along the coast on foot. This made things a little trickier. I had my own ordnance map, and consulted it, trying to figure out where they'd be walking. I decided they were doing what they said they would, which is to say, they were scouring the coastline for a bay with a tower. I parked the car by a church and waited. I figured if they saw me, I'd just have to say that I had changed my mind about coming with them and had seen them leave the

B&B. They wouldn't believe me probably, but then I didn't believe them either.

About forty-five minutes later, they were back on their bike, heading in the direction of Kirkwall. I followed at what I hoped was a safe distance. They parked in the same lot I had when I'd brought poor Percy back after our hours spent sightseeing, and then they headed for the Internet café. Once again they were doing exactly what they said they would, something I found annoying. Had they seen me or was their story absolutely genuine? I simply didn't know.

They spent an hour in the Internet café. By this time I was hungry, having passed on breakfast in the fear my stomach wasn't up for it. I was casting my eyes about for a quick place to grab a sandwich when they came out of the café, Kenny looking at his watch, and started walking quickly toward the main street of town. I followed. They went into a pub in a hotel on the harbor.

Now I didn't know what to do. To add to my discomfort, it was starting to rain, just a drizzle, really, but I'd get wet enough in time. I could sit outside in a puddle and wait for them to have lunch, I could give up and go to the Alexanders, or I could march into the bar. I could do the wide-eyed innocent routine as well as Willow. I could feign surprise with the best of them. I would ask them if they got my message that I was feeling much better and look pained that they didn't. I might even go to a phone and leave that message with their innkeeper.

That sounded like such a clever idea, I headed off immediately in search of a public telephone, and found one with no cows to be seen nearby. I just hoped that whoever the person was who took the message wouldn't note the time exactly. I then stepped into the dim light of the bar. It took me a minute to realize neither Willow nor Kenny was there. Did they have two rooms, one in the hotel and one at the B&B? That seemed excessive, if nothing else. I went to the desk and asked for Willow Laurier, but there was no one there by that name. Unfortunately I only knew her partner as Kenny, so I couldn't ask for him. I went back into the bar. I noted a back door, and took it on to a side street, a lane, really. They had given me the slip.

Once again I had several choices. I could go back to the parking lot and see if their motorcycle was still there. I could go back to the B&B if it wasn't and spend some more quality time in the hedge waiting for them to come back. Or, and this was my favored option, I could go and have lunch. I was actually starting to feel a little light-headed, and realized that if I didn't count dinner—and why would I under the circumstances?—I hadn't eaten since breakfast the previous day. I wandered down the main street and chose a pleasant looking little café. They looked full, but they told me there was an upstairs room. In it I found Kenny and Willow, talking to none other than Lester Campbell, antique dealer from George Square in Glasgow. I had no trouble looking genuinely surprised. They didn't either.

"Lara!" Willow exclaimed after a moment's confusion. "You're here."

"Hi," I said. "Am I ever glad to see you. I wondered if that was your motorcycle in the parking lot. And Lester, what an unexpected pleasure!"

"For me as well," he said, rising from his chair politely, knocking over his water glass in the process. Fortunately there wasn't much in it, but it gave us all a moment to collect ourselves.

"I left you a message," I said to Willow. "I slept for a couple of hours after I talked to you and felt much better, but you'd already left when I called."

"I'm so glad you're feeling better," Willow said.

"This is great, Lara," the adorable Kenny said, pulling out a chair. "Please join us."

"I will," I said. "I'm starving."

"Good sign," Willow said. "We seem to have stumbled on the place to be in Kirkwall, Kenny. We went to a pub first, Lara, but it was so dark we decided to try for something else, and we picked this place, and what do you know, here's Lester. And then you come in, too. I can't believe it."

I couldn't either. "How do you know each other?" I said brightly. Kenny and Willow looked discomfited. It was left to Lester to reply.

"Kenny and I met at the University."

"Interesting," I said. "Which one?"

"Glasgow," Lester said, as simultaneously Kenny offered up Edinburgh. I suppose I looked perplexed.

"Was it Edinburgh, Ken?" Lester said. At least his name was really Kenny apparently, unlike other people I'd met lately. "I suppose it must have been. I give courses at both universities from time to time, and obviously have trouble keeping them apart."

Didn't this just strain one's credulity? "Has to be," Kenny said. "I've never been to Glasgow University."

"That solves it, then," Lester said.

"You give courses, Lester?" I said. "You are a man of many talents. Antiques? History?"

"I have made something of a hobby of Viking jewelry," Lester said. "Nothing to do with the shop, but from time to time I give a lecture or two."

"He's being modest," Kenny said. "He's a real expert, unlike me who is just trying to be."

"So you're talking about . . ." Willow gave me an almost imperceptible shake of the head, but there was no mistaking her meaning. "Vikings," I said. "How fascinating. Tell me more."

"It is," Willow said. "But how do you and Lester know each other?"

"Fellow antique dealers," Lester said.

"Yes, we met in Glasgow when I happened upon Lester's shop. He was kind enough to suggest I attend a rather splendid fund-raiser at a lovely home in Glasgow."

"I think we're going to be fellow houseguests this evening, in fact," Lester said.

"Are we?" I asked.

"You're staying at the same B&B in Stromness?" Willow said. "What a coincidence!"

"Stromness?" Lester said.

Oh, dear. "I received a very nice invitation today," I said. "I ran into Maya a couple of days ago, and she's just invited me to stay with them."

"She told me last night you were coming," Lester said.

Kenny and Willow looked at me. The tables had somehow been turned here, and I was the one who was under suspicion. I didn't think that was exactly fair under the circumstances. "I think she must have meant she intended to invite me," I said. "I was just talking to her this morning."

"That must have been it," Lester agreed, but he looked doubtful.

"I see," Willow said. I expect she did, too, which was too bad, but given I didn't believe a word she was saying, maybe she shouldn't believe me either.

"The Alexanders are fabulous hosts," Lester said. "I know you'll enjoy it there. I e-mailed Robert a couple of days ago with a photo of a pocket watch I thought he'd love, and he invited me to come for a visit. I never turn down an invitation from the Alexanders."

"This would be Robert Alexander the entrepreneur, would it?" Kenny said. "The rich guy?"

"One and the same," Lester said. "They have a wonderful weekend home here."

"Very nice," Willow said, but she didn't mean it. The conversation was a little strained after that, and I didn't learn anything more of interest. Lester rattled on about antiques and Vikings, Kenny joined in on the Viking stuff, and Willow just picked quietly at her food. I concentrated on eating everything in sight.

"So, are we going to get together tomorrow as planned?" I asked brightly as we left the restaurant.

"Kenny and I were thinking of taking a day off," Willow said. "Given you'll be spending time with Lester and your hosts, maybe we should regroup the next day."

"Fine with me," I said. "Should I just come to your B&B first thing the day after tomorrow? Then we can take my car."

"Sure," Willow said, and with that we parted company. I offered Lester a ride to Hoxa, but he declined saying he had some business to attend to in town, some banking or something, and had already rented a car. I went back to the parking lot and waited awhile to see if Willow and Kenny came back. I felt I had to make a better effort at explaining myself, although of course all I'd be doing would be making a lie worse. They didn't come. I eventually gave up and drove across the Churchill Barriers to St. Margaret's Hope and

Hoxa once more. Or maybe what I was heading for was The Wasteland, the maze, and the wounded king.

My reception at the Alexanders was not quite what I was expecting, although Maya and Robert were waiting for me, and Drever the Intimidating, still in army fatigues, took my bag with exemplary speed. Unfortunately Detective Cusiter was awaiting my arrival as well.

"I'm sorry to trouble you," he said in his polite Orkney fashion, looking as if he was personally pained by any inconvenience he might be causing. "But I'm afraid I have some more questions. The Alexanders have very graciously said we can use the downstairs study."

I thought he wanted to ask me about Percy's last words, but that wasn't what had brought him to Hoxa. "You were telling us you gave Mr. Budge a ride," he began.

"I did, yes," I said.

"You picked him up on the side of the road," he said, consulting his notes.

"Yes."

"Not a safe thing to do, really, is it? Pick up a stranger? This is Orkney, of course, but I wouldn't have thought you as a tourist would want to do something like that."

"I was sure I'd seen him somewhere," I said. "I didn't regard him as a real stranger. And you know he looked kind of harmless. And his bicycle was all bent and everything."

"Very good of you, I'm sure." I didn't like his tone. There was something underneath the politeness there.

"Did you get the message I left about his last words?"

"I did. Unusual."

"I thought so, too, both at the time, and when I remembered them again. Do you have any idea what that might mean?"

"None at all," he said. There was a long pause. "I'll come to the point. We found traces of the victim's blood in your rental car."

"Oh! Well, he did grab me, and there was blood everywhere, on my clothes, on my arm. But you knew that." I was obviously still not firing on all cylinders, because I didn't immediately fathom where he was going with this. I had not been in that car since just before I'd found Percy.

"On the door side of the passenger seat," he said, as if I'd said nothing. "You didn't climb across from the passenger side, did you?"

I was tempted to say I was always trying to get in the passenger side, that and turning on the windshield wipers when I wanted to signal a turn, because I was unaccustomed to right-hand drive. "No. It must be from his bicycle accident, when I gave him a ride. He did have some bad scratches from a barbed wire fence."

"Hmm," he said, or something like that. I suppose it did sound a little lame. "Anyone you can think of that would confirm this bicycle accident?"

"His mother? He might have mentioned it to her. The bicycle repair shop? I mean he couldn't repair it himself. I even wondered if it was a write-off."

"The blood," he said. "The cuts and scratches. Did anyone see him in that state?"

"We went to Maeshowe," I said. "He went into the men's room at the Historic Scotland center there, so maybe someone would recall that."

"Hmm," he said again. "He had a bad fall, cut himself on barbed wire, was bleeding, but you decided to go sightseeing with this complete stranger."

"We struck up a conversation. It turned out he'd been to

Toronto recently, so we talked about that." There I'd said it. "He pointed out Maeshowe to me and was appalled I didn't know what it was, and insisted we go to see it. I guess he thought I should know something about his home. Then I said I'd like to see the Ring of Brodgar and the Standing Stones of Stenness and he very kindly agreed to accompany me, then we went to Skara Brae. He was very knowledge-able, and I assumed this was his way of saying thank you for the lift. I dropped him off in Kirkwall. But why are you ask-ing me this? He wasn't stabbed in my car. He was stabbed in the bunker."

"Just part of our investigation," he said.

I thought about that for a moment. "The glasses," I said. "You didn't find the glasses, and that means he was killed somewhere else and transported to that bunker. Am I right? There'd be other things, too, where the blood was and everything."

He looked a bit startled, but then he almost smiled. "I see a close personal relationship with a policeman has rubbed off on you. You may even know what I'm going to say next."

"Something about not leaving Orkney anytime soon."

"Right again. You wouldn't be thinking of it, would you?

"I guess not," I said.

"Good. That will be all for now."

"You can't possibly think there'd only be a couple of drops of blood in my car if I'd driven him around with all those stab wounds, do you? You think I propped him up in the passenger seat, hauled him up that hill and then down the steps of the bunker and on to that slab?" This was mak-ing me cranky.

"I don't think anything," he replied. "We're in the early

stages of our investigation. But we believe someone, presumably the person who stabbed him, threw Mr. Budge
down the stairs, along with his bicycle, and that Mr. Budge
dragged himself across the bunker and up onto the slab."

"Please, no!" I said, with a catch in my voice. I could
hardly tolerate such a terrible thought, and I think it must
have showed. I got this horrible idea Percy had crawled up
on that slab to get his last look at the setting sun. Ridiculous, but I couldn't shake it.

"We'll find whoever did this," Cusiter said, his expression softening slightly. Then he shook my hand and left.

Despite the welcome, my accommodations at the
Alexander residence were definitely a step up, although perhaps not as relaxing as Mrs. Brown's place. Robert immediately asked me if I played golf. I reluctantly said no, because
his homegrown driving range and putting green would be a
spectacular place to play. I was given my own little suite,
complete with fancy bathroom and a little sitting area off
the bedroom with a small sofa, a desk, and a couple of
interesting-looking chairs. Still, the fabulous antique furniture, which I promised myself I'd have a closer look at later,
took second place to the views: from the bedroom across
beautiful countryside to the sea, and from the sitting room,
a perfect, unobstructed view of the house across the way.
Maya showed me to my room.

"I want you to consider this your home," she said. "Anything you want, please help yourself. If you can't find it, just
ask. I'll give you a key so you can come and go as you please.
We have a reservation for dinner at a very nice place, and we
want you to be our guest. If you feel like coming with us,
that's great. If you'd prefer, I'll make something up for you
here. I know you've had a terrible time, and you might just

like to rest. I hope that discussion with the policeman wasn't too upsetting. You looked a little pale when he left."

"Unpleasant subject," I said, which was true, especially the part about a dying Percy dragging himself up on to the slab. On top of that, I seemed to have gone from unfortunate tourist to potential killer in the space of a day or two. I wondered if Maya would be as keen on me as a houseguest, going so far as to give me a key, if she'd known that. "I'd like to come with you to dinner." I didn't want her to think I was an invalid, because I had things to do, people to see, and I didn't want her fussing over me the whole time. "I really would like the company. It keeps my mind off what happened. I can't tell you how much I appreciate your exceedingly generous invitation."

"It was a selfish invitation, if truth be told. I'm very glad of your company, too. Robert is away from the house much of the day when we're here, and Drever always has chores that take him away for hours. I'm not that comfortable by myself now, what with that murder happening so close by. I'll be a lot happier when they catch the awful person who did it. I love it here. I just hope this doesn't spoil the place for me." I didn't tell her that Percy might have been murdered somewhere else entirely, because what difference would that make to her? The body had been found just a few minutes drive away. I didn't think this was a random killing though, a killer just roaming the neighborhood looking for someone to stab. I thought Maya pretty safe and said so.

"I suppose it wasn't a robbery, or anything," she said. "A man on his bike can't be a great target, so I guess I don't have to worry about a home invasion or anything. It must have been something else, a jilted lover or something. What do you think?"

"I'm sure you're right," I said.

"I wish I knew more people here. I'm lonely, really. Robert is, I don't know, a jealous man. I don't mean other men. He would have no cause for that. He seems to be content with just the two of us, you know. We don't have friends as a couple. There are lots of people around, like that evening we did the fund-raiser in Glasgow, but they're not friends. I haven't had a close girlfriend since Bev, Robert's first wife, died. Robert has his business associates, of course, and so he always has people to talk to, but I don't. So often I'm alone with only Drever. Please don't tell Robert, but I don't like Drever much. I sometimes think he considers part of his job to be watching me on Robert's behalf. Oh my. I'm really running off at the mouth, here, aren't I? And you've had such a dreadful time. I know I'm very fortunate. Anything my little heart desires is mine. Please forgive me. It must all sound terribly selfish."

"Not at all," I said. "I appreciate your company very much, and I hope we'll be friends. I think we are already."

"You are so nice. If you don't mind, I might just have a nap before dinner. I haven't been sleeping that well."

"A nap sounds good to me, too."

"Good. We're leaving at seven-thirty. We have two other guests, Lester whom you know, and there's someone else as well, Simon Spence, a museum consultant. He's a friend of both Lester's and Robert's."

"I look forward to it."

"I meant what I said about staying on longer. Robert can fly his plane back, and I'll take a regular flight whenever it works for you."

"Robert has his own plane?"

"He does. He loves to fly, maybe even more than golf. If

the weather's good, he might even take you up in it. Or out in his boat. He does love his toys. See you about six-thirty downstairs for cocktails."

I suppose Maya really did have a nap. I, however, borrowed some binoculars—she had, after all, told me to help myself to anything I needed—and turned them on the house across the way. I watched for some time but saw no one, just the wind blowing dried brush around the yard. It was a very dismal spot, all the more so because Orkney seems such an orderly and tidy place. Then for something to do, I turned the binoculars on Robert, who was hitting golf balls, and Drever, who kept working way out of Robert's range. I decided that Maya was right, and that Drever spent most of his time making sure every blade of grass on the green was perfect. At some point both Robert and Drever walked over the hill toward the sea together, maybe looking for golf balls.

Dinner that evening, in the dining room of the Foveran Hotel in St. Ola, was very pleasant. The food was spectacular, the conversation stimulating, although I was not exactly sparkling myself. Lester was amusing, Robert and Maya both generous hosts. Simon Spence, the museum consultant was from Edinburgh, in Orkney on a contract of some kind with Historic Scotland.

I finally managed to work in the question I needed to have answered, which is to say, what is an "orc"? Spence launched into an explanation immediately. I don't know why I hadn't noticed that "orc" was essentially part of the place name where I found myself, the "orc" in Orkney.

"The Norse called these islands *Orkneyjar*," he said. He pronounced it more or less orc-nee-yahr. "That was their interpretation of a much older name for the islands. The Celts referred to the islands in Old Gaelic, as *Insi Orc*, or 'Island of the Orcs,' which is to say young pigs or wild boar. Not that we think Gaelic was ever spoken in Orkney, although it's possible the Picts, who were here a very long time ago, spoke a type of Celtic language. It was not Gaelic, though. When the Norse, or Vikings, arrived in the ninth century, they assumed the name meant Seal Islands, because their word for seal was *orkn*. *Eyjar* means 'islands,' hence Seal Islands. But the name predates the arrival of the Vikings by hundreds and hundreds of years. The Romans knew the islands as the Orcades, for example, and the Romans were long gone by the time the Vikings showed up here. Some believe that the Picts, who were here before the Vikings, took the boar as their symbol, which would explain the name."

I told him how interesting I thought all this was, and I meant it. Bjarni the Wanderer had hidden the cauldron in the tomb of the pigs or the boar, or maybe the seals. Not that I was any further ahead in actually nailing this down, mind you, but at least I knew what the word meant, and that it was not so far-fetched in this place given the long history. Would Bjarni have thought the tomb held the bones of seals? I suppose it depended when and by whom the line had been written.

"I don't suppose you could explain why this island is called the Mainland," Maya said. "Given that it is an island, and what I would call the Mainland would be Scotland proper, the Highlands and such."

"Corruption of the Norse name for it, *Meginland*," Spence said. "Just to make it more confusing, what is now the Mainland may once have been called Hrossey, or Horse Island." That, too, was interesting, in that it showed that

Kenny the Adorable knew what he was talking about, even if that animal on his treasure map was really a camel. "You do all know that you call these islands Orkney and not the Orkneys unless you want to sound like an ignorant tourist."

"That much we figured out," Robert said. "And we know it's the Mainland, not just Mainland, as in we are touring around the Mainland."

"That is correct," Spence said. "Always good to call a place by the name preferred by those who live there."

"So the names are essentially Scandinavian, not Gaelic or whatever?" Lester asked.

"True. Norn, a Norse language was spoken here for almost a thousand years. It was supplanted by English, not Gaelic. The last official Norn document dates to the middle of the fifteenth century. Scottish earls replaced the Norse *jarls,* and Orkney became more Scottish than Scandinavian, although I can tell you people here are proud of their Norse heritage, and most place names here are of Norse origin. I understand that there were elderly people who still spoke Norn in the early nineteenth century, but the language died with them. Nobody speaks it now, and even then nobody read it. It essentially had gone out of common usage in the seventeenth century." That information, too, was interesting, and would later prove, although I didn't realize it at the time, to be very useful.

"What about Viking runes?" I asked. "I saw some in Maeshowe."

"Yes, there are several examples of runic inscriptions here. It's an early Germanic writing system, once used for magical purposes, but it was in use as a general communication for some time."

"So people here could once write something in runes."

"Certainly. That's why we get all those runic inscriptions in Maeshowe and other places here. They are not magical inscriptions though. Instead they are about rather lusty encounters of the secular kind."

"Didn't the runes say there was treasure there?" Maya asked.

"Yes, indeed. And there may have been. Unfortunately it was long gone by the time archaeologists arrived. There are some runic inscriptions right in the tomb that say the treasure was removed over three days by Hakon. The runes make it clear that the tomb was definitely well-known to the Vikings. In the Orkneyinga Saga there is a story about Harald Maddadarson of Atholl who tried a surprise attack on Orkney while Orkney Earl Rognvald was on a pilgrimage to the Holy Land. Maddadarson got caught in a bad storm and took shelter in Maeshowe, only to have two of his men go crazy while there."

"Seriously?" I said.

"Who knows? It was a tomb after all. Maybe this was the Viking equivalent of staying in a cemetery overnight for us, and they scared themselves right over the edge. It's a good story in any event."

"I have another question, Simon," Maya said. "I'm sure I should know the answer, but what exactly did St. Margaret hope for?"

Simon laughed. "Hope is a word for a cove or bay. There are two possibilities for St. Margaret, one being Margaret, the saint and queen of Scotland, the other the very young daughter of the king of Norway who died in the late thirteenth century when she was on her way to be wed to the English Prince Edward. She was only seven or something, unpleasant thought. I opt for the former."

"I wish I hadn't asked," Maya said. "I prefer 'hope' as in 'hopeful.'" I thought that was true, too, but especially for Maya, who seemed chronically hopeful, yet destined to be disappointed in some way I couldn't explain.

This had all been very interesting. I didn't know what to think about it all, insofar as mad Bjarni was concerned, but it did say that poor Percy's last words were not without precedent, except, of course, for the chalice part. What if, and this was a revolutionary thought, the skeptic, by which I meant me, was wrong and the dreamers like Willow and Kenny and possibly Percy, and even the con man looking for his big windfall, which is to say Trevor, had been right and there really was something to this Bjarni business? I tried to put such a ridiculous thought out of my head.

There was another important moment that evening, the full significance of which would not be apparent to me for a while. Maya was wearing the necklace I had coveted that evening at her home in Glasgow. We were standing in the hallway waiting for the gentlemen to join us to leave for home, and, really just making conversation, I told her I could not understand why it was around her neck and not mine. She laughed, and insisted I try it on.

"I don't know anything about it," Maya said. "I'd like to be more appreciative when Robert gives me these things, and just to be able to discuss his passion for antiques with him. He gave me the necklace on Valentine's Day a couple of years ago, and I love it. It's my favorite; simple, you know, but I always feel elegant when I wear it. I do adore it."

"You should. It looks wonderful on you. I saw a very similar one a couple of years ago. Someone was thinking about buying it for his wife. That one was Liberty and Company. This one is, too," I added, turning it over to check it out.

"It's about a hundred years old." I tried it on and admired myself in the hall mirror.

"All I know is that I like it. I'll confess something, though. I'm afraid to wear it, although I do because I know Robert would be hurt if I didn't. Quite by accident I found the bill for it. Okay, I'll be honest. I was snooping. I was afraid he was giving me something that had belonged to Bev, you know, his first wife. We were very close friends, but, you know, I just didn't want to have her jewelry. But he bought it just a short time before Valentine's Day. I was relieved until I realized that he'd paid about a hundred thousand dollars for it. I was horrified."

"Wow," I said. I meant it, too. I wouldn't have let anyone I knew pay a dime over ten thousand, maybe fifteen thousand tops. I would have thought Robert would be more discerning. There were several possible explanations for the rather startling figure. Perhaps it was simply that Maya needed glasses or that she'd been into the champagne to the extent that an extra zero appeared before her eyes, although I hadn't seen any indication here that she drank too much. She had a couple of glasses of wine with dinner, and she certainly wasn't even remotely sloshed when I found her in the garden. That evening in Glasgow could well have been an anomaly. She was essentially shy, and maybe having all those strangers in her home was a little too much for her. The third, less palatable option was that Robert had someone else for whom he was buying extraordinarily expensive necklaces, and Maya had merely assumed the invoice was for hers. I'm always a bit suspicious of the "darling this" and "darling that" type, but he did genuinely seem to adore her.

"Horrified by what, darling?" Robert said, coming up and putting his arm around his wife's shoulders.

"We're just sharing a girl story. By the way, Lara has been telling me all about the necklace you gave me," she said. "She saw one very similar in Toronto. She says it's a hundred years old."

"I expect it is, darling."

"You spoil me, Robert."

"And why wouldn't I, darling?"

At this point, I had taken the necklace off and was looking at it very carefully. It was remarkably similar to what I remembered about the piece Blair Bazillionaire had asked me to look at. I suppose one couldn't be entirely certain at a distance of a couple of years, but really, the stones were the same, and the chain, which was rather distinctive, particularly the medallions of mother-of-pearl, was what I remembered as well. I really would not have thought there would be two of these. I handed it back with a smile, though, and told her I was envious. If Blair had bought one like it, I sure hoped he hadn't paid what Robert had.

Later that night when all the lights were out in the house, at least all that I could see, I once again turned my binoculars on The Wasteland from the dark window of the sitting room off my bedroom. No light shone anywhere in the old house, although given the late hour that didn't mean anything. There were, however, lights farther out, past the driving range. It could have been a boat of some kind, or just someone walking along the shore. As nice as the place was, I didn't think I'd want to be out there by myself.

As I turned to go back to bed in the dark, I banged against a chair and heard something fall to the ground. I turned on the light, and reached to pick up a magazine that had fallen off the side table. It was then I noticed, really noticed, the chair. It was a rather unusual carved wood piece, probably by Antoni Gaudi. It looked very similar to one I had helped Blair Bazillionaire purchase, one that had once held pride of place in the holy of holies alcove in his home. We had bought it for tens of thousands less than the going rate because of a tiny cigarette burn on the seat. I tipped the lampshade up and had a really good look. It wasn't similar to Blair's chair, it was identical, right down to the tiny cigarette burn on the seat. I sat and looked at that chair for a very long time.

Chapter 9

Bjarni and his crew spent many months as guests of the man who had spared their lives, but Bjarni wasn't happy, and when it was clear they were free to go whenever they wished, announced his intention to Svein, Oddi, and Goisvintha to move on. This was the occasion of much debate in the group, with Bjarni and Oddi taking opposite sides.

"I've been thinking, Bjarni," Oddi said. "This is the most exciting place I've ever been, not that I've been very far until now. And I think I'm tired of traveling. I also can't see taking Goisvintha with us, nor can I see her back in Orkney on our farm, with those cold wet nights and the stale air, I'm thinking now I've seen better, of our houses. I've been offered some work here should I choose to stay, and I believe with your permission, Brother, I will do just that. But I'm hoping you will stay, too."

"I understand your feelings, Oddi," Bjarni said. "And were I in your position I believe I would do the same. But I have a wife and sons in Orkney that I would like to see again. I'm told there are men of the North farther east, and it is my plan to find them. Perhaps I'll find a ship making its way back, or a party going overland at least part of the way. So I'll be off and wish you and Goisvintha good fortune."

"If you're back this way," said Oddi. "I'll be very pleased to see you." And that, as they say, was that. Now laden with supplies and gifts from their generous host, Bjarni and Svein alone of the sixty or so who had sailed from Orkney, journeyed on.

Bjarni intended to go home, he really did, but he didn't get the name the Wanderer for nothing. As planned, he and Svein met up with a group of Northmen in what is now southern France. But these men were not for going back to Orkney or Norway. They told tales of fabulous riches, silks, wine, spices, and jewels to be found in a place called Mikligardr, or Great City, more wonderful still than Cordoba. Frakokk and his sons forgotten, Bjarni threw in his lot with the others, and headed for Mikligardr, known also as Constantinople, the heart of the Byzantine Empire.

It took almost a year to get there, with all of the trading and raiding to be done, but having reached Mikligardr, Bjarni was quite taken by the glories of the Byzantine Empire and decided to join the Varangian Guard. Varangian is an Old Norse word meaning "sharers of an oath," and the Varangians were Vikings, most of them from Russia, although other Vikings joined, too. While Vikings had once been a threat to Constantinople, as they were everywhere they went, by Bjarni's time that had changed. The Varangian guards were troops loyal to the emperor, guarding the palace and the armories. They were mercenaries, of course, and the pay was exceedingly good, too, with plenty of opportunity to acquire loot on the side, and so Bjarni signed up. Bjarni, it seems, was accepted by the others, being a good man with the two-handed Viking axe.

The guard was paid but once a year, and Bjarni and Svein

stayed around to collect thrice. With the pay, and his other Viking activities, Bjarni accumulated quite a fortune. He also acquired some relics. A pagan to the end, despite the fact he served the Christian emperor, he nonetheless adopted the habit of his friends in the Varangian guard, and acquired a piece of the True Cross, which he kept in a purse at his side. Still, while other guards wore a small cross around their necks, Bjarni wore the hammer of Thor. Bjarni, one might say, was hedging his bets.

Svein the Wiry wanted to go home now, and so, in many ways, did Bjarni. The problem was, they had no way of knowing whether or not Einar was still in control of Orkney. Svein suggested a spell might work and had an idea. He'd heard-tell of Vikings going to Jerusalem and swimming across the river Jordan in order to make a spell, so that's what the two men did. This was several decades before the First Crusade, you understand, of 1099, and the Fatmids, who were reasonably tolerant toward other faiths had begun to reestablish control. Bjarni, as he intended, swam across the Jordan, and upon reaching the other side, tied the brush on the river bank into a magic knot, reciting a spell as he did so. The spell was to ensure that his enemy Earl Einar would be dead by the time Bjarni got back to Orkney. That accomplished, Bjarni agreed to turn toward home.

AT SOME POINT over the next eighteen hours, Maya's lovely necklace disappeared. Police were called. There was evidence of a break-in. A couple of pairs of Robert's cufflinks and a diamond bracelet of Maya's also went missing at the same time. Lester, Simon, and I lost nothing, possibly because we didn't have anything worth stealing.

I don't think Maya suspected me of the crime, but I'm certain Robert was not as convinced of my innocence. The police, having reconstructed the event, believed that someone had been watching the house. Timing was carefully studied. We had all helped ourselves to whatever breakfast we wanted. Simon left the house first to go off to his consulting work. I went shortly after that, to follow Willow and Kenny again, although I would never admit that. Sightseeing is what I called it. Around eleven, Lester drove into Kirkwall to look for antiques, and Maya had also gone into Kirkwall to do some grocery shopping. Robert, the last to leave, had taken off just before noon to do whatever rich men do when they are ostensibly on vacation.

Maya was back before 1 PM, and from then on there was always someone in the house. It was not until later that the robbery was detected. Drever, who'd come and gone a few times during the day, discovered signs of a break-in at the back, but he'd pretty much tramped all over any evidence before he noticed it. He did, however, raise the alarm. Robert discovered his missing cufflinks, and then Maya realized the necklace was gone.

Allowing for a few minutes leeway in the time everyone came and went, there was an interval of less than an hour when the house was empty. Maya was convinced it was the people in the derelict house across the way. "It's that man," she whispered to me. "The one I told you about, the weird one. They have a perfect view of this house."

The police, in the person of Detective Cusiter, who gave me a pained look when he saw me, didn't think so. The elderly resident was in a wheelchair, and completely incapable of the crime, and he in turn swore the other man, the one that frightened Maya, had been with him all day. He said neither had seen anything untoward at the Alexander house. It seemed to me that I was the most likely suspect as far as

Cusiter was concerned. He interviewed me for some time about where I had been. I had no alibi for that one hour period. "You do find yourself in the immediate proximity of criminal events on a regular basis," was all he said when we were done.

Maya cried, of course. The rest of us went around looking somber and whispering to each other. "I have a weakness for cufflinks," Simon Spence said. "I hope they don't think I needed an extra pair or two and helped myself."

"You may recall when we left dinner last night, I was trying on the necklace," I said. "If anyone is a suspect, I'm it. I'm afraid I even have a key to the place."

"We all do," Lester said. "I'm an antique dealer. I could have stolen that necklace to sell. It's worth something, you know. Actually I suppose you do know, Lara."

"Yes." Did I detect a hint of suspicion in his voice on that last note? I didn't mention that Maya thought it was worth considerably more than it was. Lester would have flipped if he knew there was a possibility that Robert paid a hundred grand for it. As a regular adviser on antiques to the Alexanders, Lester might have taken that personally. I would have. Then again, maybe he'd sold it to Robert at the inflated price, which wouldn't speak well of him.

The person who seemed to have made up his mind about the identity of the thief was Drever the Intimidating, and the person he made pretty clear he thought was the culprit was a certain antique dealer from Toronto. Every time I turned around he was eying me with suspicion, and from that moment on, he dogged my every step.

In the middle of all this drama, Clive called. His tone was the one usually reserved for imparting juicy gossip and this time was no exception. I knew it was going to be good, too, because it had to be after midnight his time. "You aren't going to believe this, Lara," he began.

Right now I wasn't inclined to believe anyone or anything, but I didn't say so. "Try me, Clive," was what I said.

"Blair Bazillionaire is out of jail!"

"You're kidding. Did he make bail after all this time?"

"Not bail. He's out, a free man. They've dropped the charges!" He paused, waiting for me to beg for details. I begged. "He has an alibi. Someone came forward at this late date and provided it. Guess why this person didn't show up until now."

"I don't know. Married woman, maybe?"

"Bingo! You got it in one. Married woman comes forward, says the reason she didn't speak until now was because she was afraid of her husband and didn't think the charge was really going to stick, and anyway she was too embarrassed for reasons I will get to in a minute. Now she realizes she has to do what she has to do, no matter the cost, et cetera, et cetera. Rob says that's why Blair has been ragging the puck, firing his lawyer, and starting anew. He was stalling for time and probably sending secret emissaries to this woman to convince her to confess. Now, bonus points for guessing the name of the woman in question."

"I have no idea."

"Oh, come on, Lara. Get into the spirit of this."

"Camilla Parker Bowles?" I said.

Clive sniggered. "Try harder. I'll give you a really big clue. Ready? She's married to Blair's new lawyer!"

I was momentarily confused. "You don't mean Leanna Crane!"

"But I do. Don't you just love it? Blair Bazillionaire was boinking Leanna the Lush, his lawyer's wife. Dez played squash with the boys every Tuesday night, and Leanna had another type of sport she participated in at the same time. Trevor was, if you recall, killed on a Tuesday. I'm really glad the unhappy couple has paid their bill for all that work we did for them, because they're going to be in divorce court forever. And I mean forever! What was Blair thinking, retaining Dez? What did Leanna the Lush have to say when her husband came home to tell her about his new client? I tell you, rich people are not like the rest of us."

"Oh," I said. I could hardly believe my ears.

"Oh? Is that the best you can do? Can you not imagine the jokes in the hallowed halls of justice? The only people who aren't enjoying this are people like Rob, who's ticked that Blair got off. There isn't a police officer in the western hemisphere who likes Blair, but even Rob had to laugh. Dez recused himself or whatever the correct legal term is. Anyway, he quit, not that it mattered anymore. It's just too rich, I have to tell you. The whole town is abuzz. Now the police have issued a warrant for some guy called Dog or something, if it's possible anybody could be named that. He's wanted in connection with the death of Trevor Wylie, is the way the papers have put it."

"I know who that is. His name is Douglas, something or other, Sykes, if I remember correctly, and he always walks around with his Doberman."

"Hence, Dog," Clive said. "I see. You do know interesting people. Rob says you're to come home, by the way."

"I will, as soon as they let me."

"That reminds me, I'm supposed to get the name of the policeman who is working that case you're involved in. He wants to have a chat with him, brother to brother, you know. See if he can get you out of there, promising that you would return, if necessary, if they really have no reason to hold you. They don't have a good reason, do they?"

"Clive!"

"Okay, relax. What's the guy's name?"

"It's Cusiter." I had to spell it.

"What kind of a name is that?"

"Common in these parts apparently. He's here now. There's been a robbery."

"Everywhere you go there's something," Clive said.

I could hardly argue with that, but I was feeling rather odd. Blair's getting out of prison was the best news I'd had for a while, and up to that point, it would have been a spectacularly unsuccessful day. Much to my annoyance, Kenny and Willow once again seemed to have done exactly what they said they would, which is to say, take the day off. I followed them into Stromness where they took a midmorning ferry, a nice little boat named the *MV Graemsay*, which I discovered upon asking, went to the island of Hoy. They had hiking boots, carried backpacks, and stopped to buy crab sandwiches and water in a little shop near the pier. The ferry was very small, and there was no way I could be on it without their noticing, and the return ferry wasn't until about five o'clock that afternoon. I decided I was just going to have to let them go. If I'd gone, I would have had an alibi, but I wasn't equipped for a hike at that moment, so could hardly argue another coincidence. I'd wandered around Stromness for an hour or two, wondering what it was I could believe and what I couldn't before heading back to St. Margaret's Hope. I did see Drever, as a matter of fact. He drove up to the pier, apparently to meet a boat that came in. He unloaded some cargo from the back of his truck, watched it being loaded on the boat, and then took off. He didn't see me, so there was no opportunity for an alibi from him either.

This news about Blair should have cheered me up to no end. It didn't. It was partly Percy, and partly the necklace, but there was something else, and if I were to be honest with myself, it wasn't pretty. I'd justified this whole trip in my mind by saying that I was looking for details of the Mackintosh transactions to prove I was right, but that vindication, to use Percy's term, was secondary. I always managed to overlay the notion that I remained unconvinced of Blair's guilt, and that finding the source of the furniture was going to help prove that, although when it came right down to it, I really couldn't see how. Even if I could persuade myself that my true motive was making sure justice was done, then surely with Blair's release it had been, even if it was in a spectacularly unseemly way. If I really meant what I said, I should be very pleased with the result, and I was, in a way; but unless I found out about the Mackintosh, the trip had not only been completely unnecessary, but I had found Percy dying, and I could never feel the same about this whole situation again.

Maya took to her bed once Cusiter left, no doubt depressed by it all. Frankly, I was, too. I went up to my little sitting room and got out the binoculars. It was late in the afternoon, and the van was there, although I could see no one about. Now that I'd had the unpleasant little chat with myself about my true motives, I had to ask myself what on earth I was doing spying on the neighbors, with nothing more to go on than a dead man's reference to The Wasteland. I decided it was time to put this one to rest as well. I had no idea what I would say when I got there, but I took a bottle of scotch I'd purchased for Rob with me, told Lester and Simon that I was going out, and then drove along the relatively short distance to the old house.

It was more than a little intimidating. Dodging debris of various sorts, I went up to the door. It took me a second or two to get up the courage to ring the bell. When I did, dogs, presumably the ones Maya found frightening, started to bark loudly within. There was a pause before a rather imposing voice, through a speaker I hadn't noticed, said, "Speak!"

I spoke. "Hello. I'm wondering if I might speak to you."

"About what?"

"Um, well, about the man who died in the bunker you can almost see from here."

"Go away!" the voice said. There was a click. I believe I had been cut off.

I rang again. There was no response. I stuck my finger on the bell and held it there. I could hear it ringing and ringing inside. The dogs were going crazy. I would have found that intensely irritating and I hoped the man or men inside would, too.

"What?" the voice finally said.

"Before he went mad, Bjarni the Wanderer hid the chalice in the tomb of the orcs," I said rather loudly and right into the speaker. I could hear my voice through the door. There was a long pause. My finger was poised to hit the button again when a buzzer sounded, there was a click, and the door slowly swung open. I stepped into a dark hall.

It took my eyes a minute to adjust, and when they did, I took in an elderly man in a wheelchair staring at me. Beside him stood a man of about fifty or sixty, the man I'd seen helping with the wheelchair. I supposed this was "that man," the weird one Maya so distrusted. He was holding on to two dogs still barking.

"Who are you?" the man in the wheelchair yelled above the din. The dogs started to calm down.

I told him. "Might I ask your name as well?"

"My name is Sigurd Haraldsson," he said. "This is Thor, also Haraldsson. If you don't know who I am, then why are you here?" Thor giggled.

"You're going to think I'm crazy, but please hear me out. I'm here because someone I knew only briefly, but rather liked, has died, and his last words to me were the words I just recited to you, the ones about Bjarni the Wanderer. I told the police what he said, and they have ignored it. He died violently, and I think if I could understand those words I might know what happened to him."

"The man in the bunker?"

"Yes."

"And you came to me because . . . ?"

I didn't want to say that his house made me think of The Wasteland, and he of the wounded king. Worse than preposterous, it was rather insulting. "The man who died thought this place was significant to his quest."

Haraldsson harrumphed. "I suppose he was correct in that thinking." The younger man beside him giggled again. I looked more closely and could see Thor was what we would call developmentally challenged. "Thor, don't you worry," Haraldsson told him. "This young woman is not going to hurt me. You just wheel me into the parlor, and then you should either go out to your workshop or watch the telly while I talk to our guest. There are cartoons on now, and you'll enjoy them." Thor smiled and did as he was bidden, pushing the older man into a rather sparsely furnished room and gesturing to me to follow. One of the dogs left with Thor, the other lay at Sigurd's feet, and soon I could hear the noise of cartoons coming from a room toward the back of the house. Now that they had stopped barking frantically, the dogs seemed pretty harmless. They were similar, except that one had a white face, and they were both of indeterminate parentage.

"I'd really appreciate it if you could tell me about this Bjarni," I said. "I am at a loss as to where to go with this one." It hadn't yet been suggested that I should sit down, so I figured I was still on probation, but at least I'd made it past the front hall. There was only one armchair in the room, and a rather uncomfortable-looking settee. It didn't look as if they had company very often.

"Rather brave of you to come in here. Most people are afraid of me," Sigurd said.

"I guess I'm desperate. The police have me on their list of suspects in the killing."

He nodded slowly. "That must be unpleasant."

"It is. I'm also on the list of suspects in the robbery of some jewelry of Mrs. Alexander's. I didn't do that, either."

"I believe I am on the list of suspects for that theft as well, or rather Thor is. You may have gathered neither he nor I are capable of such a thing. Or rather, if Thor took it, he wouldn't have any concept of the nature of what he had done. But he was with me no matter what those people across the way have to say. What exactly are you expecting me to do about these problems of yours?" His tone was belligerent and quite unwelcoming.

"I would just like to know what this Bjarni the Wanderer business is all about. That is all. If that is too much trouble, then . . ." I turned toward the door.

"Oh, sit down. You don't strike me as the kind of young woman who murders people or steals jewelry, either, I'll give you that. I suppose you want a cup of tea in addition to sympathy."

"No tea, thanks, but you go ahead. I do have a bottle of Highland Park Single Malt," I said. "I'd be happy to share it."

"Twelve- or eighteen-year-old?" he said.

"Eighteen."

"The glasses are in the cupboard above the sink in the kitchen." I got them and poured, and after a sip or two he began. "You might as well make yourself comfortable. This is going to take some time. I don't want any interruptions, do you understand?"

"Were you a school teacher?" Sigurd reminded me very much of my grade seven math teacher, Mr. Postlethwaite, of whom I had been terrified, and probably still would be should I ever run in to him on the street.

He glared at me. "What is that supposed to mean, young woman?"

"You know, I'm not all that young any more. Why don't you call me Lara."

"I'm eighty-nine. Everybody is young to me. Yes, I was a school teacher. It was a long time ago. I've been retired twenty-nine years. I would have liked to go on with it, but my health took a turn for the worse. Are you going to listen to this or not?" I shut up. His tale began. "You're not the only person lured by the words, 'Before he went mad, Bjarni the Wanderer hid the cauldron in the tomb of the orcs.' It's an intriguing declaration to be sure, one that requires more than a little explication, and in some ways an irritating way to put finis to a story. For some, though, it is a beginning rather than an end, a statement of such promise that hopes and dreams are pinned on it, as if believing would make it so. To decide whether you come down on the side of the dreamers or the skeptics, or rather somewhere in between, you will have to go back to the beginning, and that means more than nine hundred years . . ."

It took some time all right, but it was a fascinating story. Bjarni the Wanderer was a Viking, putative founder of Sigurd Haraldsson's family, who lived in Orkney a very long time ago. This Bjarni the Wanderer, whose name was really Bjarni Haraldsson, got caught up in a political feud, backed the wrong side, and had to leave home, embarking on a journey of thousands of miles and several years' duration, hence his moniker "the Wanderer," during which he experienced any number of adventures, some more plausible than others. The saga ended with the words that I had come to know so well, about how before Bjarni went mad, he hid the cauldron in the tomb of the orcs.

Haraldsson told it straight through, stopping only to take a sip now and then from the tumbler of scotch, which I refilled when necessary. I didn't dare ask any questions until he was finished, as if my asking them would break his concentration and he would lose the thread of his story, and so I just sat there quietly as the light coming through the window dimmed, and the room grew cooler as night rolled in. It made me think he had memorized the story word for word, which maybe he had. I felt as if I were sitting around a campfire very long ago, hearing an elder tell the story of our people, enjoining us not to forget our history, to memorize the story exactly as it was told.

At last he took a deep breath. "The last line of the saga is this: 'Before he went mad, Bjarni the Wanderer hid the cauldron in the tomb of the orcs.'"

My opportunity to ask questions began. I felt as if I should put my hand up to get permission to ask them. "You believe this story is true? I know you said it wasn't inconsistent with the facts, but do you believe it?"

"I'm afraid I do. Perhaps I should clarify that. I think there really was someone by the name of Bjarni the Wanderer who traveled where and when he said he did. There is precedent for Vikings taking the route he did. Do I think some of it is exaggerated? Yes, I do. I think the part about the caliph of Muslim Spain is a later addition. Probably Bjarni was in Spain, but he never saw the caliph. Still, I believe there is a great deal of truth in Bjarni's saga. Most of the sagas of this type have at least some real history in them. Even legends often have a kernel of history in them."

"And the part about finding a cauldron and hiding it in the tomb of the orcs?"

"I believe it to be possible."

"Have you ever tried to get an expert opinion on Bjarni's saga?"

"I have, and I'm sure I'm not the only member of my family to do so over the years. I know my grandfather did. Most recently I talked to some fellow by the name of Spence, Simon Spence. He's supposed to be some kind of expert."

"I've met him. He's staying with the Alexanders, next door. He struck me as pretty knowledgeable. What did he say?"

"The Alexanders! I can't stand people who don't like animals. They poisoned Bjarni, you know. I can't prove it, but I know that fellow who likes to pretend he's still in the army, that Drever whatever his name is, did it."

I had this awful thought that this old man was crazy, thinking the neighbors had killed someone who'd lived, or maybe not, a thousand years earlier. "Bjarni?" I said.

"My dog. That's why we keep the dogs inside now, here in the house or with Thor in the barn. We used to have three, now we just have Oddi and Svein. Oddi's the one with the white face. I see you're surprised. If you had three male dogs from a litter and you were me, knowing what you do about my family, what would you call them?"

"Probably Bjarni, Oddi, and Svein. That's terrible, though, poisoning your dog."

"They didn't take to my dog relieving himself on that ridiculous golf green, I suppose, nor did they like Thor coming to get the dog, either."

"Maya Alexander is a bit frightened of your dogs."

"How intimidating do you find them now that you've been introduced?"

"Not very."

"Exactly. I drove over and tried to discuss the problem. We used to have a good relationship with Alexander. Thor even did some work for him, but Drever's there now, and he was abusive. He told me to keep my dogs and 'that retard' off the Alexander property. I tried, but the next time Bjarni got out and went over there, he died that same night."

"That retard? What a terrible thing to say."

"It is. Thor is a very gentle person, and he has many skills, even if he is at a disadvantage in some ways." He was quiet for a minute or two, before continuing. "Show me the manuscript."

"I beg your pardon."

"That's what that fellow Spence said: 'Show me the manuscript.'"

"Meaning?"

"Meaning that a copy of it, in English, indeed a copy of a copy of a copy was interesting but essentially useless. The manuscript itself would be absolutely priceless. However, we don't know where the original went. It may simply have disintegrated. Instead we passed along the translation over the centuries. Spence said that it would be extraordinary to have, if it existed. You may not be aware that the Orkneyinga saga, whilst about the earls of Orkney, was written in Iceland. Many of the famous Viking sagas were written there, the *Heimskringla*, the history of the kings of Norway, also Icelandic, not from Norway. It is the same with the *Knytlinga* saga, the history of the kings of Denmark. So we don't have an Orkney saga actually told by an Orkney man, and written here. Bjarni's saga would be extraordinary, if we had it."

"Spence wasn't interested at all?"

"He was polite. I think he wanted to believe it and he enjoyed the story. I can understand his point of view. We have nothing to show him except a stack of lined notebooks where children have practiced their handwriting. Perhaps if we'd been able to find this tomb of the orcs, particularly if there was still treasure in it, specifically a cauldron, that might lend some credence to the story, I suppose. But we've tried and failed many, many times."

"You call this a cauldron. When I heard it, it was a chalice."

"I'm more perplexed by the idea that someone outside the family would utter the words as they lay dying. I think, though, the correct word would be cauldron, although who knows? Cauldrons were very common in Viking times. They were used for cooking. On sea voyages, when they could spend time on shore, they would use them to cook meat and vegetables for the crew, so Bjarni would have started out with one, although that is not the point of the story. You get the idea that Bjarni's cauldron was different. There are many instances of magic cauldrons in mythology. The Irish have the cauldron of the god known as the Dagda, a cauldron that is never empty no matter how much food you take from it. The Northern European god Thor sought cauldrons for the feasts of his fellow deities, and the Irish Bran had one, too. It is my understanding that cauldrons were used in Iron Age rituals. They have been found in bogs and so on where they were probably thrown as part of some ceremony or sacrifice. And reading between the lines in Bjarni's story, he does seem to have come across some ritual-istic rather cult-like behavior. So I'd say cauldron. They were called *graal*, actually, these cauldrons."

"What are the chances of this cauldron's having survived all this time anyway?"

"Better than average, which is still not terribly good. Most of Scotland has very acidic soil, so artifacts don't last long, but here we have a lot of shell sand, so chances are rather better."

"For some reason I thought this was about furniture," I said. "And now it's about a pot, or a medieval manuscript, I should say. I don't want to belittle it. It's just not what I ex-pected."

"Why did you think it was about furniture?"

"I was looking for a Charles Rennie Mackintosh writing cabinet, or maybe two of them. It's a long story and I won't get into it. The short version is that someone showed me a photograph of an older woman standing in front of this piece of furniture, and this person later quoted the line about the tomb of the orcs as he died. I thought he and I were both looking for the same piece of furniture. I really don't know what I'm going on about. I just can't take all of this in right at this moment."

"You said a photo of a woman standing in front of a writing cabinet?"

"Yes, but don't worry about it."

"Get me the photo album overby, will you?" he said, waving his arm in an indeterminate direction, but more or less toward the back.

"Overby?"

"My apologies. I should have said throughby. On the desk. It's moved."

Throughby? "I'm afraid neither overby nor throughby are expressions I know," I said.

"On the desk in the back room," he said irritably. I got it. The room at the back was much more comfortable, what we'd call a family room off a large kitchen. I could see past it into what might have once been a dining room, but which now held a bed, presumably for Sigurd who would have difficulty getting upstairs. Thor looked up from the cartoons long enough to smile and wave at me. I smiled and waved back. Oddi didn't acknowledge my existence. He was sound asleep on the sofa beside Thor.

Sigurd flipped through the pages for a minute or two, and then pulled a photograph out of its sleeve. "Would this be that photograph?" he said.

It was the photo Percy had shown me, with a pleasant-looking elderly woman standing in front of a Mackintosh, or perhaps a reproduction, writing cabinet. "That's it!" I exclaimed. "The writing cabinet."

"You have eyes but cannot see, as the saying goes," he said. "Look again."

I did. The woman looked just as pleasant, the Mackintosh just as I remembered it. Then I realized what he was talking about. On the wall behind the woman and over the cabinet there was a picture in an old frame. When I took it over to the light of the window, I knew what it was. It was Willow and Kenny's treasure map. "Got it," I said. "This goes with Bjarni's saga, right?"

"That is correct."

"Is it really, really old?"

"No. It, too, is a copy, although certainly older than the notebooks in which I keep the story itself. Again, my grandfather copied something earlier. One of my less reputable uncles tried to pass it off as the original, and even one of my students set out to produce something similar, weathered it, and tried to sell it to the museum." He stopped for a moment and chuckled. "You had to have a grudging admiration for the youngster, although one could foresee a bleak future for that one."

"But the scroll in the photograph? It was sold? Stolen?"

"The latter, I regret to say. Do you know where it is?"

"Yes, I do. Please believe me, I didn't steal it."

"I didn't think you had. You have it, though?"

"No, but I know who does."

"That would be the person who stole it presumably?"

"No. That person is dead. It was found in his personal effects."

"The man found in the bunker?"

"No, someone else."

"A lot of dead people in this saga of yours. Will you see to it that it's returned to me?"

"I'll try. The people who have it think it is going to lead them to a great Viking treasure. They may not be keen on giving it up. They think that the swirls and squiggles along the bottom are an outline of a piece of coastline."

He thought about that for a minute. "That's actually an interesting idea. Amazing, isn't it, how a stranger will look at something, and see what you haven't in eighty-nine years? Longer than that. We've been looking for the treasure for hundreds of years and haven't found it. My grandfather actually built this ridiculous house that I am now incapable of managing because it is close to the place some people believe Earl Thorfinn Skull-Splitter is buried, and the saga mentions the tomb of the orcs was near that place. We don't actually know that Thorfinn is buried where we say he is, so that clue may be entirely useless. It hasn't helped us, I know that. Good luck to them, I suppose. Wouldn't a copy of the scroll do then, if the treasure is what they want?"

"I would think so. So this lovely woman in the photograph is your wife?"

"My late wife, Betty. She died about a month ago. She hadn't been well for some time. Dementia, you know. I miss her so much, but really I lost her a long time ago when that horrible disease stole her away." There was a catch in his voice.

Then it hit me, this photograph, and the fact I'd seen it first in Percy's hands. I felt kind of sick. "I am so sorry. I've been so thoughtless and stupid. Please, I didn't know." I was completely disconcerted.

"How could you know? You had never met us. She'd not had any sense of where she was for some time. It is tragic for me and for Thor, but not for her."

"I didn't mean that. Why didn't you tell me it was your grandson who was murdered? He showed me this photograph," I said. "He was looking for it."

There was a significant pause. "I do not have a grandson," he said. "Dead or alive."

"But your wife, in the photograph: he was her grandson, but not yours? Is that it?"

"Let me make myself perfectly clear. Neither I nor my dear and much missed wife, who is the woman in the picture, has a grandson. I have two sons, one of whom you have met, who has no children, nor will he ever, I suspect, and my other son has two daughters. I have great-grandchildren, but they are too young to be participating in this farce, and besides, all of the family with the exception of Thor and me, live in America. I had only two children conceived before the war, and after my war injury, a land mine explosion, let us just be polite and say I wasn't going to have any more. I loved my wife, but I wasn't much of a husband for her."

"So Magnus Budge wasn't your grandson. Do you know Magnus Budge?"

"Magnus Budge? There are a lot of Budges in Orkney, and I've taught quite a few of them. I'm not sure I recall a Magnus Budge, but my memory is not what it used to be."

"How about Percy, Arthur Percival? He used that name, too."

"Is that what he called himself?" He sat very quietly for a minute before he started to shake. I thought he was having a seizure of some kind and was about to yell for help, but then he actually guffawed. He laughed so hard, tears were rolling down his cheeks. I just stood there and watched him roar. I did not find any of this amusing.

"Come now," he said at last. "Give me a little smile. You must get it, surely. You strike me as being reasonably well-educated. Percival. Parzival. Arthur. The chalice. Think, young woman!"

All that young though I might not be, I thought as instructed: Percival, Arthur, the chalice, The Wasteland, the maze, the wounded king. "The Grail," I said at last. "The Holy Grail."

"Well done," he said. "The Quest of the Grail. In legend, the chalice from the Last Supper is brought to Britain by Joseph of Arimathea and hidden somewhere. Its story becomes bound up in Arthurian legend, with Avalon. All the Knights of Arthur's Round Table seek it, including Sir Perceval, spelled with two *e*'s, and in some versions known as Parzival, in still others Peredur. I suppose if your fellow had called himself Lancelot, or Galahad, you wouldn't have been taken in. The Grail is to be found in the castle of the wounded king, the fisher king, a castle at the center of a wasteland, its entrance obscured by a maze. No one knows where this castle might be. Perceval finds it, though, more or less by accident, makes his way through the labyrinth, and is served dinner at the table of the king. A beautiful maiden brings the Grail into the hall. But Perceval does not ask the right question, and the next day the castle and the Grail are gone. If he had asked the question, the spell would have been broken, the wounded king restored to health, and the wasteland would bloom again."

"Whom does the Grail serve?" I said.

"The question that Percival doesn't ask," he agreed, nodding. "You have redeemed yourself. I've always liked Perceval. He always seemed to me to be an average knight, unlike Lancelot who caused a lot of trouble, and Galahad who was just too pious. I suppose I'm the wounded king, am I, guardian of the Grail, also referred to as the Chalice? The wound is supposed to be of a sexual nature, hence the wasteland, so that's about right. In my case the land has been laid waste because of a brush fire, a lack of money, and my inability to keep the place up, all, I suppose, due to my injury in some way. Your Percy, Magnus, whoever, was looking for the Grail."

"Isn't everybody?" I said. I was tired and discouraged. Percy couldn't possibly have been killed because he was looking for the Holy Grail. Locked up in an institution maybe, but not murdered. "Are you looking for it, too?"

"No. My quest is much more prosaic, I regret to say. I've always felt that the tomb of the orcs and Bjarni's cauldron are nearby, but I've never been able to find them, and I don't suppose I ever will. I will have to sell this house soon, and go someplace that can deal with my medical condition and my advanced years. I should have done it long ago. Too stubborn, that's all, and I was afraid it would be too much for my wife, too confusing for her in her mental state. All I seek now is somewhere with kind people where Thor will be happy. That would be my Holy Grail."

"I'm sorry I've bothered you," I said. "Thank you for telling me about Bjarni the Wanderer. It's a wonderful story. I promise I will try very hard to persuade the people who have your scroll to return it to you. If they don't do it voluntarily, I'll think of something. Enjoy the rest of the scotch." And then I turned, patted Oddi, who got up when I did, and dragged my sorry rear end out the door.

The house was quiet when I got back. The only person who saw me come in was Drever, and I had a sense he'd been waiting for me. I was pretty sure he knew where I'd been. Perhaps he didn't like the idea of my fraternizing with the neighbors any more than he liked the dogs and Thor visiting the Alexanders' place. In my opinion it was none of his business. There was a note telling me to help myself to whatever I felt like from the kitchen. I found myself some cold salmon and a salad, and took it up to my sitting room, only to discover that in my absence the Gaudi chair was gone, replaced by another. I wondered how stupid the Alexanders thought I must be.

Chapter 10

It is here that Bjarni's tale diverges from what one might expect in a journey of this sort. In other words, it ceases to be consistent with the facts. Up until now, his journey would be similar to that of many Vikings, like Earl Rognvald, for example, who went as far as Constantinople just a hundred or so years later. But Bjarni's was different, very different from this point on.

Despite Svein's entreaties, Bjarni and Svein did not return the way they had come, nor did they go directly home. Rather, from Jerusalem they went overland to Baghdad. Baghdad under the Abbasids was the marketplace to the world, a place where the camel caravans from the east came loaded with silks and spices, and men from the north and west, including many Vikings, came to trade, where silver and gold were to be found, along with gems and pearls from the Persian Gulf. No doubt Bjarni, flush with his wages and the other loot he'd acquired in his years in the Varangian Guard, and having heard of the riches there, had some trading to do. From there Bjarni and Svein joined a camel caravan for the overland *route to Gorgon on the edge of the Caspian Sea. They crossed the Caspian, and then undertook a perilous journey on the Volga River, thence overland on the trade route that took them through what is now Poland and Germany, at that point heading for the north. It was in northern lands that something very strange occurred.*

According to the tale, Bjarni became separated from the rest of his group in a storm, not to be reunited with Svein and the others for several days. He wandered in the forest for days, foraging for food, before he came upon an encampment. He found the people there passing strange, but they fed him well, and gave him shelter. In the evening he drank with them, offered a bitter liquid from a large silver cauldron by a beautiful woman. According to Bjarni, while he was in the forest with these people, he had very strange dreams about a disembodied head that spoke to him. Brought before this head, men were stabbed and beheaded, then thrown into a stream. Bjarni, who may not have been well-educated, was not a stupid man, and he began to think that perhaps he hadn't been dreaming, and furthermore that he was to be a victim. That evening, when a drink from the communal cauldron was passed to him, he only pretended to sip it. Frenzy gripped the group, all of them but Bjarni, and soon the woman who had served him the drink began a dance around him. Bjarni decided this did not bode well. He leapt up, grabbed the cauldron, and ran with it into the forest. For three days he fled, until, exhausted and hungry, he happily came upon his companions.

All admired the cauldron, the beauty of the silver and of the designs that graced its sides and bottom. Some said it was a cauldron fit for a king, or even for a god. They marveled even more at Bjarni's tale of human sacrifice in the forest. Some were for going back to see if more silver was to be found and to put an end to these practices. Others, more cautious, told Bjarni to leave the cauldron behind, in order not to incur the wrath of the gods to whom it must surely belong. But now Bjarni was truly determined to go home, and to take the cauldron with him.

I WAS DISAPPOINTED to learn that Percy wasn't the grandson of the nice woman in the photograph, not the least because he was yet another person who'd lied to me, and the list of those who had was getting unpleasantly long. His reticence I could understand. I could even make allowances for not telling me his name. Maybe he didn't like the name Magnus Budge. His bald-faced lie about his granny I couldn't forgive, nor could I understand why he was always running away from me and refusing to answer my questions, at least right up until the end. What he wouldn't tell me in life, I was determined to find out now. I just couldn't figure out how to find his mother. Even I, who has been known to lie from time to time when I thought the occasion called for it, balked at the idea of going to St. Magnus Cathedral and fibbing to that nice clergyman who had come to the police station and worried about my cold hands.

As it turned out, it wasn't a problem. I went to Percy's funeral. The forensics expertise outwith Orkney having apparently completed its work, the police released the body. A very small ceremony was held in the very large St. Magnus Cathedral, which is a most extraordinary place, beautiful in red stone, dating to the first half of the twelfth century. Its sheer size and the centuries of history represented there, from St. Magnus himself, appropriately enough in this instance, to its builder St. Rognvald and the rest of the mighty of Orkney, rather overwhelmed the pathetic little group that came for the funeral. It also added some majesty to it, though, and I was glad for Percy and his mother, even if he hadn't been entirely honest with me. Then we all went back to Percy's mum's place for tea and little sandwiches with no crusts on them. I simply followed them home. The streak of fine weather I'd been enjoying had come to an end. A light drizzle fell, and the cathedral and the ruins of the earl's and bishop's palaces nearby were shrouded in mist, ghostly sentinels of the past.

Mrs. Budge was much better than she had been when I'd met her first. She even recognized me, which I thought was extraordinary given the state she was in the day her son died. She was pathetically grateful to me for coming, which of course made me feel even worse than I already did.

"Wasn't it a lovely service?" she said as I expressed my condolences at the door. "You are looking much better, dear," she added, taking both my hands in hers. "I've been so worried about you. I asked that policeman if you were all right, and he said he thought you were, but I'm so happy to see for myself, and it is so good of you to come today." I suddenly wanted to make a run for it, but she insisted I come in and meet the neighbors. "This is the lovely girl who found Magnus," she told the assembled mourners, all eight of them, over and over again. "She held his hand while he died. The police told me. I'm so happy he wasn't alone." The neighbors then proceeded to make a fuss over me, in a reserved Orkney way. I was acutely embarrassed by it all. It was not lost on me that in many ways I was being just as dishonest as everyone else associated with this sordid business.

"What are you going to do now, Emily?" one of the neighbors asked, as we all munched our sandwiches. They were remarkably good sandwiches, as were the home-baked cookies the neighbors had brought. "We hope you're not selling. The place won't be the same without you." The place was a very pleasant laneway well off the main street of Kirkwall. The houses were certainly neither large nor luxurious, but they were well-kept. Emily, she told me to call her Emily, showed a distinct preference for aqua and white. She obviously did not have a lot of money, the furnishings inexpensive and a bit worn, but she tried to make everything look nice.

"I'm going to rent out Magnus's room," she said. "If you know of anyone who might be interested, please tell them about it."

I spoke up immediately. "I might know someone," I said, and in a flash I realized I was actually telling the truth. "Why don't I have a look while I'm here?"

"Aren't you wonderful," Emily said, and everyone nodded their approval.

The best I could say for the room at that very moment is that it had a lot of potential. It had a bay window and a view over the neighbor's garden, which even in autumn was pretty. Right now, however, the room was something of a disaster. The bed was piled high with what I could only assume were Percy's belongings and there were two more piles on the floor. Somehow, I didn't think this was Emily's fault. Percy would have to have been pushing forty, but he had a teenager's room. There were posters, all of them for films about King Arthur. *Excalibur* seemed to be his favorite. If I remembered the film correctly, Perceval featured highly in it. A bicycle leaned against the wall.

"I know it doesn't look good right now," Emily said. "I'm clearing it up. You may think I'm callous, with Magnus just in the ground today, but I need the income, and you know, it's kept me busy. Without Magnus's help, I can't manage all the expenses. It was hard enough when he quit his job, but at least he got part-time work, which brought in some cash. I've done what the girl on the telly, you know the one who organizes everybody, tells you to. Three groups, she said: keep, sell, and bin it. When I began, I put everything into the keep pile. I couldn't bring myself to throw out anything belonging to my boy. But Sally down the street came to help me. You met Sally. She's the girl in the pink jumper." I couldn't remember what a jumper was here, maybe a sweater, and there were no girls in the room, none of them having seen fifty in a while. Still, I knew the woman she meant.

"I'm doing a bit better on the clearing up now that I'm resolved to rent the room. I'm going to send most of his clothes to charity. He only had one good suit, and he's buried in it. I am sure I can sell his bicycle."

"I thought the police had his bicycle," I said.

"They have the one he rented while this one was being repaired. The police had a look at this one, but after all the repairs they said it wasn't going to be much help. The rental place told me they'd collect the insurance on the one my boy had the day . . ." She took a lace handkerchief out of her sleeve and dabbed her eyes. I patted her arm.

"It won't be enough to keep me going," she said, when she'd composed herself. "Selling the bicycle, I mean, but it's a start. As you can see, the keep pile—that's the one on the bed—is still the biggest. It's all his favorite books, mainly, all about King Arthur and everything. He read everything he could find about King Arthur and the Round Table. He was fascinated by Arthur and the rest of the Knights, ever since he was a peedie-breeks."

"Peedie-breeks?"

"Sorry. A little child. I should be proper spoken while you're here. He loved King Arthur from the time he was a little boy in school."

"Yes," I said. "I'm thinking that the library would like those. I'll just take a look at them, shall I, and tell you what I think?"

"That would be lovely," she said. I flipped through them quickly. Percy had highlighted the references to the Grail in all of them, which was hardly a surprise anymore, but as I opened one, a piece of paper fell out. It looked like doodling, but to my eyes, it also looked like the swirls on the bottom of the scroll currently in Willow and Kenny's hands. "May I keep this?" I said.

Emily looked at it. "Of course you can," she said. "What is it? A drawing? Magnus wasn't very artistic, was he? But if you want it, I'd be happy for you to have it."

"Thank you. Which pile is that one?" I said, pointing to one in the corner. The truth of the matter was that all three piles, keep, sell, and throw out, looked the same in all respects other than size, the "keep" one being the biggest, as Emily had already noted. The one I was pointing at had a collection of bicycle clips, various eyeglass frame parts, half-empty shampoo bottles, and some other stuff I didn't recognize.

"That's the pile for the dustbin," she said. "Not much in it yet, but I'm trying. There are a couple of bicycle parts that are bent and I don't think anybody could use them. My boy hardly ever threw anything out, as you can see."

"What is that?" I said, pointing at a large object in the middle of the pile.

"I don't know. It's something Magnus brought home the

day before he died. I don't know what possessed him to bring such a dirty thing home. I didn't even want to let him bring it into the house, but he insisted. That policeman, Cusiter I think he said his name was, said it was one of the least attractive pots he'd ever seen. I wondered if I could use it for a planter. I was thinking that I could put bulbs in it for the spring, but you know I think it's too ugly even for that purpose."

I picked it up. It was a very large and dirty flat-bottomed bowl, quite deep and maybe twenty- or twenty-two inches in diameter. It was heavy. I scratched the surface, and then started brushing away at it with my hand. Someone, presumably Percy, had already started that process before I got there. "What are you doing?" Emily asked.

"I'm trying to see what's under the dirt," I said.

"Would you like to have it?" she said. "I'd be happy if you'd take it, too."

"No, Emily. You don't want to give this away or throw it out. See here," I said, pointing to an area I had scratched. "I think this might be a trace of silver, and I am going to find out about this for you. I'm an antique dealer, and I think this might be worth something."

"Would you like to buy it?" she said in a hopeful tone. "I don't know, would you pay maybe twenty pounds?"

"No, Emily. You don't understand."

"Ten pounds then?"

"Emily, you don't want to give this to me, nor sell it to me either. I am going to rent it from you for a day or two. I will give you . . ." I stopped and got out my wallet. "I will give you fifty pounds if you'll let me keep it for a few days. I'm also going to give you a receipt for it, and my business card, so there will be no question it's yours. Okay?"

"Oh, my," she said. "You must really think it's worth something."

"I think it might be," I replied. "Although I'm not sure how much you'd get for it. I think a museum might want it."

"What is it?" she said.

"It's a cauldron," I said. "A very old cauldron."

"You mean for soup, or something? It's very big."

"I'm almost certain it's silver, and just by feel I think there is a raised pattern of some kind on it. More likely it was for some ritual purpose, a very long time ago. It will need a lot of work before anyone could be sure."

"A hundred years? Two hundred?"

"Maybe a whole lot older than that."

"Oh, my," she said again. "Would the *Antiques Roadshow* be interested in it, do you think? I love that show. To think I almost threw it out."

"It doesn't look like much," I said. "Anybody could make that mistake."

"It doesn't," she agreed.

"I wonder where he found it. Do you have any idea?"

"He was always out on his bicycle," she said. "I never knew where Magnus went. He wasn't happy with my move to Kirkwall. What could I do? I couldn't look after the property when Magnus's father died. He loved South Ronaldsay, you know. That's where he lived all his life up until we moved here. We were just south of St. Margaret's Hope. Once he quit his job, he . . . You know I haven't said anything to anybody about this, but you are so nice. I have wondered if Magnus was fired. One day he was working, the next day he wasn't. He said he resigned. He said he wanted to travel, and he did, you know. He took his savings and went to America. It could be, though, that he wasn't telling his mother everything."

Percy wasn't for telling anybody everything in my experience, but I didn't say as much. "I'm sure he did go to America. What did your son do for a living?"

"He worked for a moving company. He was strong you know. He looked slight, but with all the cycling and everything he was very strong." I knew for a fact he had a strong grip, but I didn't say that either.

"By moving company, you mean he moved furniture?"

"Aye."

"He didn't say where he'd been the day he found this?"

"He was always talking in riddles. He had some strange notions. I loved him dearly but he wasn't one to share his ideas and activities. I think he said something about The Wasteland not being what he thought. I don't expect that will help you much."

"Maybe it does. Would you mind lending me a blanket or something to wrap this in and a piece of paper for the receipt? I think it's time you went back to your other guests. Please don't say anything to anyone about this. I'm going to see what I can find out about it."

"You're a lovely girl," she said. "I would have liked a daughter-in-law like you. Magnus had girlfriends from time to time, but they didn't last. He was a little too eccentric, maybe."

"Hmm," I said.

All of a sudden, Emily just sort of crumpled. She fell back on the bed, half of the pile of stuff sliding on to the floor as she did so. Then she started to cry. "I don't know who would do such a terrible thing to my boy. He was stabbed many times, you know. I suppose you do, seeing as how you were with him. The police say he wasn't stabbed in that bunker, but they have no idea where. It could be anywhere. I can't sleep, you know. I'm frightened, and I don't understand any of this. This doesn't happen here. I don't lock my door when I go out, at least I didn't before this happened. The police say it may have been someone who came in on the ferry and left, and we'll never know. How can this be? Why my Magnus?"

"I'm going to get Sally," I said, going out to the living room and signaling to the woman in the bright pink sweater. In a few minutes Emily had composed herself, and we were back eating sandwiches and drinking tea as if nothing had happened. Her friends were curious about the large object wrapped in a blanket, but Emily told them I was finding a good home for something of her son's at her request. A half hour later, feeling absolutely dreadful, I took my leave, but not without one more question. "Do you know that man standing down the road there? The one in army fatigues?"

"I've never seen him before," Emily said. "I wonder what he's doing just hanging about like that."

I knew what he was doing. He was watching me. "Is there another way out of here?" I asked. "I know who it is. I just don't want him to see me with this." Fortunately there was not only a backdoor, but a gate and a lane that took me back to the church and my car. Emily hugged me several times as I left. "You'll be hearing from me very soon," I told her. "I promise." A few minutes later, I hit the road with what I was certain was a treasure in the trunk. I sincerely hoped Drever the Intimidating, who was rapidly working his way up the scale to Drever the Scary, got very wet waiting for me to come out the front door.

I was making a lot of promises these days, both to myself and other people, even if it seemed way beyond my power to do anything at all, let alone fix it. And she was right. This kind of thing should not happen anywhere, but somehow it particularly shouldn't happen in Orkney, where the people were decent and law-abiding and really nice in a reserved way. While I was looking for a piece of furniture, or not even that, the source of a piece of furniture to resurrect my tattered reputation, a rather superficial goal to be sure, Percy, who was looking for the Holy Grail was stabbed several times some place unknown, then dumped in a bunker. It was just too awful. I knew I was getting close on the furniture. The germ of an idea of what this was all about was growing in my mind. But it didn't seem that important anymore. It would have to wait. I was going to do what little I could for some people in Orkney: Percy and Sigurd Haraldsson and Thor.

The question was where to start. The Haraldssons and Percy seemed to me to be inextricably linked by one Bjarni the Wanderer, fictional character or real historical person it mattered not. The Haraldssons were the keepers of Bjarni's saga, just as the wounded king was guardian of the Grail. The saga told the story of a cauldron of obviously great beauty, and at the time much significance, and part of that saga was a scroll that might or might not point in the direction of the hiding place of that cauldron, something called the tomb of the orcs.

Percy was not looking for a Viking cauldron. He was looking for the Holy Grail. Somehow the cauldron and the Grail were one and the same in Percy's mind. It was possible, too, I suppose. I knew just enough about the Grail legends to know that people believed the Grail existed, and that the quest for it was tied to Arthurian legend. The Grail was supposed to be somewhere in the British Isles, and at

one time had no association with what we now know as The
Holy Grail. It was a magic cauldron pure and simple. It
didn't matter if Percy was confusing two different objects or
even mythologies. Percy had shown me a photograph that I
thought was of a piece of furniture, but was really a photograph of the scroll. He had come all the way to Canada to
try to find it, so clearly it was important. Airfare wasn't
cheap, and Percy wasn't rich.

Trevor Wylie had somehow come into possession of that
scroll. Willow had found it amongst his belongings when he
died. He got it legally or otherwise, when he purchased the
furniture. Had the nice woman in the photograph, the one
with dementia, simply given it to him not realizing what she
was doing? Did he just take it off the wall at the same time he
talked her out of the furniture? I wouldn't put it past him. It
didn't matter really. Both Trevor and Sigurd's wife were dead.
The important questions right now were why would Trevor
take it? Was it just because it looked a little bit old and was
there to be taken or was Willow correct in saying that Trevor
was off to hunt for treasure? If the latter, what would make
him think it was a treasure map? Was he a Viking expert,
too? And how had Percy known about the scroll?

When I thought about it, though, I knew how Percy had
seen it. He had gone to get the Mackintosh furniture, real or
otherwise, I couldn't tell from the photograph, for Trevor. I
couldn't prove it at this moment, but I was willing to bet
that there'd be an invoice from an Orkney mover in Trevor's
files, and that mover would have been Percy's employer. I
was so busy looking for something that could be the Mackintosh, both of them, that I hadn't worried about who had
transported and shipped it. But why had Percy come looking for the scroll, if indeed that was what he had been look-

ing for? How could he have any idea as to its significance in the tale of Bjarni the Wanderer? It could still have been the cabinet he was looking for. He never said that it wasn't that I could recall. No matter which way I turned, the furniture and the scroll and therefore two murders kept intersecting in a way I did not understand.

For the sake of argument, I assumed Percy had seen the scroll, framed on the wall above the cabinet. How did he know what it was? In a way, I suppose, it didn't matter. No matter how he'd seen the scroll, I thought it very possible that Percy had found not just a cauldron, but *the* cauldron. And then Percy had been killed. Had he been killed in the tomb of the orcs? Was that why the police could find no trace of the initial scene of the crime? And if so, where was this tomb? If Percy could find it, so could I. I had seen him cycle by the Alexanders' place the day before he died. I think I would have noticed if he had a cauldron on his handlebars. He had come home that day with it, though. At least that is what Emily said, and she now seemed to be completely alert. So he had found it somewhere later that day, and my guess was Hoxa. It fit with Bjarni's saga and also with Percy's one known location that day. Did people get killed because they were looking for the Holy Grail? Surely not. Did this mean this was still about a piece of furniture? A hugely expensive piece of furniture, that is.

The day he had died, and I had forgotten this, I had seen Willow and Kenny go by on Kenny's motorcycle. They were heading for Hoxa. I hadn't seen them later. They were liars, but were they murderers, too? Did they kill Percy because he found the tomb of the orcs and the treasure before they did? Did they try to torture him into telling them where it was? I felt sick.

And Lester: where did he fit in all this? Friend and dealer to the magnificent Alexanders, he had shown up on Orkney and just happened to run into Kenny and Willow, had he? When I'd asked how they knew each other, one had said Glasgow University, the other Edinburgh. I guess they hadn't had time to get their story straight when I came upon them in that restaurant. Yes, Orkney, at least the Mainland was a small place, but was their meeting just too much of a coincidence?

I was coming to realize that I had too many questions, and that I had missed an opportunity to get answers to at least some of them. Like Perceval, I hadn't asked the right question at the right moment. But unlike Perceval, I thought I might get a second chance. First, though, I was going to keep my promise to Sigurd Haraldsson.

What had started out as drizzle was now a gathering storm. Some of the darkest clouds I've ever seen sat poised on the horizon, and the wind was beginning to howl. It was, as one of Emily's neighbors put it, "a peedie bit of a puff." The water on the roads swirled in little eddies ahead of me. I was heading for Willow's B&B when I saw Kenny's motorcycle in front of the Quoyburray Inn. They were seated once again in a corner of the bar. Celtic music was blaring through the sound system. They didn't look that happy to see me. I didn't waste any time with small talk.

"I've come to get the scroll. You have to give it back to its rightful owner. It's not yours. Trevor stole it. The true owner isn't going to look for the treasure. He gave up on that long ago, and even if he wanted to, he wouldn't be able to do it. He says you are welcome to take a copy of it, and look as long as you like. But you really do have to give it back to him."

"How do you know Trevor didn't buy it?" Willow demanded.

"Because I know it wasn't for sale." That was true, but it was still possible that Sigurd's wife had simply given it away, a bit of information I considered unnecessary for the purposes of this conversation.

"We don't have it with us."

"Then go and get it. I'll even come back with you to pick it up."

"Why should we believe you are going to give it to its rightful owner? Would it surprise you to know that Kenny and I don't find you particularly trustworthy, Lara?" Willow said. "How do we know you won't take it for yourself, because you know there is some secret code in the lining or something that will lead you to the treasure? You have not been open and honest with us."

"Stop right there, Willow. Don't you talk to me about honesty and trust. I told you I was coming to Orkney and that is exactly what I did. You, on the other hand, didn't bother to tell me you were coming here. Please don't lie to me again about the e-mail. I don't believe that, nor do I believe you were looking for me either. You could have found me if you wanted to. Heaven knows you passed me on the highway often enough. You uncovered what you thought was a treasure map and decided to find it for yourself. I do not give two hoots about your treasure, believe me. I do care about some people here who are either dead, or in desperate straits."

"I meant to send an e-mail," Willow said. "I don't know. I got so excited about this treasure map . . ."

"As for you, Kenny," I said, ignoring her. "I'm wondering what your surname is, and what your true relationship to this whole issue might be. Because it has just occurred to me as I look at you, Kenny, that you bear a certain resemblance to one Trevor Wylie. You wouldn't happen to be a relative, would you?"

Kenny blushed and nodded. "Cousin," he said, hanging his head. "Sorry."

"It's just so easy to forget to mention little details like that, isn't it? You know, I found it difficult to believe that the two of you met on the ferry, and that Willow, you would just immediately tell this stranger all about the treasure. I suppose you and Trevor stayed in touch over the years since he left Orkney, right, Kenny?"

Kenny nodded again. The proverbial cat had apparently got his tongue.

"But . . ." Willow said.

"Shut up. Let me tell you both something. I have your precious cauldron. What I don't have is the location of the tomb, and I want to find it because the person who uncovered the cauldron died the day after he found it. People here think I'm going to believe a whole bunch of coincidences, for example the one in which you just happen to run into Lester in Kirkwall, but this coincidence, and someone dying the day after he finds a treasure, doesn't wash with me."

"But . . ."

"So this is what is going to happen. This afternoon we are all going to a place I like to call The Wasteland. You are going to bring the scroll with you and you will meet the man who owns your cute little treasure map, a man whose family has kept Bjarni the Wanderer's story alive for hundreds of years. He's a disabled World War Two veteran, and he's eighty-nine years old. He is trying to look after his son who is also disabled, albeit in a different way. He will tell you the story of Bjarni the Wanderer if you let him. And then I am going to show him the cauldron, explain about the woman I have borrowed it from, and you are going to give back that scroll. If you don't, I'm going to the police to tell them you possess stolen property. Do not delude yourself into thinking that I won't. Here is the map to The Wasteland. Be there at five o'clock or else."

"But . . ." Willow protested again.

"Don't say one more word to me. I am completely disgusted with you. You are as bad as Trevor ever was. And by the way, it is a camel." Then I stomped out of the place, slamming the door so hard I rattled the windows. It was not my finest hour, but I was far too angry to care. I didn't even bother to wave to Drever the Scary, who clearly had learned tracking skills in the army, as I left. Maya said she thought Drever was always watching her. I knew for certain he was spying on me, and right now he was going to have to hurry to keep up with me.

Chapter 11

By the time Bjarni and Svein landed in Orkney, they had been away for six or seven years. You would think Bjarni would be happy to learn that his magic spell had worked, that Earl Einar was dead, the young Earl, Thorfinn, now ruling Orkney. But the changes in the world at large were none compared to those in his own small ambit, at least as far as Bjarni was concerned. Frakokk, thinking him dead after all this time, had married again, a farmer from Rousay. Bjarni's sons, now strapping youths, did not remember him, and his lands had been dispersed to others. Oddi was gone, of course, never to return to Orkney. A church had been built and all attended, and the men were not inclined to go raiding anymore. There were still Vikings who would fight, and who still went raiding in England, but 1066 was not that far off, when at the Battle of Stamford Bridge an army of Vikings under Harald Hardrada fell to the Anglo-Saxon king, Harald Godwinson, who was defeated in turn at the Battle of Hastings by the Norman and a descendant of Vikings himself, William the Conqueror. The Viking Age was coming to a close.

*Bjarni did what many of us would do under the circumstances.
He drank himself into insensibility. The drink just made him belligerent, and he decided to trick and then kill his wife's new husband, in order to win her and his lands back. He'd brought her
silks from Constantinople and jewels from Baghdad, but she would
have none of it. Bjarni tried to lure the farmer, whose name was
Kali to a broch on South Ronaldsay where Thorfinn Skull-Splitter,
Earl of Orkney, was said to be buried. He told Kali that he knew
of treasure hidden in an ancient tomb nearby, the one known as the
tomb of the orcs: gold and silver arm rings, cloak brooches, the finest
of swords, and of course, there was the lure of the silver cauldron
that many had seen and wondered at. That night, Bjarni armed
with his Viking axe and knife, and with the silver cauldron with
him for safekeeping, hid near the broch and waited for Kali to appear.*

*Unbenownst to Bjarni, some kin of Kali's heard of the plot and
warned the man. Kali was all for confronting Bjarni but Frakokk
wouldn't allow it, and so Kali stayed home with his eye on the door
lest Bjarni, thwarted in his plan, come to get him. But Bjarni
never did.*

I HAD NO trouble finding the Howe of Hoxa on my map,
the place where Thorfinn Skull-Splitter is supposed to be
buried. It was not that far from where I was, drying out in
my little sitting room at the Alexanders. Sigurd's grandfather had chosen the site for his castle well. If indeed there
was a tomb of the orcs, then it should be nearby. Sigurd had
been surprised by Kenny's idea that the swirls on the bottom of the scroll represented a section of coastline. I
thought of all the tombs into which I'd slithered with Percy
and later. I could see how they would get lost in the land-

scape. The terrain was rolling hills, and after many thousands of years, the tombs would just be grassed over. They were still turning up. One had turned up on a dairy farm and not that long ago. There might still be a tomb of the orcs to be found.

So where was it? I looked toward the sea from my window, but the fog had rolled in, and if there were a shoreline there, you wouldn't know it right at that moment. I left a note for Lester, and then headed out once again for The Wasteland. I wanted to be there good and early.

There was no answer to my ring at the house. There were also no barking dogs. The van was out front, so that pretty much meant they had to be home. Maybe Sigurd was having a rest. Maybe he didn't want to talk to me, but he might if he knew why I was there. I slid a note I'd written in my room through the mail slot. It informed him that I had told the people who had the scroll to come to the house at five. I sincerely hoped Sigurd was there, and that he'd get the note very soon. It was twenty to five. There was no sign of Willow and Kenny.

I thought I could see a light in the barn through the gloom and wondered if Thor might be there. The wind was really howling as I made my way along a muddy path toward it. I pushed the door open and stepped in. The barking started the moment I touched the door handle. I stood still as Oddi and Svein circled for a moment, but they seemed to remember me, and quickly went back into the gloom. "Thor? Are you in here? It's Lara. Remember me?" There was no sound, but I was almost certain he was hiding. I flipped a switch by the door.

Thor was nowhere to be seen. What there was to see, however, almost made me laugh out loud. It seemed to me that ever since I'd left home, when I was looking for furniture I found something about a tomb. Now I was looking for a tomb, and what had I found? Nothing less than the source of the furniture that had started this whole business! Before me was revealed a workshop, or perhaps more accurately an artist's studio. Sketches and designs were pinned to the beams, and the wonderful smell of fresh wood permeated the space.

Looking around I realized that I, like Sir Perceval, Knight of the Round Table, had failed to ask the right question the first time I'd come. I had not asked about the writing cabinet in the photograph, so entranced had I been by Bjarni's saga, the scroll, and the possibilities they presented. I did not ask whence the cabinet in the photograph came; I did not ask where it went. But standing here I now knew who had made it. Thor may not have had many advantages, as far as raw intelligence went, but he made some of the most beautiful furniture I have ever seen, each piece made by hand, every joint cut to fit perfectly, every surface so beautifully planed and sanded and polished it felt like silk to my touch. I had thought I had come to Orkney looking for a forger, but I had found instead a master craftsman, someone inadvertently, I was certain, drawn into the murky world of art and antiquities fraud. I had not asked if Sigurd Haraldsson knew Trevor Wylie.

Thor had been working on a beautiful piece of furniture. The specs and drawings were pinned above his workbench. He was making a Mackintosh writing cabinet. I guess he'd sold the one he'd made earlier, and he was going to make another for the house or perhaps to sell. If it weren't for the fact that Trevor was murdered, it would have been funny.

"This is wonderful, Thor," I said loudly, hoping he could

hear me. "Yours is some of the most beautiful cabinetwork I have ever seen. You should be very proud of it." It was possible I heard the tiniest creak in the loft. "I know Trevor Wylie liked it, too."

Now I had another question. Where had Thor gotten the copy of the specs for the writing cabinet? The owner of the original, of course, but who would that be? An answer to all my questions was rapidly forming. I would have liked to talk to Thor, although I wasn't sure he'd be able to answer my questions, and in any event, my heartfelt compliments met no response. "Thor," I called out again. "I'm going up to the house to talk to your father. I have asked the people who have your family's scroll to bring it back. They'll be here in a few minutes. I'd really like to talk to you about your wonderful furniture later." I looked at my watch. It was ten to five. There was still no response from Thor, although I remained convinced he was there, and when I went outside, there was no sign of Willow and Kenny either. My threat about reporting them to the police as the recipients of stolen goods had been just that, a threat. If they didn't show up, I didn't know what I was going to do.

I started toward the house, now thoroughly drenched and cold. I decided I was going to have to lean on the bell until Sigurd opened the door again. As I dashed through the rain, I looked down toward the shore, and in the fog thought I saw someone making their way along in front of the Alexanders' place. I wondered if I'd been wrong about Thor being in the barn, and that instead he was out walking. Or could it be Willow or Kenny? Their motorcycle was nowhere to be seen. The figure vanished into the mist. I followed, cutting through the hedge that separated Sigurd's place from the Alexanders'. The shadowy figure was gone.

From my vantage point I scanned the area. In such treeless terrain it was difficult to hide, let alone disappear. Still no one. Where had that person gone?

I was about to return to Haraldsson's house to wait for Willow and Kenny when the mist cleared a little by the water. I stared at it for a minute, then began rummaging in my bag for the scribbles I'd taken from Percy's room. The rain tore at the paper the minute I opened it, and with water in my eyes, I was having trouble seeing it very well, but I held it up as best I could, and looked back at the shoreline. It was difficult to tell, but I thought perhaps Percy had been scribbling this shoreline. I walked a little farther across the Alexanders' property in the general direction of Robert's putting green and driving range. It was a work of art, really, ridiculous though it might be. It seemed to me it would have been easier to go to a real golf course, but that obviously wasn't Robert's way.

"It can't be," I believe I said out loud, as I began running toward the putting green. In a minute I was standing on the top of the mound that marked the end of the driving range. I walked quickly around it, but saw nothing. If Percy had found a tomb here, there had to be an entrance of some sort. At the top there was a small pipe protruding from the ground, a watering system for the course. A tarpaulin lay around it, with a garden hose coiled there. I yanked away the hose and the tarpaulin to reveal a large metal plate. It all looked very ordinary, just part of the irrigation system, ordinary, that is, unless you were looking for the entrance to a tomb. This was a hatch. I pulled at it for a minute, before I realized that it ran on a track. I had to sit on the dismally wet ground and brace my feet against the edge of it. In a second or two it started to slide back to reveal an old iron ladder leading down into the dark.

I descended past large stone slabs, into the inky darkness. At the bottom of the ladder there was actually a light switch. This tomb had been put to use rather more recently and by someone other than Bjarni the Wanderer. A stone tunnel led off to one side. I crouched over and made my way toward the light that seemed to come from a chamber beyond. At the end of the tunnel I was able to stand up. If there had been any question in my mind as to whether or not this was a tomb, that doubt was dispelled by the pile of skulls and bones stacked in a side chamber to my right.

So excited was I to find this tomb, that it took me a few minutes to accurately assess the situation in which I found myself. My first clue as to the precariousness of my position was the sight of the Gaudi chair that had once graced my sitting room. There was a small plastic bag on top of it which I didn't bother to open because I pretty much knew what it would contain: Maya's necklace, bracelet, and perhaps some cufflinks of Robert's. Apparently Drever was not only scary, but a thief, pure and simple, stealing from his employers.

But then I entered a second side chamber to find that it contained two large wooden crates. It took a minute to use the small crowbar sitting on top of one to pry it open, see what was in it, and to close it up again. One quick look at the contents told me that Percy's death was not really about furniture or a cauldron. It was about the quest itself and where it had taken him. As I turned, something else caught my eye, and the sight of it made me sick. A skull stared out from a niche in the room, as if it were an icon in a little shrine. This skull wore eyeglasses, one arm of which was held with a safety pin, one lens cracked and smeared with what must have been dried blood.

I had seen enough to know that Percy had died here. I had seen enough to know what was going on. I had seen enough to know that I had to get very far away from this place if I didn't want to end up like Percy on a concrete slab in a bunker on Hoxa Head. I crouched down and headed back along the stone passageway as fast as I could, but I could hear the sound of the hatch closing as I hit the bottom rung of the ladder and looked up to see Drever Clark smiling down at me.

I still had the crowbar, and I did the only thing I could think of. I hauled myself up a few more steps and smashed at his fingers on the edge of the hatch, hitting as hard as I possibly could. I heard a grunt of pain, and for a moment the hatch stopped moving. It was long enough for me to get up and out, but not long enough to get away. Drever had recovered sufficiently to hit me with the hose. I stumbled, then tried to run, but slipped in the mud. The next thing I knew Drever was standing over me with a shovel. "Say good-bye," he said. He was still smiling.

As the shovel came down, I tried to put my arms over my head, but somewhere in my frantic brain I knew it wouldn't save me. Suddenly there was a frightening sound, more howl than anything else. Drever stopped, the shovel in midair, as two dogs went airborne, straight for his neck. He went down in a scream of pain, Oddi and Svein all over him. There was blood everywhere. I just lay there for a minute, stunned, unable to think what to do. Then I heard a voice calling my name. "Run, Lara," Willow yelled. "We have your back."

I staggered to my feet, then turned to see Robert Alexander, gun in hand, sprinting across the lawn toward me. Willow was running from the direction of the hedge, Kenny a few yards behind her. Thor was just ducking through the hole in the hedge right behind Kenny. Robert stopped and took aim just as Willow hurled herself at him. She grabbed him from behind and held on. Robert fired, but missed, then shrugged Willow off, and smashed her head so hard with the butt of the gun that she was unconscious before she hit the ground. Then Robert turned the gun on her.

"No!" Kenny screamed, lunging at Robert, who in turn staggered and fell back. The gun flew out of Robert's hand and arched through the sky. In a second, Kenny had his hands around Robert's neck and was throttling him. I started for the other gun, but Thor beat me to it.

"Bad man," he shouted looking at Drever and waving the gun around.

It was bedlam. The wind was howling, the dogs were snarling, Drever was screaming, Kenny was sobbing, and Thor kept shouting, "Bad man, bad man," over and over. Over by The Wasteland, Sigurd was gesturing and calling out to Thor, I suppose, but he couldn't be heard over the din. The only people who were silent were Willow, lying cold and lifeless, the dark hair framing her pale, pale face now matted with blood and mud, and me, whose vocal cords had unaccountably shut down completely. I kept trying to say something, but could make no sound.

There was another shot, and we froze where we were and turned to look. "Stop!" Maya Alexander screamed. She was standing few yards away, a shotgun in her hands. Unlike Thor, she looked as if she knew exactly how to use it. Stop we did, every single one of us, maybe even the wind. For a moment there was a deathlike silence, as if the whole world were holding its breath. Then Robert straightened up and almost smiled.

"Give me the gun, darling," Robert said. Maya still stood there, gun in hand, waving it back and forth as if to keep it fixed on all us. "Maya, darling? The gun, please."

The tiny rational part of my brain that was still functioning, the part charged with the onerous responsibility of trying to ensure my survival said, "Say something now or it's over." The shotgun was pointed at me.

"Don't give him the gun, Maya. Your husband and Drever are drug dealers. You can go and see for yourself. They are hiding drugs in an old tomb under the putting green. They killed the man in the bunker. His spectacles are still down there. I think his blood is, too. They stabbed him and then they dumped him in the bunker. He crawled up on to the slab before he died, Maya. He died slowly. The murderer you fear is right in your house."

"The gun, darling," Robert said. "Just give me the gun and I will get this situation under control."

"Bad man," Thor repeated, pointing the gun at Drever.

"Maya!" Robert said in a tone that brooked no opposition. "The gun!"

"Don't, Maya, please," I said.

Maya took a deep breath. Mascara was running in rivulets down her cheeks, rain or tears or both. "Drugs? Tell me this isn't true, Robert."

"Of course it isn't true, darling," he said, taking a step toward her. Maya took a step back, but he was gaining ground.

"Drugs?" she repeated. "Bev died of a drug overdose. I knew you and Drever were up to something. But drugs? It couldn't be drugs, could it? Bev was my best friend! I thought you were the perfect couple!"

"You and I are the perfect couple," Robert said. "Now, then, the gun."

"No, Maya," I said. "He will kill us all."

Robert took another step toward her, Maya another step back. She was looking back and forth at each of us, waving the gun wildly at everyone. Now only a few feet separated Maya from her husband.

"She's lying. You know that, and you know what to do, darling," Robert said, lunging at her. Maya stumbled back, took aim, pulled the trigger, and blew Robert away.

Chapter 12

Bjarni's saga is about to come to an end, but perhaps not the way we would expect it. The truth is we don't know, and probably never will, what happened that night, out by the grave of Thorfinn Skull-Splitter, out in the tomb of the orcs. What we do know is that Bjarni was found the next day in a field near the broch where he'd waited for Kali. He was dead, although there wasn't a mark on him. Kali, of course, was a suspect, but he had what we'd now call an alibi, although one might view it with some suspicion: Frakokk and his kin swore Kali never left the house. There were those who believed Bjarni had been frightened to death, had run from the tomb mad with fear. Others believed he'd drunk from the magic cauldron, or had been carried off by the people from the forest, or struck down by the god to whom the cauldron belonged. Everyone looked for the cauldron, but none could find it. Some said if you could find it, you'd know what happened to Bjarni. Most agreed with Svein the poet that before he went mad, Bjarni the Wanderer hid the cauldron in the tomb of the orcs. Neither the tomb nor the cauldron has ever been found.

BLAIR BAZILLIONAIRE WAS sitting in one of his many vehicles when I got there. I didn't even recognize the car. I've been told since by Clive and Rob that it was a Maybach sedan, worth something over three hundred and fifty thousand. For all I know that's where all rich men go when they have nothing else to do—they sit in their ridiculously expensive cars. Still, compared to a Charles Rennie Mackintosh writing cabinet, it's a steal, particularly if a very stupid antique dealer ships you a fake one. I tried to take some comfort from that, but I couldn't. I just couldn't find closure on this one. Nothing could make me feel better. Everything was bothering me, even my home. Toronto hadn't changed any when I got back, but in some fundamental way, I had. The city was sophisticated, noisy, gritty, hurried, cars everywhere, people too rushed to be even polite, and I didn't know what to do with it. I was awash in a sort of creeping melancholy not knowing where to turn. I even suggested to Clive that we sell the business, quit while we were ahead. All he said was, "Define ahead."

Standing there, it occurred to me that Blair liked sitting in his car because it was quiet. It was relatively pleasant in his secluded and leafy neighborhood. From his driveway, the cacophony of the city had been reduced to a hum, punctuated by the soft wail of a siren somewhere in the distance. *Maybe*, I thought, *that's what money really buys: silence.* He rolled down the window as I approached.

"Hey, babe," he said. "I've been planning to call you. What's cookin'?"

"I know you killed Trevor Wylie," I said.

"Do you now?"

"Yes."

"Can you prove it? Not that it matters. The judge threw

the case out. I have an airtight alibi, one that will be believed because of the—shall we say embarrassing?—
circumstances attached to it. I suppose I'll have to marry her
though. Anyway, they're looking for some guy called Dog.
They won't be arresting me for this one again."

"I guess not," I said. I was feeling very tired at that moment, even though I'd done little else but sleep since I got
home; I was also oddly disinterested, given the subject at
hand.

"Don't guess, babe. Know it."

"Okay, I know it. But you did do it." A slight breeze rus-
tled the leaves of the trees, masking the siren that grew
closer.

"Maybe I did." He was smirking. "Maybe he irritated the
hell out of me. Maybe he just picked the wrong guy to rip
off."

"Maybe," I agreed. "That was quite the legal maneuver
you pulled, hiring Dez Crane when you were having an affair with his wife."

"Had to get her to come forward somehow, didn't I,
babe?"

"She didn't come forward voluntarily?"

"Hell, no! I had to force the issue, didn't I? She didn't
give me much choice. She was going to let me fry rather
than tell her husband about our affair. I fired my legal coun-
sel, hired Dez, and then had the distinct pleasure of telling
him I had an alibi, which was to say that I was with his wife.
It was worth it just to see the expression on his face."

"You'll probably be reprimanded for that ploy."

"Would it surprise you to know I don't care? I'm on top
of the world right now, babe. Tell me why I shouldn't be."

"How about because you're going to be charged with

drug trafficking and money laundering? You know, sort of like Al Capone: they couldn't get him for all the murders, so they got him for tax evasion. I suppose that will have to do." Now Blair wasn't looking quite so smug.

"You don't know what you're talking about."

"Actually I do know something about money laundering," I said. "It comes with being close to a police officer. Money laundering is, as my partner is always telling me, really very simple, in theory anyway. It's all about either over-valuing or undervaluing something in order to move money around, money obtained, of course, from illicit activities. Robert Alexander, drug dealer and generally scum, someone who had a sense of . . . shall we say irony? . . . so profound he could donate money to help those whose misery he had personally caused, was in possession of some of your furniture and a necklace of yours. He paid way too much for them. By furniture I am referring to a chair by Antoni Gaudi, a sideboard by Victor Horta, and a Liberty and Company garnet and pearl necklace. Their combined worth is a hundred and fifty thousand tops. Alexander paid you well over a million, minus a small commission to Trevor Wylie."

"You don't say."

"I do say. I saw them, and Robert Alexander was stupid enough to try and make sure I didn't have a good look, once he realized I did know all about them, by moving the chair and pretending to steal the necklace. I have to say that really irked me. Then there is my personal favorite, the Charles Rennie Mackintosh writing cabinet. This is the flip side, the undervaluing of an object. There was a real one, belonging to Robert Alexander. Alexander still owed you money, so he shipped it, again via Trevor to you. The reason there is no record of a transaction between you and Trevor is that you didn't pay for the Mackintosh writing cabinet at all. It was actually a payment to you. Alexander owed you a few million for drugs, and all that cash crossing international boundaries and all, well, it is just so inconvenient. So he sent you something you wanted, a Charles Rennie Mackintosh writing cabinet valued at ten thousand on the books, but worth something in the millions, and presto you're paid. No fuss, no muss, no bribing of bank officials, no setting up of bogus businesses.

"All you needed was someone to make the transfer happen, which is to say Trevor Wylie, rather vulnerable given his gambling debts, and the violent individual to whom he owed money. Even you and Alexander must have seemed to be an improvement over the guy with the Doberman. You should have kept the transaction just between you and Trevor, but you wanted someone like me to verify that the object in question was worth what Robert Alexander said it was. The trouble, of course, is that you didn't actually receive your payment, because Trevor was an idiot. He thought he could outfox and outrun one of the most ruthless men around. He showed you the real cabinet, then sold it to someone else, giving you instead a reproduction made in Orkney by a man who almost certainly would not understand nor condone the purpose to which Trevor was putting his work."

"I'm thinking you've been working too hard. Your brain is overheated. I'd like to help. How about a little Porsche sports car, silver, something like that, a gift from me to you? You'd look pretty good tooling around in that. And of course, you can count on all my business from now on."

"No, thanks," I said. Apparently Blair thought everything could be solved with a car.

"Not extravagant enough for you?" he said. "Okay, name your fee. You might as well take something for your trouble, because you can't prove any of this."

"I believe I can. I recognize that a million here or there is nothing in the drug business, small potatoes and all that, but now that we know what to look for, I'm sure we can find lots more. Maybe furniture isn't your favorite modus operandi for moving money around, either, but you did it a couple of times, and it's a start. I know this is only the tip of the iceberg. I've already seen the paperwork on the Gaudi chair, the one Alexander paid almost a million for even though it wasn't worth a tenth of that, while I was helping the police go through Trevor's files, even if I didn't know what I was seeing at the time. There'll be similar paperwork for the Horta and eventually the real Mackintosh is going to turn up."

"You won't be able to prove conclusively that the Gaudi or the Horta were mine."

"Yes, I will. There'll be photographs for insurance purposes."

"I didn't insure them," he gloated.

"I'm not talking about *your* insurance, Blair. I'm talking about *ours*. McClintoch and Swain photographs all pieces it has in its possession worth over about five thousand at the request of our insurance company. We staple the photo to our copy of the invoice when it's sold, and believe me our files are in very good shape. So, yes, there's a very clear photograph of the Gaudi chair complete with cigarette burn, and the Horta, too. I'll be very happy to testify to that effect. We don't have the necklace because you didn't buy it through us, but I do know where you got it. I believe they will have what is needed there, too. Even if they don't, I expect your ex-wife will remember it well. The really wonderful thing about this furniture is that it links you to Robert Alexander, now a known drug kingpin. One link in the chain is broken, and you're next."

"It's your word against mine, and you're just an antique dealer," he said, reaching over and opening his glove compartment.

"Actually it's the police's forensic accountant, Anna Chan, whose word it is you're up against, not mine. If you're going to take out a gun, I wouldn't if I were you. It will only make it worse," I said, as the sirens grew much louder, and a number of law enforcement officials jumped out of the cedar hedge in which I, too, had hidden some weeks before. I had been able to tell them exactly where to stand. Six police cars swept up the driveway.

"It's over, Blair. They've recorded all this."

"Step away from the car, Lara," Rob ordered, something I was only too happy to do. Within minutes Blair was on his feet, cuffed, and Rob was informing him of his rights.

"You'll pay for this, babe," Blair said, almost spitting at me.

"The person who will pay here is you, Baldwin," Detective Singh said. "Our colleagues in the Northern Constabulary have Drever Clark in custody, with enough evidence to convict him, and Robert Alexander, too, had he lived to be in court, and you're not going anywhere for a long time. As Ms. McClintoch says, it's over. Anything else you'd like to say to this rat before we take him away, Lara? This is your last chance before you see him in court."

"No," I replied, but there was. As I watched Blair's head

recede into the distance in the back seat of that police car, I suddenly felt better.

"Don't call me babe!" I yelled at the top of my voice. The malaise I was feeling suddenly lifted. I was going to pull through.

Epilogue

And there you have it, Bjarni's story. You can see why there are
those who think there is treasure to be found. Bjarni's travels took
him to places both exotic and spiritual. People draw their own con-
clusions as to what Bjarni found, and indeed what has been lost. If
it is gold and jewels from Constantinople or Baghdad you seek, or
gifts worthy of a caliph of Spain, or religious icons of incomparable
worth, then Bjarni's saga gives you cause for hope. I was always
amazed at the theories my students would invent, in terms of what
happened to Bjarni, and what the real treasure might be. It seemed
to stimulate their creativity in ways that other lessons did not, perhaps because there was no proof, and therefore their imaginations
could roam at will. My grandfather was convinced that a piece of
the True Cross acquired by Bjarni during his stint in the
Varangian Guard would be found in the tomb of the orcs, along
with the pagan cauldron. If that is what you choose to believe, the
evidence is there.

You can decide for yourself if you think the saga is true. Some *consider Bjarni's story absolute rubbish. I am not one of those. Can I prove it? No. Does that matter? It does to some, those who would see and hold the evidence, but not to me. I suppose if I could find the tomb of the orcs, then that would go some distance toward silencing the skeptics. If I could find the cauldron, those who now scoff would at least be forced to listen and consider what the saga reveals. But in truth it doesn't matter. I know what happened. When I sit here watching a storm blow through, or the sunset turn the sea and sky to purple, or a soft mist clinging to the dark slopes of Hoy across the water, I know I'm hearing the same wind, watching the same mist and sky and sea that Bjarni did. We both have Orkney in our blood. That's what matters to me.*

IN ORKNEY THEY believe that Thorfinn Skull-Splitter, earl of Orkney, father of Hlodovir, grandfather of Earl Sigurd the Stout, the man to whom Bjarni the Wanderer gave his loyalty and trust, was buried in 976 in the Howe of Hoxa, a crumbling prehistoric broch or tower filled now with weeds and stones. If the Skull-Splitter, one of the first Orkney Vikings to die in his bed rather than in battle, really is there, he has a very good view for all eternity. I know, because I set out to find the spot before I left for home. It seemed fitting somehow, given the way this all started, that I should spend a moment at Skull-Splitter's grave.

As I stood in what remains of the broch looking out over the clear blue waters of Scapa Flow, or rather what Thorfinn would have known as Skalpeid-floi, I thought about how it is impossible for us to know if the moment in time in which we find ourselves is the cusp of a glorious era, or merely its dismal, if not catastrophic, end. Politicians try to persuade us that through them lies a brilliant and prosperous future, doomsayers may warn that the rot has set in and the end is near, but when it comes right down to it, we can never know.

Bjarni certainly didn't know that his time was over, that he and his people, once rulers of the northern seas, would become frozen in time as mere nuisances at best, violent thugs at worst, in the onward march of civilization. Bjarni thought he'd come back to find his world the same as it had ever been, that if anyone had changed it was he with his great adventures, and a magnificent silver cauldron to prove it. He was perhaps no more nor less realistic than those who came after him, those seeking the cauldron, or a chalice, or even the Holy Grail, imbuing the object with spiritual significance way beyond its physical presence. But it was a pot, useful perhaps for food and drink, and even, in the beauty of its workmanship, an object to inspire. Still, it was a pot.

Both Trevor and Percy saw the scroll framed above the reproduction Mackintosh. They both knew what they were looking at, because they'd both been in one of Sigurd's classes more than thirty years before. Percy, like so many of Sigurd's students, loved the tale, and when he later came to read Arthurian legend, he put the two stories together in his mind, saw connections that weren't there, and determined to find the Grail.

Percy's quest took him far afield. He must have realized what had happened to the scroll, because he followed Trevor to Toronto to get it. I like to think he would have returned it had he found it, but I'm not really sure. What I do know is that his quest took him to the tomb of the orcs. He was stabbed there, according to police who found traces of his blood, and the knife with Drever's prints on it. I don't know whether he went back a second time to see what else there was to be found and was discovered there by Drever just as I was, or whether Drever or Robert enticed him back to his death.

I still have mixed feelings about Percy. If there was anyone whose time was long past, it was he. I believe that it was Percy who hid in my shop after it closed for the day, and then ransacked the place looking for the scroll. He didn't trust me, not then anyway, but I didn't trust him either. I think that explains why he was always running away from me, because he thought I was about to accuse him of that crime. I also think he wanted to tell me what he had done the day we went touring together. As far as the shop is concerned, he didn't steal anything, he didn't break anything. I am trying to just close the door on that one.

Unlike Percy, Trevor helped himself to the scroll. Either that or Betty Haraldsson, lost in her dementia, gave it to a fellow she doubtless thought was charming. No doubt Trevor thought he was on the cusp of some great new life. He'd found his own grail, and it had nothing to do with a cauldron. Instead his time was up: he was on his way down the basement stairs.

Trevor apparently was born a rogue. There were a lot of questions I failed to ask at Sigurd's house that first afternoon. Sigurd told me that one of his students faked a scroll and tried to sell it to the museum. I did not ask that student's name, but could it possibly have been the man who ended up dead as a result of having tried to fake something again? Sigurd confirmed later when, unlike Perceval, I got a second chance to ask questions that it had in fact been Trevor. Trevor was sent to a strict boarding school in Glasgow in order to avoid more serious charges. He left both school and Scotland as soon as he could, which may explain why he never talked about Orkney.

As the police have pieced it together, Trevor was forced to help Robert and Blair move their furniture back and forth because of his gambling debts. He got the real Mackintosh from Alexander, who had purchased it many years earlier from Lester, made up a phony invoice and had it shipped, probably for a relatively small commission, one that would not even come close to paying off his gambling debts.

Sometimes I try to imagine how Trevor felt when he first saw the reproduction that Thor had made. It must have seemed a godsend, as a plan to solve all his problems began to form. I expect it was Alexander who told Trevor about Thor, never guessing the purpose to which he would put that information. Trevor purchased Thor's reproduction, made up another bogus invoice and separately shipped both that and the real Mackintosh to his store. I think he did some work on the fake to make sure the wear on the drawer and legs matched, at least from a distance, that of the original. He showed Blair the real one, got my approval, however tentative, but delivered the fake. Then he turned around and sold the first one a second time, planning to simply take the money and run. He didn't make it.

The question was where had the real Mackintosh gone? I told the police what I thought, and they paid a visit to Desmond Crane, search warrant in hand, and found the Mackintosh writing cabinet in a room hidden behind a fake bookcase. The Mackintosh's lock, I can tell you, was just fine. Blair must have been feeling pretty smug about getting to the Mackintosh before Dez did, while he was having an affair with Dez's wife. Dez, who didn't know about Leanna and Blair, must have been feeling pretty smug about owning the real one, too. Neither of them is feeling particularly cocky now. You have to wonder why someone like Crane would pay that much money for something he couldn't show to anybody, but as Clive is always pointing out, rich people are not like you and me. True collectors aren't either. I suppose it was enough for Crane just to possess it, but for some reason that fact depressed me. I mean if the rot is setting in, this surely is a sign.

In addition to the Mackintosh, police found a number of objects including a pair of bronze candlesticks from McClintoch & Swain that Desmond hadn't paid for. Or rather he hadn't paid us. He'd paid the thieves who'd stolen them in the first place. Antiques thought lost forever by other dealers in town turned up, too, which also proves, I suppose, that even people with pots of money like to get stuff cheap. Crane swears he had no idea he was purchasing stolen goods. I don't know whether anyone will be able to prove otherwise or not. At least the break-ins seem to have come to an end.

I sincerely hope the era of men like Robert Alexander, Blair Baldwin, and Drever Clark is fast coming to a close. The Churchill Barriers that I crossed so often while in Orkney were built during World War Two to provide safe haven from German U-boats for the British fleet in Scapa Flow. They could not stop people like Alexander, however, who used his army connections, including Drever, to find a source for heroin in Afghanistan, and to bring it in to Scotland via Orkney. Heroin is a terrible scourge there, particularly in Edinburgh, according to Rob, and Alexander and Drever must share some of the blame for that. The police here believe that Blair was a major player in cocaine in

Toronto, and he and Alexander had begun to have unpleasant business dealings.

An international team has been struck to piece this all together, including, I'm proud to say, my sweetie, lovely man that he is. Rob wasn't thrilled with my participation in Blair's arrest, but we both did what we had to do. It seems clear that Blair is also going to jail for a long time, not, as I hoped, for the murder of Trevor Wylie, but for money laundering and drug dealing. So far that's the best anybody can do, but they're working on it.

Robert Alexander died virtually instantly at Maya's hands, and Drever has been charged with Percy's murder and numerous drug offenses. Drever isn't looking nearly as good as he used to after his encounter with Oddi and Svein. Ask me if I care. Actually, I shouldn't say that. I do care, very, very much what happens to people like him. It does seem rather fitting though, that in a way, and after about a thousand years, Oddi and Svein took their revenge on Bjarni's killer.

The body of one Douglas "Dog" Sykes was found in a field north of the city a few weeks after I got home. There was no sign of his Doberman, and no identification or money on him. The police had believed he robbed Trevor of the money he received from the second sale of the Mackintosh, then was robbed and killed in turn. That theory held until over a million dollars was found in a locker, the key to which was hidden in Trevor's shop. Now the police have turned their attention back to Blair.

Leanna the Lush, then, is key to the resolution of who killed Trevor. Right now she and Dez are in divorce court. I would not want to be in Leanna's shoes for anything. She provided her lover Blair with an alibi, probably sincerely convinced he was innocent, only to find him arrested on a different set of charges. Technically this leaves an axe murderer at large, but the police aren't looking too hard for one, convinced that Blair was guilty of that crime, too, and that Leanna was lying. I think she was, too, but I am not entirely convinced she knows it. She always seemed a little befuddled to me, and her powers of observation suspect. She doesn't seem to have noticed, for example, that both her husband and her lover had identical pieces of furniture, but maybe Dez wouldn't let even his wife see it. I think it's possible that Blair killed Trevor, and then met Leanna for their usual assignation, and somewhere in the back of her mind, she chose to forget he was not there the whole time. But even if she is lying outright, what should she do? If she retracts her statement about Blair's whereabouts during the time period Trevor died, she might find herself up on a perjury charge. If she doesn't, she can hardly be staying mum because she continues to believe Blair is an upstanding citizen. Dez has made it very clear he won't take her back.

Sigurd Haraldsson moved into a nursing home where I believe he is comfortable. The Wasteland is up for sale. He writes to me from time to time in an increasingly shaky hand, and I'm always glad to hear from him. His move was made possible by the fact that Thor is living in Percy's room in Emily Budge's home. I introduced them, I'm pleased to say. Emily lets Thor use the basement for his workshop, and he has made her home very beautiful, as the photographs she sends me attest, and he has no trouble coming up with the rent. It is no crime to make a fake. It is only a crime if it is offered for sale as the genuine article, if there is a real attempt to deceive. It seemed to me, though, that Thor's talent could be put to better purpose. I talked to some architects I know, and when they need custom furniture, they send the plans to Thor. His work is exceptional, worth the extra cost for the freight.

Thor apparently is happy living with Emily. I can believe it. Emily will be fussing over him all the time, serving him those lovely sandwiches with no crusts with his tea. Emily, at the age of sixty-four, got her driver's license, bless her, and she drives Thor over to see his father several times a week in the van that Sigurd gave her. She also takes Thor to visit Svein and Oddi who now belong to a pleasant farm family who let the dogs run free, and who are always happy to see Thor.

Willow has recovered completely, although she had a really severe concussion that worried us all. She and Kenny plan to marry. They're going to live in Edinburgh and spend as much time as possible in Orkney. I envy them that. I've had to admit that much of what she told me was true. Oh, there were exaggerations and omissions and questionable explanations, but at the heart of it, she didn't lie. I suppose there are parallels here to Bjarni's story, and the necessity to work hard to find the nugget of truth amid the fiction. In Willow's case, I proved not particularly adept at separating the wheat from the chaff. The truth of it is this: she discovered that Trevor had a relative in Orkney when the legal process to determine who was to inherit the proceeds from the sale of the contents of Trevor's store got underway. As she had in fact told me she would, she decided to go and see this relative of Trevor's, that is to say Kenny, and make a plea for some of the money. She didn't tell me because she was going to Edinburgh, not Orkney and didn't expect to see me.

It was the scroll that changed her plans. She found it, and

rightly determining it came from Scotland, took it with her. Kenny, who could read runic script, told her what it said, and the two of them headed for Orkney. They didn't meet on the ferry, but according to Willow that is where they fell head over heels in love. She didn't tell me any of this because she was rather embarrassed about it at first, and then there was a period of time in which we both viewed each other with suspicion. I think it would be good if Willow got the million dollars found in the safety deposit box, because after all, Trevor did sell the real Mackintosh, and Dez really paid for it. I think it will be some time before that is decided, though, but I don't think Willow will be overly upset if she doesn't see any of it.

Kenny really did know Lester from the university. Lester was investigated for months, but no involvement in Alexander's drug business was found. Lester told me that he hadn't revealed to me that he had sold a Mackintosh writing cabinet to Robert that first day we met in his shop, because he believed that what his clients did or did not purchase and for how much was a confidential matter, and you know I have to agree with him. He did what he could to help me by suggesting I go to the gala, and by introducing me to Robert and Maya. It did have the required result eventually, and he has apologized about it a hundred times. He had no idea Robert had sent the writing cabinet to Blair.

What is to happen to the cauldron is still up in the air. Under the law of Treasure Trove in Scotland, objects like the cauldron have to be reported, and authorities will decide on their disposition. Simon Spence tells me it is an extraordinary find. In it scientists found traces of a hallucinogenic substance, which may explain what happened to Bjarni in the tomb. Spence believes it was used in rituals in ancient times, one in which sacrificial victims were beheaded. The severed head that speaks was an important symbol in ancient mythology, according to Simon.

As far as Bjarni's saga itself is concerned, though, it raises more questions than it answers. The cauldron, which scientists believe does indeed come from Northern Europe, predates Bjarni by at least a thousand years. The tomb in which Percy found it—and soil analysis does place the cauldron in that tomb—is three thousand years older than that. Does that mean that when Bjarni's saga was first written down a fragment of a much earlier tale insinuated itself into the story? Did Bjarni come upon an isolated cult that was still practicing rituals from a much earlier time? Did he simply find, or perhaps more likely, steal the cauldron and make up the story about his capture in the forest to explain his extended absence to his traveling companions? We will never know.

Despite that, Spence is coming around to believing much of Bjarni's tale, even if no one will ever prove it, in no small measure because of a runic inscription found in the tomb of the orcs that essentially says "Bjarni Haraldsson was here." It's possible that someone in relatively recent times saw the runic inscription and perhaps even the cauldron and invented a story to go with them, rather than the other way around, so Bjarni's story remains one that you can believe or not as you choose.

The cauldron is priceless, of course, not that Emily Budge or Sigurd will ever see any money from it. Neither of them seems terribly upset about this, bless their hearts. They just want to see that it is placed somewhere it will be appreciated. They have agreed that if it is donated, the donor recognition will be to both Sigurd and Thor Haralds-

son and Magnus Budge. It is very beautiful, now that con-
servators have had at it. Much of the silver gilt is still there,
and there are embossed panels that show a scene in a forest
with stags and a disembodied head that looks as if it is
about to speak. Bjarni's story gains more credence with me
every day.

Maya Alexander was not charged in her husband's death.
We all testified that it was self-defense and that she had indeed saved us all. She is back in New York, Maya Hausman
now, having gone back to her maiden name, something I'd
have done in a flash, too, if I had found myself in her situation. She's looking for a job, given her late husband's assets
are all frozen. It was not my powers of persuasion that convinced her to believe me and not her husband that fateful
day. It was not even Willow lying in the mud unconscious.
Instead, it was one of those moments when everything one
has been trying to pretend doesn't exist just cannot be ignored any longer. In Maya's mind, her friend Bev and
Robert were the perfect couple, and it is possible that Maya
was always secretly in love with her best friend's husband.
Bev tried to confide in her, but Maya either could not, or
would not, hear what Bev had to say. On that fateful day in
the rain, suddenly everything Maya feared was exposed, the
message was crystal clear. And, as Robert put it, she knew
what she had to do. It was perhaps not what he had in mind.
She says one of her real regrets, other than not realizing
what was happening to her friend, and what kind of poor
excuse for a human being Robert was, is that she will never
feel able to go back to Orkney. The place, she says, has gotten under her skin.

I can understand that. Despite all that had happened in
Orkney, I kept thinking of its rolling countryside, the soft

touch of the air, the clouds coming down to kiss the green slopes, the shining water of St. Margaret's Hope, where children play, and even the wild fury of the wind and the sea. Most of all I think of the kindness of strangers. Percy said he was looking for salvation there. I doubt salvation was his. He said I went to Orkney to seek vindication, and I think I can say with some justification that I found it. But more than that, I gained a profound sense of history as a continuous stream, as a living presence in our lives. I'm happy to have breathed the same air, felt the same rain, and watched the same sunsets as Percy, Sigurd, Thor, and yes, Bjarni the Wanderer. If there is treasure to be found in Orkney, I believe that is where it lies.

Turn the page for a preview of
the next Archaeological Mystery
by Lyn Hamilton

The Chinese Alchemist

Coming from
Berkley Prime Crime
in April 2007!

Prologue

───

I used to believe that brigands lurked in the bamboo forests at the edge of our garden, and that a ghost haunted the well. It was Auntie Chang who told me about the brigands. I expect she said that to frighten me, to make sure I did not stray far from home. It may be, though, that she especially didn't want me to go to that part of our property. The brigands didn't worry me. When I grew up, I planned to be a brave soldier in the service of the Emperor, just like Number Two Brother. Brigands would have cause to fear me.

The ghost was a different matter. She was an ugly woman with disheveled hair and eyes that burned through you. I knew that because Auntie Chang had seen the ghost and was very frightened. She said it is someone whose hun *had escaped the body, and that the ghost could not rest until the proper rites were performed and the corpse's mouth sealed with jade so the hun could not escape.*

Sometimes I dreamed that Number One Sister had joined the brigands in the bamboo, that the eerie knocking sound bamboo makes as the wind blows through it was Number One Sister send-

ing me a message. Number One Sister, you see, had simply vanished from my life. One day she was there, the next morning she was gone.

If Number One Sister was not with the brigands, then she had run away to the Gay Quarter to become a dancer. I thought that would be exciting, too. I decided that when I was older and able to make my way about the city as I pleased, I'd look for her there. She would be wearing gowns of the finest silk in the latest fashion, with jade and pearls and kingfisher feathers, and all the men would cheer as she danced and sang. She sang and danced very well, that I knew, having watched her when she thought she was alone. When I found her, I would cheer, too.

I missed my sister. She was the only one who would play in the gardens with me, and she also let me watch while she put her hair up in elaborate tall bindings. Her favorite styles were flower bindings, where she wove peonies into her hair. When she was married, she told me, she would be able to go into the streets with her hair made up so. She was also the only member of the family who would play with me in the snow, the rest of them preferring to huddle behind screens to cut the drafts or hold their hands to braziers for warmth. I was grateful for these moments with my sister. Number One Brother was too busy studying for his civil service examinations to pay any attention to me. He was angry when I interrupted him. He told me his future depended on success in the examinations. I didn't know why he would say that when he could be a brigand instead. Number Two Brother simply ignored me.

The drums of the Imperial Palace are now sounding. Soon the drums of the city will do the same, and the doors of the wards will shut for the night. It was on one such night that Number One Sister did not return until dawn. Our father waited by the gates all night long, afraid that she would be found outside and beaten by the Gold Bird Guard, *twenty blows of the rod for remaining out-side our ward during the night.*

It was shortly after that event that Number One Sister disap-peared for good. I did not understand why she didn't say goodbye.

Chapter One

THE FIRST SIGN that there was something amiss came in the form of a phone call from someone suggesting he was ready to install fire-detection equipment in my home. I said there must be some mistake, even though he had quite correctly asked for Lara McClintoch. He disagreed. He had my name, address, and phone number. I said I already had smoke detectors, thank you very much. The next day, another man called to say he wanted to book a time to pour the new concrete in my basement. I have rather lovely Mexican tiles, all in good repair in my basement. Both men spoke with a foreign accent I couldn't pinpoint and sounded as if they had socks in their mouths. Within a few hours of casually, or perhaps not so casually, mentioning these calls to my partner, Rob Luczka, a sergeant in the Royal Canadian Mounted Police, I found myself living in a hotel.

It seems that Rob, of whom I am inordinately fond, had seriously annoyed members of a gang that was terrorizing the merchants of downtown Chinatown. These thugs called themselves Golden Lotus, which just goes to prove you should never judge an organization by its name. I suppose that is his job, annoying bad guys. Still, I had never thought it would have much to do with me, other than the fact that I occasionally worry myself sick about him when he's off on some assignment.

"Why exactly am I here?" I said in a tone I seem to acquire when I'm unnerved. I was finding this a tad stressful, all that slapping stuff into a suitcase and running around the house to see that everything was turned off so that my smoke detectors would not have to be put to good use through some fault of my own, as opposed to malfeasance on the part of men with socks in their mouths.

"You are here because some very nasty people have figured out that you are a person of some importance to me," he said. "They probably know that because I live right next door and spend a lot of time going out my gate and in yours for sleepovers. Now if you'd let me knock down the wall between our two houses so I would not have to brave rain, snow, sleet, and hostile neighborhood dogs to pay a visit, they might not have known that."

"If this is a ploy to get me to move in with you, it isn't exactly working."

"No? They were trying to tell you they are going to burn your house down with you in it. Either that or kill you by some other means and bury you in your own basement."

"Burn my house down!" I said. "They can't do that. Our cottages were built in 1887 and are protected under the Ontario Heritage Act!"

"The Heritage Act! I wonder why the brains at Headquarters didn't think of that. These lowlifes extort, rob, and kill at a whim, and so far we haven't been able to stop them.

But then, just like that, you come up with the Heritage Act."

I looked at him for a moment. Rob, unlike me, is hardly ever sarcastic. "You're really worried about this, aren't you?" I said.

"I wouldn't want you to think I cared," he said, looking away.

"I'd never think that. Jennifer is safe, isn't she?"

"I don't think these guys from Golden Lotus would go to Taiwan to find her, no. That at least is working in our favor." Jennifer, Rob's daughter, was teaching English in Taiwan for a year. We worried about her, of course, but right now Taiwan sounded better than Toronto where her personal safety was concerned.

"Good. Everything will be fine. Now, what's my name again?"

"Charlyn Krahn," he said. "We're Herb and Charlyn Krahn. Please try to remember to sign all chits that way."

"Are the Krahns paying for this?" I said.

"They are, indeed. Nice of them. I even have a credit card with Herb's name on it, compliments of my employer."

"So what happens now? This is a short version of the witness protection program, right? Which is to say, how long do we get to lounge about in this hotel? Can I go to work, even if you can't?"

"It is the considered opinion of my superiors that, no, as an undercover officer I am to stay out of sight, and yes, you can go into the shop. Someone will be keeping an eye on the place and if there's any sign of trouble, then we'll reassess. I know you don't want to leave the redoubtable Clive in charge for too long."

Clive Swain is my ex-husband and my partner in an antiques business called McClintoch & Swain. And no, I don't like to leave Clive alone in the shop for too long. I usually return from my buying trips to find the store completely rearranged and not always, which is to say almost never, to my liking. "As for how long, it shouldn't take long. My brothers in the force will take care of these people," Rob said.

"What does take care of these people mean?"

"Whatever it takes," he said. "In the meantime, we're having an all expenses paid holiday. Now let's see what's on the room service menu."

As pleasant as an all expenses paid stay in a pretty nice hotel, with someone cooking and cleaning and even making the bed every day, sounds, I can tell you it is amusing for about forty-eight hours. After that it gets a little claustrophobic, the room service fare starts to taste like prison food, assuming prison food tastes the way I think it does, and generally your roommate begins to get tiresome. I believe the feeling was mutual. If we ever move in together, the place will have to be very large, something on the scale of, say, Versailles.

So it was that what I consider to be my acutely sensitive nose for dissimilitude was not working as it should, so eager was I to get out of the place. What I saw as a godsend, but was really a trap, which if not set for me, certainly caught me in its snare, came in the form of a call to the shop on a fine autumn day from one Dorothy Matthews, known to her friends as Dory.

"I have a favor to ask," she began.

"Ask away," I said.

"It's more of a proposal than a favor, although I would be exceedingly grateful if you would undertake it for me. I suppose I'm actually asking two favors. Would you consider having lunch with me at my home? I need to show you something, and my arthritis is acting up today. Taking it to you at McClintoch & Swain, no matter how much I might enjoy it once I got there, would be difficult. Would one o'clock work for you?"

"I'll be there," I said.

The maid was setting out a plate of sandwiches and some fruit when I arrived shortly after one. Dory was in an armchair, a cane at her side, and she greeted me warmly. I first met Dory when I was researching Chinese bronzes for a client of McClintoch & Swain. At that time, Dory was the curator of the Cottingham Museum's Asian galleries, having been lured there from her position at one of Canada's most prestigious galleries by Major Cottingham when he first opened a museum to house his private collection. Within five years, the Cottingham's Asian galleries had not only expanded, but had earned an international reputation, all thanks to Dory. Everything I know about Chinese art and antiquities, I learned from Dory Matthews.

People who knew Dory by reputation only, as a preeminent scholar of Chinese history and art, were surprised to meet her in person, not expecting the Asian woman in front of them. She got Dory from her English mother, and Matthews from her husband, the industrialist George Norfolk Matthews. Born Dorothy Zhang, or more accurately Zhang Dorothy in 1944 in Beijing, she was taken to England by her mother in 1949 as the Communists took power, eventually settling in Canada. Getting out of China was a harrowing experience she told me. In the chaos of the times, as many people tried to leave the country before the Communist forces of Mao Zedong took over, she and her mother became separated from her father. She never saw him again. She was led to believe that her father had survived but had never joined them, choosing instead to become a part of the People's Republic of China. She believed that at one time, at least, he held a senior position in Mao's Communist China, having been a loyal supporter of Mao, most notably having accompanied Mao on the Long March in 1934. This was one of the most famous strategic retreats in history, a five-thousand-mile march that took just over a year, but which enabled Mao to break through the Koumintang lines and eventually push the Koumintang and their leader, Chiang Kai Shek, off the Chinese Mainland to Taiwan, then called Formosa. Dory thought she might even have had other siblings in China, a half brother or half sister, although she never tried to find them. Dory's mother remarried, whether or not exactly legally neither I nor perhaps Dory was ever entirely sure. I think she probably just said her Chinese union wasn't legal and carried on.

When we were alone, and I was tucking into my lunch— I noticed she wasn't eating—she began to talk. "You are aware, I'm sure, that it is not really ethical for a curator to personally collect in the area in which he or she works. My husband has collected for some years, and I gave him advice as often as I could, but never when the object he wanted could be considered Asian art. But now that I am under no such restriction, I feel that I can get into the market, if I wish to do so. Would you agree?"

"Sure," I said. "Why not?"

"Good," she said. "I was worried what you would think about that."

"Why would you? I'm assuming you're not trying to smuggle antiquities out of some country or buy on the black market."

She was silent for a moment. "Do you know how my stepfather made his fortune?" she said at last.

I decided I'd better stop stuffing my face with the lovely

homemade sandwiches, such a nice change from hotel fare, and pay attention, as this conversation did not seem to be following a nicely logical path, and there were some undercurrents, possibly disturbing ones. "Didn't you tell me he imported china and porcelain, some of it from Occupied Japan, after the war, or was it Hong Kong?"

"Both," she said. "That's how he made his living. He made his fortune by importing very high-end Chinese antiquities, by which I mean very old Imperial treasures, sometimes even older than that, a lot of them smuggled out of China and into Hong Kong where it joined his regular shipments. He used contacts of my mother's to do so, a high party cadre in Mao's regime, someone I have come to believe was my father. If so, my father had no compunction feathering his nest by selling whatever he could get his hands on, and in his position that was quite a bit, and my stepfather had no compunction expediting its passage out of the country and making a good deal of money for himself as well."

"I can understand why this would bother you for any number of reasons," I said carefully. "I'm not sure, though, what you mean by smuggled. It really depends when the objects came out of China as you know only too well. There was a period when a lot of antiques and antiquities were considered decadent Imperialist trappings by the Communist Party, and nobody cared if they were taken out of the country or even destroyed."

"It may have been legally acceptable, but it was never morally acceptable," Dory said. "So is what I am about to ask you to do legal? Of course it is. Ethical? I suppose that depends on what I propose to do with what you get for me if, that is, you agree to do it. I promised to show you something. Would you mind going over to the walnut cabinet? On the lower left side there is something wrapped in cloth.

I want you to bring it here so that we can look at it together."

"It" was an exquisite rectangular silver box with a hinged and rounded lid of a shape sometimes referred to as a casket. Incised on the top was a bird, and a scene showing a number of women together in a garden wrapped around the four sides. "May I open it?" I asked. I believe I was whispering.

Dory nodded. Inside along the sides and bottom were Chinese characters. I couldn't read them, but I thought perhaps Dory could. I closed it carefully.

"Beautiful," I said. "Very old." I waited for her to say something.

"T'ang dynasty," she said. "You know when that was, of course."

"Don't tell me," I said. "I'll remember. T'ang dynasty is, just a minute, 618 to 907. Capital was Chang'an, essentially where the city of Xi'an is now. It was preceded by the Sui dynasty and followed by the Five Dynasties Era and then the Song, Yuan, Ming, and Qing dynasties in that order. How am I doing?"

Dory smiled. "For a time I thought you would never learn! I know you regarded me as a stubborn old bat for making you memorize all the dynasties, but really if you don't know your dynasties, you don't know your Chinese history, and for sure you don't know your Chinese antiques."

"Not so. I never thought you were a stubborn old bat, and furthermore, I like to think I'm your most accomplished student," I said, and she actually laughed, something I hadn't heard her do much lately.

"I think you may well be," she said.

I looked at it a little longer. "Beautiful workmanship," I said. "I've never seen anything remotely like it. But what is it exactly you want me to do, Dory?"

Rather than answering me directly, she slowly and painfully reached for something in a magazine rack to one side of her chair and set in front of me the catalogue for the annual Oriental auction at Molesworth & Cox in New York. A yellow sticky marked a page on which was shown another silver box.

"You're selling it," I said. "No, just a minute." I eyed the box in front of me. It was about six inches long, four inches wide, and maybe six or seven inches high measured to the top of the domed lid. "The one for sale looks very similar but I think it's slightly smaller all 'round."

"Very observant," Dory said. "And you are quite right. They are almost identical, although I believe the text inside is different, the scene depicted on the outside is as well, and mine is larger. I think there is a series of boxes designed to fit inside each other, like those Russian dolls. There will be a third in silver even bigger than this one, and possibly a fourth box in wood rather than silver, the largest, at least that is what my stepfather said, but of course the wood is unlikely to have survived. The silver, in the proper circumstances, would."

"You want me to go to New York next week to bid on this box for you," I said. My heart soared. I'd still be staying in a hotel, of course, but it would be a different hotel. Even better, I wouldn't have to look over my shoulder for gangsters every time I left it, nor would I be tripping over Rob's feet every time I turned around.

"Would you consider doing just that? I would pay your expenses of course, plus something for your time, and I would pay you a commission if we get it."

"Sure," I said. "I'll see if Alex will come in to the shop to help Clive out for a few days. I'd like to go early and get a good look at this at the preview to make sure it's authentic before we buy it."

"You should go right away," Dory said. "But is it authentic? Almost certainly. You see this silver box in front of us is one of three that my stepfather smuggled to Hong Kong, and thence to North America where they were auctioned off one at a time in the mid–nineteen seventies. I expect my stepfather believed that he could get a better price if he sold them separately, although I'm not so sure he was right. George, my husband, bought it at auction about ten years ago . . .

"Inside the box is a process for making something," Dory said. "It tells you to heat the ingredients, unspecified, in a sealed container for thirty-six hours, and then to partake of the resulting substance for seven days. George interpreted it as a process for making drugs, and that is why he acquired it. It's Chinese, so he didn't discuss it with me for reasons I have already explained. I recognized it as soon as I set eyes on it however. I saw the three boxes when my stepfather got them. I fell in love with them, but he sold them over my protests. George found this one, a second has turned up in New York that I plan to purchase through you, and I hope to find the third before I die. George and I may be the only people, along with you now, that know that this is part of a nesting set. When I find all three of them, I plan to give them to the Shaanxi History Museum in Xi'an, China. I want them to go home."

IT WAS UNSEASONABLY warm in New York when I got there. The Molesworth & Cox Oriental auction was the first of the season and had attracted a lot of attention. There were some wonderful objects in the show, and the people at the auction house were justifiably proud, managing to get some play in the *New York Times*. Unhappily, the silver box was one of the objects featured, almost certainly ensuring I would have more competition for it.

THURSDAY EVENING I was in my favorite position at the back of the room, waiting for the silver box to come up. I had my paddle and was ready to raise it as required. I was also calling up my killer instincts. Something that was easy enough for me to do. I just thought of those thugs who were planning to fire bomb my heritage cottage with me in it.

It was after a break in the proceedings, about midway through the auction that the situation changed significantly. The announcement came from the auctioneer, Gerald Cox, the Cox of Molesworth & Cox, who told us that an object had been withdrawn.

"I'm afraid the timing of this is highly unusual," Cox said. "Item eighty-three, a silver coffret dating to the reign of T'ang Emperor Xuanzong has just been withdrawn by its owner."

I took a deep breath and phoned the news to Dory, hearing her sharp intake of breath. "I'm sorry," I said. I could feel her disappointment coming across the phone line.

"It's not for you to apologize," she said quietly. "There'll be another time."

There wasn't another time for Dory, though, because ten days later she was dead.